"If you don't like being left behind, then why are you trying to do it to me?"

Winnie watched stone-faced as Lauren's lips parted, then slowly hardened into an angry line. "Left behind?" Lauren sputtered. "*I* have left *you* behind? Pardon me, Win, but I seem to remember inviting you to spend the entire summer with us in a beautiful beach house. We all got in the Jeep *together*. Remember? Then we drove nine hundred miles. . . ."

"You and Mel are so wrapped up in TV-land, you seem to forget I'm even *here*," Winnie said hotly.

"You are completely out of line," Lauren said with quiet fury. She took a breath and let her violet eyes bore directly into Winnie's. "What's going on with you? First you make a scene about Liza and Travis—then you start in on me and Mel and our jobs!"

Winnie glared at her.

"If you want a boyfriend or a job, Win," Lauren growled, "why don't you go out and find one, instead of blaming and ranting at us?"

Don't miss these books
in the exciting FRESHMAN DORM series:

FRESHMAN BEACH PARTY

LINDA A. COONEY

HarperPaperbacks
A Division of HarperCollins*Publishers*

This is a work of fiction. The characters, incidents, and dialogues are products of the author's imagination and are not to be construed as real. Any resemblance to actual events or persons, living or dead, is entirely coincidental.

HarperPaperbacks   *A Division of* HarperCollins*Publishers*
10 East 53rd Street, New York, N.Y. 10022

Copyright © 1994 by Linda Alper and Kevin Cooney
Cover art copyright © 1994 Daniel Weiss Associates, Inc.

Cover illustration by Tony Greco

First printing: June 1994

Printed in the United States of America

HarperPaperbacks and colophon are trademarks of HarperCollins*Publishers*

❖ 10 9 8 7 6 5 4 3 2 1

One

auren swam through the warm water, her eyes fixed on the powdery white sand of Crescent Beach. She felt the mighty ocean swell beneath her, then kicked harder, plunging her arms into the surf. The wave caught her perfectly, its white crest breaking over her head. Her body surged forward, and she let herself feel the powerful ocean sending her back to shore.

"California," Lauren whispered to herself, and a thrill stirred deep inside her. She squinted against the brightness of the water as it swirled around her waist. It seemed impossible that only two days ago she and her friends Winnie Gottlieb, Liza Ruff, and Melissa McDormand, were back at the University of

Springfield's mountain campus, taking the last of their final exams. Their freshman year in college was finally over.

And now they were in Crescent Beach for the whole summer—together.

Lauren breathed in the salty seaweed smells of the beach, her head spinning with excitement. Squinting across the water, she spotted Winnie performing cartwheels across the wet sand. Melissa was doing warm-up stretches. She frowned. And Liza? Where was Liza? Lauren felt someone grab her around the waist from behind, nearly knocking her over.

"One day in southern California and she's already looking like a spaced-out sun kitten," Liza's deep voice blared into her ear. "Get this woman some mineral water and a massage!"

"Liza!" Lauren screamed, giving in to the fizzy excitement that was overtaking her. But Liza began kicking away, clinging to a huge inflated dinosaur. Flamboyant, flame-haired, Brooklyn-born Liza was a performing-arts major, determined to become a star. It didn't matter to Liza that tacky swim toys were practically banned at Crescent Beach. What mattered to Liza was staying visible at all times—you never knew where a talent scout might be lurking, especially in southern California.

"Look out, Lauren and Liza!" Winnie's high-pitched warning sailed across the water. Lauren looked up and laughed. Winnie was exactly the right kind of friend to bring to California. In her fruit-covered sun hat and huge earrings, she looked like a small tropical tree growing out of the sand. "Melissa McDormand is out of the starting block."

Melissa looked dangerous in her red Speedo tank suit as she leaped a series of invisible hurdles into the foamy water. When she neared Lauren and Liza, she knifed the side of her hand into the water, drenching them.

"Fight, fight," Melissa yelled, her coppery hair blazing in the sun.

"I'm in. I'm in," Winnie screeched from the beach, whipping off her sunglasses. Her short, spiky hair looked as if it had been run through a salad spinner, and her tiny body was barely covered by what was probably the skimpiest bikini permitted by law in southern California.

Lauren whipped up the blue water with her arms. The salty surf and the sun made her body tingle. She splashed Liza, then sent a powerful water curve right into Melissa's astonished face.

"Lauren Turnbell-Smythe," Winnie shrieked happily, staggering toward her, "I think I liked you better last fall when you were just a shy little thing wearing your mom's East Coast tweeds and pearls."

Lauren laughed back, splashing her. Her arms dripped, and her bathing suit clung cool and wet to her body. "Never fear, Winifred. Somewhere deep inside, the pearls and the good manners are still there, waiting for a bad moment to emerge. Just give me a little time and—monster preppy will return!" Lauren lunged playfully for Winnie, but a huge wave overtook all four of them at once, plummeting them back toward the soft, sandy beach. Exhausted, Lauren led the way, running back to their beach towels.

"This place is paradise," Winnie groaned, collapsing onto her towel. "I never want to see another mountain or snowstorm in my life."

Lauren lay stomach-down on her warm beach towel, savoring her summer freedom. The waves crested clean and white against the glinting blue Pacific. The sun burned on her back. Lauren thought her heart would burst. The Crescent Colony. They were here! They were really here.

"I've never met your exceptionally rich parents, Lauren," Liza teased. She was lying faceup on her Little Mermaid beach towel, fanning her raspberry-red nails through the air. "But I do love them. And when I'm an even richer, not to mention famous, Hollywood entertainer, I'm going to tell them what wonderful, unselfish people they were for handing this fab-u-loh-so house over to us for the summer."

Lauren bit the inside of her lip and smiled, digging her hands into the soft sand on each side of her towel. She let the grains sift through her fingers. Unselfish, her parents were not. Sure, they had bought the multi-million-dollar house and immediately handed it over to Lauren for the summer. But they definitely had their reasons.

Winnie giggled and pulled out a bottle of suntan oil. "You don't get it, do you, Liza? It's not Lauren's parents we need to be grateful to. There's one guy we can all thank for this summer."

Melissa rolled over and gave Lauren a sly look. "He's dark-haired and handsome, in his scruffy-rebellious-reporter way. And his name is Dash Ramireeeeeeeeezzzzzz."

Winnie began coating herself with the suntan oil. "And Lauren's parents' strategy for dealing with him worked."

Lauren felt a pang. Dash had wanted her to come with him to New York this summer. He'd landed volunteer jobs for both of them on a small weekly newspaper. But her parents had hit the roof when she mentioned the plan. Still, when they offered her the beach house as a tempting alternative, she hadn't hotly rejected it, as she would have six months ago. Instead, she'd graciously accepted. After all, she'd rebelled against her parents enough this year to last a lifetime. And how strong was her relationship with Dash if it couldn't withstand a ten-week separation? And, after the year she'd had, she deserved a break.

"Winnie!" Melissa broke in. "You make it sound like Lauren sold out. Why would anybody choose to swelter in New York City all summer when she could live at the beach and have an internship on *The April Webster Show*?"

Lauren's heartbeat quickened. *The April Webster*

Show was the hottest new daytime talk show, and Lauren's mother just happened to be old friends with one of its executive producers, who'd hired Lauren for an unpaid summer internship. Sure, she'd probably be a lowly gofer all summer, fetching coffee and delivering scripts. But there was a chance she might do a little research, too. She might actually get to work with April Webster herself.

"I could kiss Lauren's parents on the lips anyway," Liza declared, rising and heading for the beach house, a soft-gray wooden residence with a wide deck that stood on stilts over the sand. "Because I'm going to get my big break on television this summer, I can feeeeeel it. Anybody want a soda?"

"Bring the shovel, too," Lauren called out. "We'll start our campfire."

Lauren glanced over at Melissa, who was nervously sifting sand between her freckled fingers. "Liza's so confident, I could throw up," Melissa sighed dejectedly.

"Get out," Winnie reassured her. "Liza's a walking, talking sea of insecurity."

Lauren agreed, cupping her chin in her hands and staring at Liza's receding purple-sequined swimsuit. "She just hides it under a ton of pancake makeup and distracts you with her authentic Brooklyn chutzpah."

Melissa shrugged, her freckled face scrunched up into a sulk that Lauren had seen a thousand times when they were roommates. After Lauren's major midyear breakup with Dash, and Melissa's canceled wedding to Brooks Baldwin, they'd spent weeks brooding and overeating together. "Well, I'm not an actress," Melissa complained. "I'm just Melissa McDormand. The hayseed from Springfield who's never been anyplace bigger than Portland, Oregon."

Winnie reached over and tickled her in the ribs. "Look at you. You're a straight-A premed student on a track scholarship. And I remember that trip you took to Portland. That's when you left the entire northwest university track conference in the dust."

"Yeah," Lauren murmured. "I really hate you, Melissa."

Melissa's green eyes flashed. "It's easy for you to talk, Lauren. A ritzy Crescent Beach house is nothing to you. You've been to New York, Paris, London . . ."

Lauren rolled her eyes. Melissa. From the outside she looked tough, smart, and totally together. Her lean body had never carried an ounce of fat. Her life was a model of discipline, fitness, and academic excellence. Inside, though, Melissa wasn't as strong as she looked. Mel relied completely on her achievements for her sense of self-worth. She didn't make friends easily. And change was hard for her.

Melissa straightened out one leg and dropped into a deep runner's stretch. "If I don't find a job in about forty-eight hours, I'm D-E-D, dead. I can't afford to be here, Lauren. I should be back in

Springfield slinging hamburgers for sophomore-year expense money."

Winnie turned to her. "So should I, Mel. But I'm so wrung out after last year, I can't even get it together to decide what color to paint my toenails. Sometimes I think my brain is permanently fried."

Lauren sat up and put her arm around Melissa's strong shoulders. "I'm taking you to the studio with me tomorrow. *The April Webster Show*'s got to have something."

"Right." Melissa frowned as Liza returned with a large shovel, a few newspapers, and a bundle of kindling wood.

"Come on, girls." Liza dumped the wood and posed with her sandal on the shovel. "Let's get this baby fired up."

Melissa looked around. "Are campfires allowed here, Lauren? I mean, look at all these multi-million-dollar homes."

Lauren shrugged. "We're within twenty feet of our deck. Sure, it's allowed. It's just that no one on this beach but us knows how to have fun."

"What if someone complains?" Melissa fretted. "Maybe we should move a little farther from the deck, actually. You know, since it's wood . . ."

"Stop worrying," Lauren soothed, standing up and taking the shovel from Liza. Melissa's fears had probably propelled her through a thousand track meets and final exams, but it wasn't going to get her anywhere this summer. "We'll find you a job tomorrow. You'll probably make a ton of money this summer. L.A. is la-la land, Melissa. The land of big bucks."

"Bucks," Liza snorted, wadding up a final sheet of newspaper and stacking a tepee of kindling around it. "Is that all anyone has on the brain around here?" She waved her hand dismissively toward the tasteful homes and shiny foreign cars parked in the driveways. "All these people have money—and so what? So they can sit on a soft cushion and stare out at the water? They'd give their right arm for a little excitement and adventure."

"Are you planning to create a little excitement for my parents' new neighbors, Liza?"

Liza struck a match and sat back with a dreamy look as the campfire began to blaze. "Don't worry, Lauren. It's just that I'm looking for something more. I'm looking for fame. I'm looking for art. I'm looking for love. If I can have that, you can keep the cars and houses."

Melissa began nibbling on her nails, frowning. "And what do you plan to live on until you reach nirvana, Liza?"

"Money," Liza said hotly, poking the fire with a stick and opening a plastic package of marshmallows. "A little bit of money. Just enough to get me by until I hit gold in Hollywood, girlfriends. I'll get a part-time job, then use my extra time for auditions and schmoozing with directors and producers."

Winnie fingered her banana earrings and nodded sadly. "Liza's right. Money isn't everything."

"You've never had to live without it," Melissa retorted, raking back her hair with her fingers.

"Okay," Winnie shot back, "so my hotshot shrink mother sends me money, Mel. But you don't have the exclusive right to everyone's sympathy. I'm tired, and I'm planning to veg out on this beach all summer. And I'm not going to do anything more demanding than work on my tan and stare at the guys. And I hope nobody's planning to hassle me about it."

Lauren bit her lip. Winnie probably had the right idea. After all, she'd been through enough pain in the last year to last anyone a lifetime. First she had practically eloped with Josh in the winter. Then she had become pregnant, only to suffer a miscarriage. That had plunged her into a deep depression, and soon she and Josh had separated. Lauren had always admired Winnie's spunk and courage, but she felt sorry for her, too.

"'Guys,'" she repeated, eager to change the subject. "Imagine a whole summer not having to actually deal with a guy."

Melissa collapsed back onto the sand. "I'm still adjusting. But Denny and I decided it was probably good to spend some time apart."

"Denny's going to miss you," Lauren said with a gentle nudge, though she was beginning to realize that the summer might be even harder on Mel. Though Denny Markam was confined to a wheelchair, his disability had given him strength and independence. Probably more than Mel had at the moment.

"Good thing you came with a racing suit, Mel," Liza cracked. "The way you're looking lately, you'll need it to make a fast break from the lecherous groping of the local surfer boys."

Melissa smiled thinly and flicked the sand with her toe. "This place is definitely full of hunky guys. But I've never been on a summer-long vacation before. I'm not sure I get how this fling stuff works. Say you meet a guy. How do you know he's not a serial killer or drug addict?"

Winnie moaned and perked up her spiky hair with her nails, squinting into the setting sun. "Flings. Fling is the Chinese word for stupid. And I'm not stupid anymore, folks. Just call me sensible, single, boring Winnie Gottlieb. No fling advice given, none taken."

Liza plunged a stick into a sticky marshmallow and held it over the flames. "Music to my ears, Win," she began carefully. "So you won't be looking up your old flame Travis while you're down here in L.A.?"

Lauren let a smile escape the corner of her mouth. Winnie had met Travis Bennett, an American, in Europe the summer before her freshman year. He'd actually followed her to the U of S in the fall, but she'd already become involved with Josh, so Travis had headed for Hollywood, where he had vague plans to make it as a musician. Then Liza had visited L.A. earlier in the year on a TV audition, and Winnie had suggested she look up Travis. From all reports Liza and Travis had hit it off very well.

"Travis and I are ancient history," Winnie sighed. "We're so ancient, we go back to the Roman Empire . . . the Egyptian pyramids . . ."

Liza whooped and made a fist, her marshmallow suddenly catching fire and lighting up the circle of faces in the dimming light. "Yes!"

"What about Waldo, Liza?" Winnie said quietly, lining three marshmallow puffs in a row on her stick. "I thought Waldo and Liza were destined to make movies together."

Liza made a weary face, delicately licking a single finger at a time. Waldo was a U of S big man on campus, an eccentric night owl who made offbeat movies and liked to star Liza in his projects. "We're finished. I get tired just thinking about him. The guy never sleeps, and lives on coffee and junk food," she said, popping a roasted marshmallow into her mouth. "How can anybody live that way? He drives me nuts."

Lauren, Melissa, and Winnie exchanged glances. "Sooooo." Lauren nudged Liza. "Have you called Travis yet?"

Liza shook her head and looked soulfully out to sea. Her face dropped into gloomy darkness. "Yes, but he wasn't home. One of his housemates said he wasn't driving limos anymore, though. He's got some new gig." She pressed a glossy nail to her cheek. "Where was it? Something on Melrose Avenue called The Palace. I don't know. It's probably some kind of clerking or fry-cook job to tide him over until he lands a recording contract."

Lauren opened her eyes wide and lifted herself up, digging her elbows into her sandy towel. "Did you say The Palace?"

Liza shrugged and tugged at her wet bathing suit. "So?"

"Liza!" Lauren felt herself nearly exploding with excitement. She stood up on her knees and planted her hands on her hips. "The Palace! It's the hottest music club in L.A."

"It is?" Liza said in a tiny voice, her red mouth dropping open.

Lauren was trying to catch her breath. "It's a huge, glitzy joint on Melrose Avenue, and you have to practically be Sylvester Stallone's mother to get a table. Anyone with a gig at The Palace on Melrose is on his way. He may already have a recording contract."

"Oh."

Winnie looked at Liza as if she were crazy. "Aren't you going to say anything? React? Speak? As in 'share thoughts'?"

Liza slowly clamped her hand to her forehead with drama and sank back on her heels, her eyes filled with tears. "What can I say? He probably won't give me the time of day now."

Melissa stared too, in disbelief. "You're crazy. You just said you wanted to spend the summer schmoozing. And now you've got the perfect high-powered contact."

"Travis isn't a contact," Liza wailed, her shiny lower lip quivering. She collapsed onto her towel. "He's a guy I like. And now I won't have a chance against all those gorgeous music groupies who must be hanging all over him like Christmas decorations. He's probably got a head as fat as a ham by now."

"Travis isn't like that," Winnie said with unabashed loyalty. "He's a faithful, loving guy."

Liza's crestfallen look began to subside. She shrugged. "You think so? Yeah, maybe you're right. But success does funny things to people. Take it from me."

"So drop by The Palace tomorrow night and find out if it's changed him," Winnie suggested, carefully studying Liza with a sidelong glance.

Fully and rapidly recovered, as usual, Liza leaned back and dragged her oversize beach bag into the circle of friends. After yanking out several tattered scarves, a plastic squirt gun, a half-empty pack of gum, and a broken tube of lipstick, she finally located a worn map, which she smoothed out on her towel. "Famous people," she sighed.

"Uh-oh," Winnie cracked. "Liza's studying her Map of the Stars again."

"Look." Melissa pointed to a spot on the map. "There's The Palace on Melrose. It must be a landmark."

Lauren couldn't help laughing. "Look." She

pointed to an imaginary spot in the middle of the map. "There's the three-story 1930's mission-style stucco mansion owned by Hollywood's own singing and acting sensation, Liza Ruff!"

Liza regarded her gravely.

"And look!" Lauren couldn't help herself. "There's the fabulous beachside compound owned by Lauren Turnbell-Smythe—the woman behind the success of *The April Webster Show*!"

"Lauren!" Melissa giggled, jerking her marsh-mallow suddenly away from the flames.

"To fame and personal—like, uh—totally mega summer fulfillment," Lauren toasted, faking her best Valley Girl accent.

"To the beach." Winnie lifted her cup.

"To whatever comes," Melissa joined in, rolling her eyes.

"Yeah!" Liza upturned her cup and drank its contents in one characteristically dramatic gulp. "Whatever we've got coming, Oh god of fame and fortune—we're ready for it."

Two
·················

"That man has a python wrapped around his neck," Winnie shrieked out of the Jeep's window as it cruised down the unspeakably hip Melrose Avenue.

Liza bit the tip of her shiny nail, her feelings swinging wildly between excitement and excruciating terror.

At this very moment, Lauren, Melissa, and Winnie were delivering her to The Palace. Since learning about the music club, Liza had managed to convince herself that in the few short months they'd been apart, Travis had catapulted out of her league. Maybe he was a really big-time star now, who would pretend she didn't exist. Or maybe, when they met, he would scoop her up in his arms passionately, in front of all the stars and wannabes at the hottest club in Hollywood, automatically confirming her place in his heart and in the glittering firmament that was L.A.

Hoooooonk! Winnie and even Melissa laughed as the sudden noise made Liza jump and she dropped with a thud back to reality.

Trying to relax, she savored the warm breeze that caressed her hair as the Jeep made its way through the stop-and-go traffic, crisscrossed by jay-walking pedestrians, bicyclists, and guys on skate-boards. Glittery darkness settled over the boulevard, like a party just getting under way. The sidewalks were thick with beautiful people—strolling and toss-ing their heads, as if L.A. were the only place to be, and Melrose Avenue was the center of it all.

Liza looked down nervously at her skintight pur-ple leather skirt and midriff chiffon top that flut-tered in the mildest breeze. Her heart began to pump; her mouth was dry. Travis. All she had to do was think about Travis, and her body went berserk. He was famous. He was successful. A thousand girls were cooing over his shaggy brown hair. Swooning over his sky-blue eyes. It was one thing to walk through the front door of The Palace and hunt him down. It was another to be unequivocally rejected. Was she really prepared?

She leaned her head back and thought. Last spring, when she'd met Travis in L.A., he'd been the first boy who'd ever completely accepted her—just the way she was. He hadn't laughed at the wild clothes she liked to wear or her crazy skits and impersonations. He hadn't made fun of her soaring ambitions. He was the first person who'd ever made her feel as if she belonged—really belonged—to someone. She knew even then that she loved Travis. She would always love him. No matter what happened this summer.

"You look really good," Lauren said, glancing briefly away from the traffic to pat her on the knee.

Liza bit her lip. She used to think Lauren was a stuck-up snob. The only reason Liza knew her at all was because she'd roomed with Winnie's best friend, Faith Crowley, who was also one of Lauren's friends. But even though Lauren was a little on the intense side—being a writer and all—she had a big heart.

"Thanks," Liza said, trying to sound upbeat. "I picked up this little number at a sorority garage sale. The top's supposed to be a nightie, but I thought it had nightclub written all over it."

The smell of spicy cooking, espresso, and car fumes made Liza want to jump out of the car and walk. Impatient, she flicked on an AM radio station.

". . . because he's finally allowed his inner child to say yes, instead of pushing him into the prison of no," a melodious radio voice was preaching.

Lauren reached over and turned it up, giggling. "Yes. Hey, Win," she yelled over her shoulder, "this is the shrink I've been telling you about."

"Who?" Winnie yelled back over the blaring CD player in the convertible next to them.

Lauren stepped on the gas and laughed. "Dr. Angela Pressman. She's KQET's nightly call-in psychologist. Very popular. Likes to pepper her advice with gossip about various stars she's counseled."

"Hello, I'm Dr. Angela Pressman. You're on the air. How can I help you tonight?"

"Um. Dr. Pressman?" The voice of an insecure young man came on. "Uh—like—I don't really want to give my name out, but I just landed a major role on a network sitcom. . . ."

"Congratulations," Dr. Pressman said cheerfully.

Liza's ears pricked up.

"Uh—yeah—but like things aren't the same now. I mean, like, I'm making the big bucks and everything, but I've got people on my back all the time now. Go there. Say this. Sign here. I'm flippin' out, man. I guess—I—like—can't handle it."

"Get a life," Melissa said with disgust.

"Give him a break," Winnie snapped.

"Yeah." Liza sighed, jealous. "Celebrities have a right to be miserable too."

"What I hear you saying is this," Dr. Pressman said matter-of-factly. "The fame and fortune you've longed for has finally arrived. But you've just discovered the hidden price tag. The huge price you must pay for this gift . . ."

Liza gulped and stared ahead. What price did Travis have to pay?

"It's time to find a place within you where your inner child can be at peace," Dr. Pressman said with firmness. "You can find a place for intimacy—for nurturing—even if it means eventually giving up the things you thought were important. . . ."

Liza closed her eyes. Travis wasn't like the guy on the radio, was he? The Travis she knew was grounded. He already knew about intimacy and nurturing. He was the most wonderful, tender, giving person she'd ever met. Liza felt her eyes grow hot with tears. Travis would have laughed at the deal makers and bean counters of Hollywood. The music was the important thing. Travis just wanted to touch people with his music.

The Jeep suddenly slowed as the Melrose Avenue traffic thickened, and the sound of music from a hundred convertibles converged on Liza's ears. To the left a row of hot-pink-and-green neon palm trees flashed against the sky.

"There it is—The Palace on Melrose," Lauren said suddenly, her voice betraying her excitement. "And look at the line."

Liza gasped. A splashy purple sign flashed "The Palace" against the night. Below sat the club itself, a large, square building with a rough brick-and-glass front. The sidewalk was teeming with people.

Travis. They're waiting to see Travis—just like me. Liza looked desperately at the club's street number, which quivered in black lights above the door.

"Cool," Winnie breathed. "Very cool."

"Wait," Liza said abruptly, digging into her purse. "Two-zero-seventeen?"

"That's what it says." Lauren reached over and opened Liza's door. "Now, go get 'em. Drop names. Hustle. Flatter. Do what it takes to get into that dressing room of his."

Liza found the slip of paper in her purse and stared at it, her neck taut with tension. She looked around in wild confusion. It was all wrong. She looked back, then ahead. "This isn't the right address," she cried. "It's at least four blocks ahead. Two-four-seventy."

Lauren frowned. "Really? But it looks like we're leaving the hot part—"

"Drive," Liza ordered, her heart thumping. She slammed the door shut as Lauren stepped on the gas and veered back into the traffic.

Liza didn't realize she was biting her nails until she tasted the polish in her mouth. The car was moving faster now, and a few moments later Liza saw it—a building shaped like a miniature fairy-tale palace looming on their right. Dotted with tiny triangular flags, it had undersize towers and a slightly grungy red carpet that spilled from the fluorescent-lit entrance to the sidewalk.

"Maybe Travis doesn't work at a music club!" Liza exclaimed, her heart strangely light. She looked up at the sign and checked the street number again. "Maybe his roommate meant Palace Burgers."

"No," Winnie blurted.

Liza felt her neck muscles relax. She took a deep breath. "Smell those hamburgers and fat-dunked french fries."

Lauren's violet eyes looked guilty. "Gee, Liza . . . if you're right, I'm sorry I got your hopes up. . . ."

Liza sat still for a moment, trying to quiet her heart as a huge wave of relief washed over her. She wanted success for Travis. Of course she did. But she wanted to pick up with him just where they'd left off. She wanted them to succeed together, side by side. She could handle Palace Burgers. She could definitely handle it.

"Wait here," Liza said quietly. She stepped out of the Jeep, full of renewed hope. Travis was still struggling, just like her. He was still within her reach.

"I'll come with you," she heard Winnie yell behind her as she sailed up the stairs and shoved open the front glass door. Once inside, Liza looked around, catching her breath. Palace Burgers was a bustling, not-too-grungy burger joint, filled with plush booths and decorated with shields and crossed swords. The serving crew wore Elizabethan belted tunics and little felt caps with feathers sticking out the top.

"Poor Travis," Winnie was babbling. "This is definitely not his style."

"Excuse me," Liza whispered, ignoring Winnie and scurrying past a crowd of people lined up along a velvet rope. Just then she saw a familiar form slapping a stack of preformed beef patties onto a steel grill.

Liza gasped and covered her mouth with one hand.

Travis. It was Travis. Her good, patient, down-to-earth Travis. Still struggling. Still hoping. Still believing. Just as she was.

"Travis?" Winnie was saying in a low, disbelieving voice behind her. "Flipping burgers?"

Travis turned slightly, and Liza could see his clear blue eyes studying a customer order over the grill. She caught her breath as she took in the reality of the scene. His sweet, soulful brow was glistening with sweat. His ponytail stuck out of the back of a corny chef's hat that was shaped like a crown. Now that she could see things as they really were, she knew her feelings hadn't changed at all.

You are the most beautiful thing I've ever seen in my life, Travis Bennett.

"Travis?" Liza whispered, inching forward, her heart swelling partly in joy, partly in pain. Sure, Travis was a struggling artist. But what was he doing in a burger joint? He was a musician. A songwriter. A rare and gentle talent. Was this all the world could offer someone like Travis Bennett?

"Are you in line?" a woman's voice broke into her thoughts.

Liza shook her head and wiped away a tear, letting the crowd jostle her for a moment before she heard Travis behind the counter—singing. Singing? She looked up in shock. In the split second since she'd looked away, Travis had turned to face the line of hungry customers. Wearing a playful smile, he'd placed his hand dramatically on his chest and had begun singing a folksy Renaissance ballad about a lonely maiden in a tower.

"That's Travis for you," Winnie said with a catch in her voice as Travis made a quick turn away from his audience to flip a line of sizzling burgers.

Liza began to laugh through her tears. Suddenly everything about last spring with Travis came back to her. There was his funny, lopsided grin. The goofy way he wiggled his eyebrows. The brightness of his smile that seemed to light up everything in the room. She watched in amazement as Travis turned to the crowd and finished the tune, sliding his hip up on the counter and motioning for the customers to join him. Dozens began singing. Travis's song apparently was a regular Palace Burgers act. Tears spilled down Liza's face as he finished, then yanked off his crown hat and bowed. He grinned at the applause and was about to return to his meat patties when he glanced her way.

"Travis!" Liza suddenly burst out.

She watched as his face froze. Then his eyes locked on to hers. She felt her heart beating wildly in her chest. He was just standing there, his lips slightly parted, as if he, too, needed a moment to believe it was really she. Then he put both hands on his head and let his mouth melt into a radiant smile.

"Liza!" Travis yelled over the crowd. "Liza!" he shouted again, leaping over the counter. He rushed toward her. "Liza!" he repeated softly, his eyes glued

to hers, weaving his way through the crowd of customers. As he drew near, he slipped his hands up her
arms and gripped her shoulders, staring joyfully into
her eyes. "You're back. What are you doing here?"

Liza nodded wordlessly, unable to speak. Travis's
eyes were shining so sweetly. It was as if everything
else in the world had vanished. The people in the
restaurant. The time they'd spent apart. All that
mattered was that they were together again, at last.
She tugged silently at the tie of his apron, her
mouth trembling, not knowing what to say or do.
But she didn't really care. Because for the first time
in her life, Liza realized that there was someone who
felt exactly the way she did.

His face drew near, and then Travis kissed her
gently on the lips. A long, blissful moment passed as
Liza hung on to the kiss, moving closer to him until
she could feel his heart beating beneath his purple-
and-gold Palace Burgers uniform.

"Yeah!" someone in the crowd suddenly shouted.
Liza gave the room a dazed look of disbelief as the
crowd burst into another round of applause.

Winnie hurried out of Palace Burgers alone and
jumped into the backseat of the idling Jeep, slamming the door.

"Travis and Liza," Winnie muttered in disgust.
Her mind kept flipping back to Paris, where she and
Travis had met. Travis had been her first real love.
What they had was special and private and gentle.

What they had could never be experienced by a pudgy airhead like Liza.

Pudgy airhead? Was she really thinking these thoughts about her friend?

"Well?" Lauren asked, looking casually over her shoulder. "Was he there? Did Liza find him?"

"Oh, yeah," Winnie said shortly, staring down at her Snow White and the Seven Dwarves charm bracelet. "It was all very touching. They're stuck together like two wads of chewed gum. Soulful, sensitive Travis and loudmouth Liza. Hey, the perfect couple."

Lauren and Melissa looked at each other wordlessly. "Sounds perfect to me," Lauren finally said, bursting into giggles.

Winnie couldn't believe it. She'd just watched her first love fall into the arms of Liza Ruff, someone he had no business being with. She was clearly upset. Couldn't her friends see that? Did Lauren and Mel think she was some kind of unfeeling robot? Did they even consider her a friend?

As the two young women chattered mindlessly away in the front seat, Winnie clamped her hands over her ears. "Stop!"

"What?" Lauren and Mel said in unison, looking back.

Winnie's lower lip trembled. She shifted. "Look, I'm sorry, but I just saw Travis."

"Oh," Lauren said with a confused look. "Yeah. You did. Um. Look. Is this upsetting you?"

"Lauren, he was the first boy I ever loved," Winnie shot back, whipping out her seat belt and buckling it. "Do you think he had two words to say to me inside that divey restaurant? No."

Melissa and Lauren looked at Winnie for a moment, unable to react as they began to comprehend. "Sorry, Win," Melissa said quietly, looking awkward.

"Yeah, sure," Winnie replied, shifting in her seat. She looked down at her sandals and suddenly felt completely alone.

Tears fell slowly from Winnie's eyes. She wondered how her hometown friends KC Angeletti and Faith Crowley would have reacted. They probably would have given her a hug, listened to her. They would have understood. Now, without them for the first time in ages, she felt homesick and abandoned. She stared at the front door of Palace Burgers, when it suddenly flew open. She watched as Liza skipped out, her hair flying, a giddy grin plastered across her face.

"I'm in love, I'm in love, I'm in love with a won—der—ful GUUUUUY!" Liza's foghorn voice blared into the night. She jumped in next to Winnie and slammed the door.

"So, it went okay?" Lauren deadpanned, releasing the hand brake and pulling back into the traffic.

Liza clasped her hands over her chest and slumped in the seat next to Winnie. "He's picking me up tomorrow night," she said, with a dreamy look back at the restaurant's neon sign. "He never forgot me. He's flipping frozen cow at Palace Burgers, but he's still working on his music and he still has hope."

"Yes," Lauren and Melissa said in unison, reaching back to slap Liza's upturned palms.

Winnie, feeling her eyes grow hot, turned and looked out the window. Everyone had somebody or something to hold on to. Except her. And only months before, her life had been filled with people and purpose. She had her husband, Josh. Her baby on the way. Her friends. Her life. How had everything changed so fast?

Winnie sighed as the Jeep sped through the cool night, her companions' laughter only making her heart grow sadly, unbearably heavy.

Three

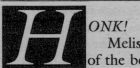*ONK!*

Melissa hesitated at the front door of the beach house. The air smelled of salt and seaweed. The waves thundered in, and the warm beach beckoned.

HONK! HONK!

Fear and dread swept through her. It was nine o'clock Monday morning, and she absolutely had to begin looking for a job.

"Come on," Lauren yelled out the car window.

Melissa took one last longing look at the ocean. As Lauren had promised, Melissa was tagging along to the TV studio, hoping to get lucky with a job of her own. But all she wanted to do now was go back to her bedroom, crawl under the covers, and sleep until noon.

"Grab your blazer," Lauren shouted.

"O-*kay*," Melissa said softly, reaching back to grab a light jacket out of the closet, then slamming the front door.

As she climbed into the Jeep, Lauren flipped down the visor and checked out her lipstick in the makeup mirror. She was wearing her belted khaki skirt and lemon-yellow blazer, looking important. "I know you don't want to come, Mel. But they've got to actually *see* you if you're going to have any chance at all."

"Right," Melissa mumbled, slipping on her sunglasses and pulling a baseball cap down over her eyes as Lauren headed up the hill toward the coastal highway. Everything in southern California was so *bright*.

Mel was used to mountain forests—and dark libraries, where she hunched over her chemistry textbooks. There was something about this place that made her feel like a bug under a microscope. Suddenly she didn't want to be seen at all.

Lauren drummed on the steering wheel happily as they began heading south into Santa Monica, where *The April Webster Show* TV studio was located. From the road they could see the light sparkling off the ocean and the sea gulls hovering along the sandy cliffs. After a few minutes the road widened, and Lauren began anxiously checking for the right exit ramp.

Melissa wiped a sheen of perspiration from her forehead. Lauren looked so cool and together. After all, she'd lived in New York and had traveled all over the world. And she knew Lauren was right. Lauren knew her better than she knew herself. But she didn't feel like facing anything right now. Instead, she flicked on the car radio.

". . . and there's major gridlock on all highways and surface streets . . ." a voice was chattering.

Lauren switched it off, then gave Melissa a sympathetic look. "Uh—Mel, I'd say you look like you just fell into a snake pit. Try relaxing. Just enjoy the scene. You don't have to be a part of it."

"I can't," Melissa said quietly. Up ahead computerized freeway signs were warning of a traffic accident. She shut her eyes, then looked up at the ceiling of the Jeep, which Lauren had attached so they wouldn't look like wind-tunnel refugees when they arrived at the studio. "Look, this is all too new, okay? Change is hard for me—you know—after last year."

Lauren nodded.

Melissa didn't like to think about last year. Brooks had asked her to marry him, then deserted her at the altar. After that she'd sunk into grief and despair, even flirting with steroids to boost her performance on the track. It was all behind her now, but it made her realize how vulnerable she was under her thin armor of straight A's and record-breaking track times. Nothing she'd achieved back home mattered now. She was a stranger in L.A.

Lauren turned on her blinker and left the freeway. A long ramp hurtled them down into the thick Santa Monica traffic. Horns honked. Exhaust fumes rose. Billboards advertised new television shows. "I think you're going to get used to it," Lauren said confidently. "You're stronger than you think, and we're going to be there for you."

Melissa looked away, trying not to cry. A row of lush palms stood on each side of the four-lane boulevard, which was lined with office buildings, small restaurants, and parking lots.

"There it is," Lauren said softly, pushing her sunglasses up on her nose and slowing down.

They drove past a group of two-story windowless buildings that took up two square blocks. Plastered on the side facing them was a huge billboard with a splashy picture of April Webster throwing back her head and laughing into a microphone. Under the picture was painted in huge block letters the word *APRIL!*

"I'm getting goose bumps," Lauren admitted.

Halfway down the block Lauren braked and turned into a small entrance with a sign that read Santa Monica Television City. After flashing her pass at a man inside a security hut, they drove inside and saw that it was a huge compound, made up of large hangarlike buildings surrounded by parking lots and temporary trailers.

"There it is!" Lauren cried as they passed an

awning over a small Spanish-style stucco building whose awning proclaimed *The April Webster Show.* "I wonder where I'm supposed to park."

"There's one," Melissa called out, pointing toward a scraggly tree.

Soon they stood in a small, empty reception area. A gray carpet covered the floor, and a large photograph of April hung over a peach-colored couch. Down a hall they could hear laughing and talking. Quickly smoothing her hair into place, Lauren headed down the hall, which was decorated with bright tapestries and textiles and posters of April. Melissa followed after Lauren's example, frantically whipping off the baseball cap and feeling to make sure her hair wasn't too badly out of place. As they turned the corner, they interrupted two women with clipboards in the middle of a heated discussion.

"Um—excuse me," Lauren said. "I'm looking for Elaine Crouse."

One woman with extremely short red hair nodded distractedly and pointed down the hall. "Take your first right, then second left. She's three doors down on the right."

Lauren dashed down the hall, and Melissa continued to follow, feeling more out of place by the second. Walls opened up into dressing rooms, makeup rooms, and a vast wardrobe room filled with racks of suits.

Lauren stopped and turned back, panicked.

"There is no second left. Wait here. I'm going back to ask."

Melissa nodded. A moment later a crew carrying cables, lights, and other equipment she couldn't identify hurried by her. "Make way, please," one of them boomed, and though Melissa was surprised at his cheerful, offhand politeness, she was self-conscious and embarrassed to be in the way. A swinging door stood behind her, the only way she *could* "make way," so she ducked through it. A rush of noise poured over her. Melissa narrowed her eyes in the dim light and turned. She was at the edge of a cavernous studio. Ahead of her, a brightly lit set seemed to float in the darkness. Cameras on huge wheeled carts were positioned throughout the room.

"Yeah—okay—I want to give this one more shot," a woman's deep voice called over a speaker. Melissa stepped back, trembling. She didn't have much time for daytime talk shows at home, but she recognized that voice. It was the voice of April Webster. Quickly Melissa slipped into the shadows behind a bank of bleachers, desperately hoping no one had seen her.

"Okay, April," a frizzy-haired woman with a clipboard and a headset barked.

Melissa stared. It looked like a show rehearsal. April Webster climbed the steps to the set and stood there casually, holding a piece of paper and studying it. Slim but tall, a larger-than-life presence even without the help of television cameras, she wore a sleek, chic aquamarine silk suit that complemented her dark complexion, and a traditional African head-wrap that looked equally chic, as though the suit were designed to go with it. A heavy gold necklace and sparkling diamond bracelet suggested how successful her television show had become. Her wardrobe was eclipsed only by her own energy, which radiated into the studio like a million-watt light bulb. Lighting technicians, stage managers, and young women wearing headsets dashed back and forth, but she seemed to be completely composed.

"Yeah." April suddenly looked up from the paper, which she'd apparently been memorizing. Her face broke into a cheerful but slightly stressed-out smile that Melissa liked. "I'm going to run through this a few times."

"Shoot," the girl replied, walking off, clamping her headset to one ear as if she'd received a distant order.

"His name is Walker Ingham," April began rehearsing her introduction for the day's show. She stopped and took a brief sip of coffee from a Styrofoam cup. "It's not a name familiar to most people in America—yet. But in Hollywood's gold-plated circles, he's given new meaning and spiritual depth to the lives of many entertainers who once thought they had it all."

"Is that too long, April?" the frizzy-haired girl interrupted. "The writers wanted to know."

April gave her a patient look and unbuttoned the front of her suit. "This'll work."

Melissa stared in fascination. But when April's intense brown eyes suddenly scanned the room, Melissa shrank back, terrified of being swept into April's own circle of energy. Spotting a small doorway into a waiting room off the studio, Melissa edged through it unnoticed. The room was empty, but two television monitors were positioned over the couches. The monitors showed the set from two different angles and were turned on. From the waiting room anyone could watch April rehearsing.

"Ingham's incredible fund-raising abilities have benefited the poor and the desperate around the world—from the projects of south Los Angeles to the famine-ravaged countries of eastern Africa," April continued. Melissa frowned. She must be really out of it. She'd never heard of the guy. "For the next hour we'll be talking with Walker Ingham. How does he raise millions? The amazing secret is that he doesn't even have to ask—because he is literally changing the lives of his followers. Through a strict regime of meditation, diet, and Spartan living, the Ingham Institute is teaching many of Hollywood's most powerful to accept their success and return at least some of their fabulous wealth to the less fortunate. Ladies and gentlemen, please give a warm welcome to Mr. Walker Ingham!"

"Okay," Melissa heard the frizzy-haired girl say briskly, "about forty-five seconds. Good. Okay."

"Mmmmm," April replied, chewing on the end of a pencil. "Let's change *fabulous wealth* to *cold, hard cash*. It's sounds more realistic. I'm going to run it through again."

"Okay, April," the girl said cheerily.

A door behind her opened and Melissa jumped.

"*There* you are," Lauren burst out, rushing into the waiting room, followed by a stern-looking man in a suit and two women in flapping linen jackets and razor-new haircuts. "Look, I'll be right back. Elaine's supposed to be in her office in a sec." She rushed out again.

Melissa sat on one of the couches. For all she knew, she was doomed to spend the rest of the day in the waiting room, pretending she was a potted plant.

"*Okay!* Finally!" A thin, early-fiftyish woman with sleek blond hair and a black skirt blew into the room, followed by Lauren. Melissa sat up taller as Lauren gave her a short nod and motioned for her to join them. "I've got advertising down my neck on next week's lineup, and if I don't get to my masseuse this week, I'm going to have a *permanent headache.*"

"Um, Elaine," Lauren spoke up as the woman collapsed onto a nearby couch. "This is my friend Melissa McDormand. Melissa, this is Elaine Crouse. She produces *The April Webster Show.*"

Melissa started to get up.

"Don't get up," Elaine barked, yanking open a

manila file and waving her away. "Great to meet you. *Now*." The woman turned back to Lauren. She flipped back a wedge of hair, waved at a passing technician, and read a memo all at the same time. "Your job is basically to do anything we ask. I know that sounds terrible and fascist and it is. But this is what we need. We need you to dig for files. Bring the coffee. Find props. Check spelling. Make last-minute phone calls when the research department screws up. In other words, you're a lapdog, but you might get something out of it, and if you don't— don't complain to me like the last intern did, because he gave me a migraine that lasted two days."

Melissa cringed. The woman was talking at such a frantic pace, she could barely understand what she was saying. Lauren, however, seemed perfectly calm.

"I can handle it, Elaine," Lauren said with a polished smile.

"Fine." Elaine stood up, stuck her hand out for a single shake, and started to bolt back out the door. "Check in with research."

Melissa's heart sank. Elaine was rushing away and Lauren hadn't mentioned anything about a job.

"Elaine, there's one more thing," Lauren called out boldly, giving Melissa a determined, sideways glance. "Melissa is job-hunting in the L.A. area this summer. Who should she ask about openings on this show?"

Elaine gave Lauren an irritated look and opened her mouth to say something. The next moment, however, there was a sound at the door, and April Webster came storming in, waving a sheet of paper.

"Elaine!" April boomed, her perfume suddenly flooding the room. Melissa's eyes opened wide. Everything about April Webster was large and shiny. Even the powerfully chic Elaine seemed to shrink in her presence. "'Stray Animals—How Two Families Cope with the Devastation of Rabies,'" April read a short blurb on a piece of paper. "Rabies? Rabies for one, solid *hour*? Elaine—this is crazy. People are going to be reaching for their remotes faster than you can say *doggie*. This is *not* appealing. This is *not* young. This is not the way to attract all those kids home from school for the summer."

Elaine's face went sharp. "But you wanted an animal spot. . . ."

"I wanted something *fun*," April roared back, slapping the blurb down on a table. "Something *darling*—like—like people who dress up their poodles. Or—or movie-star animals. Yes. Round up a bunch of famous animals. All the big family-film hits have pet dogs in them. *Get* them. *Bring* them here. Find out why people fall in love with them. . . ."

Elaine was scribbling something down, looking harassed. "Okay, April. I'll send a proposal over to Arnold's Animal Stars right now by bike messenger—oh, hell," she snapped. "I hired a messenger, and the bubble brain hasn't shown up yet."

"Get another one!" April boomed. "Santa Monica is full of people on bicycles!"

Melissa felt a nudge in her side. "Volunteer," Lauren whispered. "It's perfect. You're in great shape. You can stay in training."

Panicked, Melissa bit her lip and stared numbly at Lauren. Bike messenger? There was no way she'd find her way around Santa Monica.

"Melissa will be your new bike messenger. She's an excellent athlete, and she's available right now," Lauren said swiftly, nudging Melissa forward.

"Okay—fine," Elaine said distractedly, glancing at April, who was already involved in another conversation and was drifting back into the studio. "Check with Della at the front desk. She'll tell you where to go."

One hour later Melissa was standing in the glaring sunshine outside *The April Webster Show* offices. A shiny cross-training bike was perched between her legs, a beeper was hooked to her belt, and a map of Santa Monica Television City was spread out over the handlebars. In her pack was Elaine's envelope for Arnold's Animal Stars.

Melissa pushed off and pumped swiftly through the maze of parking lots, trailers, and buzzing golf carts. The famous animal trainer's shop was just across the street from the north end of the studio compound. But the compound itself was vast. Terrified, Melissa dodged careening sports cars, fast-moving equipment trucks, and huge groups of tourists. After a panicky trip she finally spotted Arnold's.

Wiping her forehead with the back of her hand, Melissa walked through Arnold's metal gate off the sidewalk. Once inside she realized she was in a quiet courtyard, shaded by leafy trees. A small building with an ornate, star-studded "Arnold's Animal Stars" sign next to the door was just ahead. Quickly she pushed her bike foward. To her left a row of spacious kennels appeared. In the corner of one was a magnificent German shepherd.

"Hi, good doggie, doggie," Melissa said off-handedly, relieved to have reached her destination. She made a cheerful kissing noise with her lips.

Suddenly, without warning, the German shepherd jumped to his feet and lunged at the fence, missing Melissa's thigh by inches. Melissa toppled over with her bike and crashed onto the cement pathway. She looked in horror at the dog's fangs and dripping saliva. It almost looked as if its powerful forelegs were capable of wrenching the gate off the kennel fence. Closing her eyes, Melissa felt a pain in her leg and all the breath leaving her body.

"Stop, Gretchen," an elderly voice barked in the distance. She heard a distant door slam and awkwardly tried to scramble to her feet. A short, gray-haired man wearing an open-neck fuchsia shirt ran toward her. "Down. Bad."

Melissa let her breath out again as the dog instantly hunkered back in its corner.

"Please forgive the dog." The man spoke with a slight accent. He extended his hand to help her up.

"You must have inadvertently given him a signal. He was only acting."

"Yeah," Melissa gasped. "I made a little kissing sound." She reached into her pack and handed him the envelope from Elaine.

"Ah," the man exclaimed, looking at the return address. "This is good news. Publicity is always good." He turned and gave the dog a slight hand signal. The dog leaped happily forward and licked his hand through the cage.

"Thank you, miss," he said. He dug into his pocket and pulled out a twenty-dollar bill, pressing it into Melissa's hand. "Maybe we'll see you soon."

"Thank you," Melissa said breathlessly, looking down at the tip. She was shocked at the man's unexpected monetary acknowledgment.

Then a thought occurred to her: Maybe it *wasn't* strangely generous for this man to be tipping her twenty dollars. Maybe it happened to bike messengers all the time. Suddenly Melissa's summer was looking up—way up.

Four

heck with the control booth right away, Lauren," an assistant producer was barking. "Make sure they've got the correct spelling of Walker Ingham's health center in Zimbabwe. It's W-E-B-E-K-E-M-A-M-B-U."

Lauren scribbled down the spelling and nodded. A thrill shot through her. She was quick. She was smart. They were definitely going to love her this summer. "Got it."

"Check with janitorial about the gum on the floor of aisle seven too, Lauren," the woman shouted, grasping her telephone receiver. "April lost her shoe yesterday on it. Almost busted her fanny in front of the entire universe."

"Right," Lauren replied, rushing out of the room. She stopped momentarily in the hall and brushed a wisp of hair out of her eyes. She'd started her *April Webster* internship only three hours ago, but already her head was jumping with a million tiny, interesting details. The taping of April's show with Walker Ingham was scheduled to begin in less than an hour.

Racing down the hall to the control booth, Lauren weaved her way through wardrobe racks, technicians, and harried-looking assistants. So far she'd run at least a dozen errands: checking with wardrobe on the color of Ingham's shirt, buying coffee and doughnuts for the show's producer and five assistants, making twenty copies of April's script, and faxing a show proposal to the agent of a famous child star. After opening a door that said No Admittance, Lauren walked up a narrow staircase and reached a dark room. A bank of small television screens was surrounded by dials and switches. A large soundproof window looked out over the studio.

"Um, excuse me," Lauren said softly. Two guys and a woman in jeans and a tanktop were sitting in swivel chairs, chuckling over a tape running in one of the monitors.

"Hey, a new face," one of the guys said brightly, flipping a bank of switches and twirling in his seat. Lauren recognized him as the show's director. "Don't tell me. You're Elaine's new summer slave."

Lauren grinned, liking him immediately. She liked everyone on the show so far.

"That's right."

"That Elaine," the girl in the tank top drawled. "Actually, she's a kitten underneath that layer of Max Factor. You'll have fun. The last one did. Got some big job in New York."

Lauren handed the first guy the correct spelling of Webekemambu. She gave the girl a grateful smile. "Thanks."

"Thank you too," the director said cheerfully, flipping up a computer screen on which the show's credits and subtitles were created. "Lookin' good. Would you tell Elaine we're still waiting for the ten-minute tape on Ingham's self-help seminars? We might need to use it if the show lags."

"Sure," Lauren replied. By the end of the week she'd probably be hanging out on Melrose Avenue with these very cool people. Talking shop. Swapping stories. She suddenly felt giddy. Sighing with happiness, she turned and headed down the stairway.

A moment later she was passing one of the makeup rooms when a flash of aquamarine silk caught her eye. Quickly she realized it was April, and the slender man in the makeup chair she recognized from brochures as Walker Ingham.

"Come on in here, dear," she heard April's voice calling.

Lauren froze. She took a few steps backward and looked in the door. April, who was sitting cross-legged on a couch, looked more relaxed than she'd been in the morning. She gave Lauren a friendly point and gazed up at the ceiling.

"Elaine's new intern, right?" April said hurriedly, as if she were trying to remember her name but couldn't. "Look. Welcome to the show. We'll talk later. Can you hang out a sec? I've got something for you."

Lauren felt the blood rush to her head, but she tried to act casual as she leaned into the doorjamb. Her first day on the job, and April wanted her to hang out? Was she dreaming? "Sure," Lauren said swiftly.

"Okay." April sat back in her couch and made a steeple with her long, ringed fingers. In the makeup chair Walker Ingham was being coated with pancake foundation by a woman wearing a white coat. "One of the questions I'll be asking is the obvious one, Walker. Why does Hollywood find you so appealing? I mean, the people you reach are people who are literally *hounded* on a daily basis for their money and their talent."

Lauren watched as Walker Ingham's face turned thoughtful. A serene-looking man in his early fifties, Walker had short-clipped gray hair, blue eyes, and a squarish jaw. His full mouth softened his features and gave him a certain appeal that Lauren decided was almost sexy. Wearing a long-sleeved gray T-shirt, jeans, and running shoes, Walker was a small, slim man who looked as if he worked out every day. "Because

I give these people something they need very badly," he said quietly.

April looked at him, then shifted in her seat. Lauren could see that even in the presence of this famous woman, Walker was somehow more powerful. His blue eyes looked like two mesmerizing, glowing stones. "What's that—that you, uh, give them?"

"I give them permission to celebrate and honor their success as human beings," Walker replied simply.

"Sooooo." April looked up to the ceiling. "You're saying that most of these people can't do this on their own?"

"Most of the celebrities are miserable when I first meet with them. You see, many of them struggled to get to the mountaintop. Once there, they look down and can't forget the sweltering masses below. They feel guilt. They feel unimaginable pain and loneliness. What I give them is a way out. I do the good deeds they don't have time for—but which they can easily afford. I offer a trusted channel for their innate generosity."

April nodded vigorously, her intense brown eyes fixed on him like glue. "So the medical clinics, the orphanages, the schools and food banks—they're good for the world. . . ."

"But, you see, they're also good for the people who make millions entertaining us with their art," Walker interrupted. "They have gifts. And the world has chosen to reward these particular gifts with great riches."

"So you take the millions . . ." April began.

Walker's blue eyes flooded with concern. He shook his head vigorously. "Oh, no, April. I don't personally benefit. In fact, I live quite simply. I serve only as a medium through which the money flows into these wonderful, helping organizations throughout the world."

Lauren knitted her eyebrows and reflected. She'd been preparing herself for a summer filled with power-hungry egos. The entertainment industry was famous for them. But this guy was different.

April extended her hand and touched Walker's knee, obviously moved. "And you're an inspiration to a lot of people, Walker. We're going to have a great show. Just relax, be yourself, and let me know if you need anything during the commercial breaks. . . ."

"Five minutes." Elaine popped her head in with a pleasant smile. "Anything I can get you before you go on, Walker? Last-minute snack or perhaps a glass of wine?"

Walker stood up from his makeup chair and stretched his arms forward. "Thank you, Elaine," Walker replied with a pleasant smile. "I had a late breakfast, and I don't drink alcohol. But I would appreciate a glass of vegetable juice after the show. I'll probably need it."

Lauren watched as Elaine opened her mouth to agree, then let her eyes drift into a momentary panic. It was clear that vegetable juice was probably the one thing *The April Webster Show*'s refrigerator lacked.

"I'll take care of that, Elaine," Lauren quickly offered.

Elaine's face broke into an expression of relieved victory. She placed her manicured hand on Lauren's shoulder and beamed at April and Walker. "Lauren Turnbell-Smythe," she said with mock severity. "Remember that name. This girl is going places. Thanks, Lauren."

Quickly Lauren ducked out of the room, grabbed her purse, and rushed for the parking lot. Her chest felt as if it were going to burst with happiness. Her first day on the job, and it was apparent she'd scored big-time points with Elaine.

Once outside, Lauren stepped quickly across the parking lot, digging into her wallet for spare cash and keys. But when she looked up again, she saw a young guy with dark hair hovering over the Jeep. She stared in horror as he worked at her door handles and peered through her windshield. The guy looked like some kind of thief who'd sneaked into the lot, eager to plunder the rich supply of fancy vehicles.

Every muscle in her body turned rigid.

"What am I going to do?" Lauren whispered to herself. She stopped on the hot pavement, trying desperately to think. Her self-defense-class training suddenly leaped into the forefront of her brain.

Focus the anger that is within you. You are not a

victim. You are powerful. Take your basic defense position. Let your elbow drive the fist forward. . . .

Seething with anger, Lauren stormed forward, though her gut instinct slowed her for an instant. The guy, who was now trying to jiggle the door open, didn't look like a thief. He looked more like an attractive spy who wanted something from inside her car. Wearing a navy sport coat, orange T-shirt, jeans, and running shoes, Lauren could tell he'd dressed to fit into the Television City scene. She stepped forward, not knowing whether to deliver one of her famous elbow jabs or an ear twist. She paused; the guy was still looking intently into her car. His hair, slightly long and curling, was brushed back. He wore a pair of clear-framed glasses, and his face was attractive and well shaped—handsome, even.

Finally Lauren took a breath. She was ten feet from him, and he hadn't even noticed her.

"What are you doing to my Jeep!" Lauren finally burst out.

The guy turned, only slightly startled, then narrowed his dark-brown eyes in anger. "This is *your* Jeep?" he spit back, jutting out his chin and rubbing the back of his neck in frustration. "Who are *you*?"

"I'm Lauren Turnbell-Smythe," she breathed hotly. "I'm a new staffer with *The April Webster Show*, and this is my Jeep you're trying to get into."

The guy's hard look faltered slightly. He stuffed his hands into his jeans pockets, looking a little embarrassed. "Who told you to park here?" he asked.

Then, with an expression of anger and utter frustration, he looked toward the sky and resignedly shook his head. "They don't even have the decency to tell me first," he muttered. Slowly, he began walking away toward the security hut.

Lauren squinted at his back, totally confused. "No one *told* me to park here," she finally called out. "I—um—I'm Elaine Crouse's new summer intern."

He broke into a relieved smile, raking his fingers through his dark hair. "I think L.A. is finally starting to get to me," he explained in his rapid, East Coast voice. He extended his hand. Lauren noticed his long fingers and leather watchband. "Look—I'm Max Cantor. I'm a researcher with April's show."

Lauren felt totally confused. "Well—then—why were you trying to get into my car?"

Max knelt down and pointed under the Jeep's front wheels. Lauren ducked down too and looked. Then she felt sick. There, on the pavement, was stenciled the name Max Cantor. She'd stolen his parking spot.

"Um . . ." Lauren began uncomfortably. "Look, I'm sorry. I'll move it right now. Elaine wants me to . . ."

Max took a step toward her, fiddling with his watchband as if he were also a little nervous. He was a lot taller than Lauren was; his body was graceful and lanky, his movements quick and spare, as if he didn't have a moment to waste. His dark eyes had lost their menacing look; now they looked alive.

"No, wait. I'm sorry. It's just that . . . well, I guess you could say that I've turned into an incurable paranoid. You know what I mean."

Lauren gave him a quizzical look. "I'm afraid I don't."

Max shrugged and leaned against the Jeep, drumming his fingers along its top. "Look, I'm from New York City; that's enough to permanently put a kid on edge." He looked at her and grinned. "Then I moved to L.A. and started working in television—the destruction was complete."

Lauren smiled back. "I lived in New York for a long time. And now I'm here. So I'm headed off the same cliff?"

His eyes lit up. "Another one! Another stranger in a strange land."

She watched quizzically as he reached into his coat pocket and drew out a tiny tape recorder. Giving her a quick smile, he flicked it on and spoke into it. "Monday. June twentieth. Today I thought I'd been fired."

"Fired . . . ?"

Max let out a short laugh and clicked off the recorder. "Happens all the time around here. The studio wants to get rid of someone—but doesn't have the guts to tell the person face-to-face. So they hire a replacement and assign them your old parking spot. You come in one morning and *bingo*, there's a strange car in your spot. You get the message pretty quickly."

"That's horrible," Lauren replied, shocked.

"Yeah," Max said with a grin. "It is."

"And . . . so . . . you actually thought I was your . . ."

Max nodded, starting to laugh. "Yeah . . . my hotshot replacement." He eyed her and held out two fingers, as if measuring her. "Let's see." He began a rapid-fire analysis that left Lauren breathless. "You look like you might be from New York. Yeah. Just pried away from *The Bill Monahan Show* after your big coup landing Elizabeth Taylor's inner child. You booked the kid for the show and the ratings went through the roof."

Lauren burst out laughing. Suddenly she realized they were both just standing in the middle of the lot, silently smiling at each other. "Um," she finally said, "I've got to run an errand for Elaine."

Max jingled his keys. "You can get a parking pass at the security hut."

"Okay."

"See you at work," he added. "My job consists of thinking up loony ideas for the show, then researching them. So let me know if you have any crazy inspirations. Really. Nothing's too cheap. Nothing's too far-fetched. Just lay it on me."

Lauren stuck her key into the ignition and grinned back over her shoulder. "Flashes of amazing brilliance. Sure. Glad to."

She backed up the Jeep and headed out of the lot, returning Max's friendly wave. Then she merged onto the busy Santa Monica Boulevard traffic.

But she barely noticed the traffic. Or the smog. Or the guy in the left lane honking at her. She was too busy thinking about Los Angeles. It was definitely the most exciting town on the face of the earth.

Five

ravis and Liza," Lauren was calling out, whipping her camera off her shoulder and bending her knees as she took their picture. "Smile and say cheese."

Liza smiled widely, then lifted her head from Travis's shoulder as Lauren turned and scurried away with the others down the jam-packed Santa Monica oceanfront.

Travis turned and faced Liza, his blue eyes taking her in as if she were the most beautiful girl he'd ever seen. One side of his mouth lifted in a soft, dizzy smile. Then he slipped his arm around her back. Liza relaxed and let her knees buckle. And as she fell back, he kissed her on the mouth, sending bolts of electricity through her body.

"Hurry *up,* you two," Lauren yelled over the crowds from the top of the steps leading to the beach. "We're heading for the waves. Meet you down there."

"Okay," Liza called back, trying to stand upright again. Her head was light. Her heart was crazy with happiness. The last week, in fact, had been one big wonderful melt. Since her reunion with Travis at Palace Burgers Saturday night, they'd been together practically every waking moment he wasn't at work. And today Travis had the day off.

Arm in arm, they strolled down the colorful walkway. Liza loved this beach. Unlike boring, tasteful Malibu a few miles north, *this* beach was like one huge, wonderful, sweaty carnival.

"This place makes me feel—so—*free,*" Liza suddenly declared over the passing boom of rap music. She hugged Travis tighter.

"I know," Travis agreed, hiking his guitar case up on his brown shoulder. He'd tied a red bandanna around his head, but his dark scraggly hair fell a few inches down his neck. "That's what this place is all about. Being free. Letting your mind wander as you stare out at the ocean. It's a place for artists and free spirits."

"Like you and me," Liza breathed, standing on tiptoe and kissing him on the cheek. Glancing off to her left, she could see Lauren, Winnie, and Melissa spreading out their towels on the sand. Gulls hovered. The waves crashed. And the sun shone down like hot butter on her skin. When she and Travis reached the other three, Liza spread out her own towel, then lay down on her stomach, feeling the hot burn of the sun on her back. A moment later Travis was settled cross-legged next to her, picking slowly on his guitar.

She sat up and lazily watched a coed volleyball game up the beach. Next to her Winnie had clamped on her Walkman and was staring sullenly out to sea. Beside Winnie, Melissa and Lauren chattered about their jobs on *The April Webster Show.*

". . . then Elaine sent me to this place called Hollywood Enhancements," Melissa was going on, unable to control her laughter. "So I locked the bike and went in and it looked like some kind of *doctor's office,* you know, like a clinic. And I guess they specialize in female *baldness.*"

Liza gave them a half smile, marveling at how L.A. had softened uptight Lauren and Melissa. Then she rolled over in the other direction to stare at Travis.

Behind her Lauren was shrieking with laughter. "Do you think it's a show proposal? Or do you think—Elaine's got—some sort of problem with . . ."

". . . *baldness,*" Melissa finished, turning over on her side and gasping for breath between laughter.

"Hey, guess how much I've earned in tips alone over the last five days." Melissa said finally.

Liza made an exasperated face. Money. Money.

Money. Is that all anyone thought about? "Okay. How much?"

"A hundred fifty dollars," Melissa said slowly, as if she could hardly believe it. "People spend money like water down here. It's unbelievable."

"And you're perfectly positioned to scrape up a few of the delicious scraps," Lauren said with satisfaction, brushing sand off her knees and reaching for a thick novel. "Why not? It goes to a good cause, doesn't it? One day you'll have your medical degree and you'll be treating all their sports injuries."

"Mmmmm," Melissa began to tease. "And one day you and Max Cantor will be running *The April Webster Show*."

"Good," Liza broke in, looking past stone-faced Winnie. "If you do, I'll give you first crack at interviewing me when I get my first TV show."

Lauren threw a balled-up T-shirt at her. "Oh, yeah, right. I'll run the show with him. But it's not going to happen anytime soon. I've barely talked to him since I stole his parking space last Monday."

Liza made a face and turned toward Travis. She'd overheard enough gossip from her girlfriends to last her a while. Travis's soft voice was cooing in her ear. The music stopped briefly as he reached out and stroked her back. She closed her eyes, giving in to his lazy warmth. The sun poured down on her shoulders. The breeze lifted her hair.

"Relax," Travis murmured. "You're in California now. It's hang time. *Nobody knows where the wind blows,"* he began to sing softly into her ear. *"Nobody knows where the love goes. . . ."*

"Travis," Liza whispered, rolling over from her knees to her side. As Travis laid the guitar gently aside, he drew her close and pressed her body to his. "That's so beautiful. . . ."

"I wrote it for you, Liza," Travis murmured, nuzzling her ear, his legs slowly entwining with hers as he rolled her back again. And then, as he dropped his lips on hers, she had that feeling again of being completely alone with Travis on a sea of warm, sensual . . .

"Okay, I'm outta here." Winnie's voice startled Liza out of her dreamlike state.

Liza pulled away from Travis and quickly sat up. "What?"

Winnie ripped the Walkman from her head and threw it down on her beach towel. Her face was filled with rage, and her tiny bikinied body seemed to be vibrating with anger. For a moment Liza thought Winnie's hair was actually standing on end.

"I'm getting out of here," Winnie repeated, her dark eyes flashing like two blobs of molten lava. "That is—unless you two can manage to untangle your oil-slick bodies for a few precious seconds. Long enough to keep us all from *gagging to death*!"

"Hey, Win," Travis tried to apologize. "Liza and I will go somewhere else, okay? Look, you're our friend."

But Winnie was already busily digging into her

purse for cash. "You are *not* my friends," Winnie snarled back, tears forming in her eyes. "You are insensitive, sex-crazed maniacs who care about nothing but yourselves and your own pleasure. And now, if you'll excuse me, I'm going to rent some of those roller skates—while you two are prying yourselves apart."

Liza bit her lip, stung by Winnie's comments. Maybe she and Travis *were* getting a little carried away. She kept forgetting that Travis had been Winnie's first love when they met in Europe the summer before. She had suspected as much for a long time, and Lauren had confirmed her suspicions a few days ago. If Winnie felt lonely and vulnerable, perhaps she didn't need to be reminded of Europe at all.

Travis sat down and shook his head. He buried his face in his hands.

While Winnie stomped off, Liza stared ahead, not knowing what to say. "Gee," she finally muttered, casting a guilty sideways glance in Lauren and Mel's direction, "I guess Travis and I should have left. I didn't know. . . ."

"Winnie's had a really bad year and she's jumpier than ever." Lauren said. "Sometimes I think she doesn't know what to do with her life anymore."

Mel shook her head. "She's brainier than all of us put together. It seems like such a waste. I mean, what if Winnie's summer turns out to be one big self-pity party?"

Lauren shook her head. "People are like onions,

Mel—most have maybe twenty layers of tough skin protecting them. I'd say Winnie has two layers right now—maybe three. Who knows? If we give her a chance, maybe she'll grow a few more this summer."

Liza looked at her. "That's the craziest thing I've ever heard in my life. You aren't by any chance a writer, are you, miss?"

Lauren giggled and threw sand at her legs. Melissa aimed a potato-chip bag at her.

"Okay," Liza said good-naturedly. "When all else fails, get yourself a job, gal. I'm going to check out the cafés and ice-cream stands up there. Who knows? Maybe there's a part-time job waiting for me."

Travis was stuffing his towel into a nylon pack. "I've got a better idea." He put his hands on Liza's milky-white shoulders. "I've got a friend who's been delivering singing telegrams for a company called Sing It! You know. You get hired to come to someone's doorstep and sing 'Happy Birthday'. Or 'Happy Anniversary,' or whatever. Anyway, it's for people who want to send something more than a card."

Liza could feel her face light up. "Happy birthday to *you*," she cooed, Marilyn Monroe style, pressing the palms of her hands into her thighs and jutting her chest forward. "Happy birth-day to *you*. Happy *birth*-day, Mr. Pro*du*-cer. . . ."

"You got it," Travis said, laughing. "In fact, that's why Sing It! has an opening. My friend got discovered when he delivered an Elvis-style singing telegram to the head of Movie City Productions. Now he's got a part on a new TV sitcom."

"Oh, my God. Oh, my God. Oh, my God. Oh, my God. Oh, my God," Liza began blabbering, grabbing her beach bag and searching for her cosmetic pouch. Her head felt as if someone had thrown confetti inside it. "Travis, why didn't you say something about this before? I can do this. I know I can. I can do this. I can do this."

"You're wigging, Liza." Travis gave her a patient look. "And that's why I didn't tell you before. All we're going to do is see if we can get an audition. It's just a moment in time, like any other. Relax."

But Liza couldn't hear him. When it came to big breaks, Travis could probably take it or leave it. He'd been in Los Angeles for nearly a year. But she was different. She was desperate for a break.

A few moments later Liza and Travis were racing up the beach headed for Travis's beat-up van. Yanking open the passenger door, she brushed the seat with her hand before sitting down. Travis's van was always stuffed with ancient amplifiers, speaker wire, power cords, and rolls of dusty duct tape. The next moment they were headed straight down Santa Monica Boulevard, singing at the top of their lungs. Halfway into town Travis spotted a party-goods store called Celebrations on the right side of the road.

"The Sing It! company is in the back," Travis explained, pulling the van into a gravelly back alley, overhung with dusty trees.

Inside, there was a tiny office with blue carpeting and black-and-white photos of famous comedians in a line along the walls. A bell dinged as they walked in, and a woman with long ringlets, wearing a white jumpsuit, popped through a door. "Hi," she said with an absent look, checking a list on a clipboard. "Are you Sanders or Andersson?"

Liza froze. They had to let them in. They just *had* to. "Um, I'm Ruff. Liza Ruff—and Bennett. Travis Bennett."

The woman frowned and ran a pencil down the list. "Not here." She shrugged and gave them a spacey smile. "Whatever works. You're here and you're on."

"We're on," Travis repeated.

The woman's eyes traveled the length of Travis's body, then she grinned, revealing two rows of sparkling white teeth. "It's cool. We thought we were done with auditions. But we can handle a couple more."

Travis gripped Liza's hand. "Great. Why don't you go first, Liza?"

Liza gulped, threw back her head, and marched forward, wiggling her fingers in farewell over her shoulder. "Wish me luck."

A door led into a large, dingy room that had been turned into an audition and rehearsal space. A piano stood in the corner, and a table in the back held a coffee machine. Facing the piano were a group of folding chairs, where two middle-aged guys sat, huddled over a piece of paper. Liza drew in her breath and waited politely. Silently she said a prayer. Working for the Sing It! company was just the break she was looking for. Now if she could just pull off this one little audition.

"Yo." One of the men waved at her briefly before bending back down into his conversation. "Just a minute, doll."

Liza fluffed her hair and tried to act casual. A few moments later they were motioning for her to come forward. One of the men sat down at the piano. "Okay. The audition is pretty straightforward. You're gonna sing 'Happy Birthday To You,' I'll accompany. But you've gotta tell me how to play it. Use your imagination. Just let it flow."

Liza felt weak. She tried to let things flow. Finally she closed her eyes, walked up to the piano, and leaned seductively against the top. Her blood was starting to fizz with excitement. "Okay, hon," she purred, staring straight into the guy's eyes. "Gimme a quick tempo. Nice and quick. Let's sing it like Judy Garland would have in a good mood." Slowly, Liza began snapping her fingers. She winked. *"Happy birthday—to yooooou. Happy birthday—to yooooou. . . ."* Gradually, Liza moved away from the piano and glued her eyes provocatively on the guy in the chair. She felt solid and happy, as if she were in exactly the right place at exactly the right time. Continuing to sing, she did a small tap dance, made a few off-the-cuff remarks, then ended with her hands stretched upward and head flung back, belting out the final notes.

To her amazement both of the guys clapped and smiled. "Great, great," one guy said with enthusiasm, getting up from his chair and shaking her hand. "I'm Maury Sedgwick, and this is my partner, Norm Lyle. We're the co-owners. How 'bout running through the same tune again a couple of times?"

"Hit it, Norm," Liza suddenly burst out. "Give it a throbbing disco underbeat. It's Madonna. It's rockin'. *Happy birthday—oh I love it baby—to you— Come on, baby, baby, baby. . . .*"

"Yeah!" Maury called out, as Liza began undulating her hips, looking bored and sexy at the same time.

By the time Liza had sung "Happy Birthday" like Axl Rose, James Brown, Cher, Bette Midler, and Ella Fitzgerald, she had the job.

"You're on, babe," Maury said, shaking her hand and nodding eagerly. "They're gonna eat you up. Christy will handle your paperwork, and we'll start sending you on assignment just as soon as we can."

"Thank you," Liza said breathlessly, racing back to the waiting room where Travis was sitting, strumming his guitar and practicing a few lines. "I got it," she practically screamed, flinging her arms around his neck.

Travis's face shone, as if someone had just turned a light on inside of him. "I knew you could do it."

"Mr. Bennett," Christy interrupted, "your turn."

Liza kissed him on the mouth, then watched him go through the door into the audition room. Through the wall she could hear the quiet strum of his guitar, and the sweet sound of his voice. Her heart began to pound. Unlike her, Travis was a true musician. A composer. A creative free spirit who was bound to make it even bigger than she was.

Suddenly Liza heard the music stop. There was the sound of a short conversation, then the creak of the door opening. Travis walked out and closed the door, wearing a forced smile. His eyes looked tired, almost dull. Quietly, he slipped the guitar strap off his shoulder and lowered his instrument into the case.

"What happened?" Liza asked carefully. There were unfamiliar little lines between his eyes.

An embarrassed flush crept across his face. But he gave her a brave look and shrugged. "They like my voice, but not the gig. Said I didn't have enough pizzazz."

Liza felt as if she were going to choke. *She* got a job, and wonderful, talented Travis *didn't?* It was impossible. "But that's *crazy*," Liza burst out, pulling on his shoulder. "It's just not . . ."

Travis turned, winked, and smiled. She loved the creases in his cheeks when he smiled like that. It made her feel as if she could melt into a little pool right at his feet. "I'm okay, Liza. Really I am."

Six

innie's thighs pumped her roller blades forward.

A few minutes earlier she'd rented them on the Santa Monica Beach boardwalk. Now she was out on the wide, windy path past the cafés and street vendors, swinging her arms to the beat of her stride. For a moment she felt determined and free, as if she'd left her anger back at the beach. As if she actually knew where she was going.

"Good-bye," Winnie breathed out with each pump of her roller blades. "Good-bye forever. You have behaved badly, Travis. You were mine first, after all. And you, Liza—you must be punished for your massive ego and extreme insensitivity. . . ."

"Wait up, Win," she could hear Lauren's voice behind her. "You're going to burn up the pavement at this rate."

Winnie looked back, remembering her friends. After Liza and Travis had left for their Sing It! auditions, Melissa and Lauren had decided to join her for a skate down the beachfront. Melissa pushed confidently ahead, her coppery hair blowing against the blue sky. Lauren, on the other hand, looked eager, but definitely uneasy.

"Renting skates was a great idea, Win," Melissa shouted, breezing past her. Winnie slowed and let Lauren pass her too.

"Thanks, Win," Lauren said cheerfully, wobbling ahead.

Winnie made a face after Lauren passed.

"Now those two can chow down on every last morsel of *April Webster* gossip," Winnie whispered to herself.

"*Yahoo,*" Melissa began yelling up ahead. Winnie watched as she began to twirl, balancing perfectly on one muscular leg, then the other. What was wrong with Mel, anyway? What happened to good ol' seriously depressed, control-freak Mel? For a while, back there at the U of S, Melissa was the one person Winnie could always count on to be at least as whacked-out as she was.

Winnie had secretly hoped she and Mel would be partners in misery this summer. Ambitious Lauren and Liza certainly weren't candidates for any serious pigging out and daytime TV watching. Not now, anyway. Mel was definitely the one.

She slowed as she neared Lauren and Mel, who were stopped for a water-bottle break.

". . . so they can shoot the show and have enough time to remove the nutcase phone calls and occasional audience weirdo," Lauren was explaining intently. She paused to bend her neck back and squirt a stream of water into her mouth.

Melissa was nodding. "Amazing how they do that . . ."

Winnie felt sick. She wanted nothing more than to be far away from these two cheerful Pollyannas with their TV gossip. Lauren and Melissa's constant chatter about *The April Webster Show* was making her feel as left out as Travis and Liza's continual necking had.

Lauren was especially irritating, Winnie decided, her mind now ablaze. After all, less than a year ago Lauren was an overweight sorority mouse who scarcely had the nerve to ask someone for the time of day. If Faith hadn't be there holding her hand all year, Lauren would probably be shopping with her mother right now, somewhere in Connecticut. Instead Lauren was here in California, determined to ignore her.

"But—anyway—the Walker Ingham interview went really well," Lauren was chattering on, trying not to pant. "Elaine said ratings were superhigh, so they're going to try to get him back as soon as possible."

Winnie made a few lazy turns, then pulled out ahead as Lauren was putting away her water bottle.

"Hey, speedo!" Lauren called out happily.

Winnie set her jaw and sped forward, trying to lose them. Why was Lauren trying to be so nice to her? It was such a strained, obvious effort. It was embarrassing. The wind flattened her hair and made her eyes tear up.

Meanwhile the path was narrowing. It led away from the developed areas and curved along the beach until it was practically right under the tall cliffs that soared over the ocean. Winnie shaded her eyes, slowed, and looked up at the row of huge homes balanced over the water. Large and white, they almost looked like seabirds perched in the wind, ready to drop. She stared. Halfway down the row was the most spectacular home of all. A three-tiered stucco mansion, it spilled down over green landscaping to the edge of the cliff and a fenced area that was obviously a huge deck or pool. Blue-and-white-striped awnings fluttered over the windows. A row of shaggy palms framed the property line.

"Beautiful, isn't it?" Lauren was saying behind her.

"What?" Winnie said, looking briefly over her shoulder.

Lauren rolled lazily forward. "That big mansion with the awnings. That's where Walker Ingham lives. Max Cantor told me to look for it if we came out here today."

"*Are you serious?*" Melissa answered in a stunned

voice, coming up from behind. "Walker Ingham is telling everyone in Hollywood to live simply. Isn't the mansion-on-the-hill lifestyle a little hypocritical?"

"He doesn't own the mansion," Lauren said serenely, stopping and gazing in awe at the white structure. "He rents a small room in it, with a view of the ocean."

Melissa looked puzzled. "Who owns it, then?"

"Oliver Sikes," Lauren explained, pointing the toe of her roller blade, getting ready to push out. "He's a major, heavy-duty movie producer. Big bucks. Walker Ingham's number-one disciple."

"Must be nice," Winnie said tartly, turning abruptly and suddenly taking off back toward the Santa Monica beachfront.

"What?" Lauren called after her.

Winnie felt her anger inexplicably rising again. It was almost like the rise and fall of the waves on the beach. She was feeling a new emotion every few minutes. First anger, then brief relief, then anger again—white-hot and worse than ever. "Must be nice to know so much, too, Lauren," she shouted over her shoulder. Racing ahead, Winnie sped past a group of guys on high-tech bikes and a woman jogging with her infant in a racing stroller. She could hear Mel and Lauren calling for her, but she didn't want to stop.

"Slow down, Winnie," Mel yelled from behind, catching up. "Wait for Lauren."

Winnie slowed and looked over her shoulder as

Lauren approached. Pink-faced and panting, she wore a puzzled expression on her face. "Wait up," Lauren yelled.

"Wait up?" Winnie snapped, stopping her skates and glaring back at Lauren. "Are you trying to tell me you don't like being left *behind*?"

Pointing the toes of her roller blades together, Lauren came to a wobbly stop. "Huh?"

"Left *behind*," Winnie repeated. "If you don't like being left behind, then why are you trying to do it to me?"

Winnie watched stone-faced as Lauren's lips parted, then slowly hardened into an angry line. "Left behind?" Lauren sputtered. "*I* have left *you* behind? Pardon me, Win, but I seem to remember inviting you to spend the entire summer with us in a beautiful beach house. We all got in the Jeep *together*. Remember? Then we drove nine hundred miles. . . ."

"People desert each other in many different ways," Winnie spat back.

Lauren's face was turning red and incredulous.

"You and Mel are so wrapped up in TV-land, you seem to forget I'm even *here*," Winnie said hotly.

"You are completely out of line," Lauren said with quiet fury. She took a breath and let her violet eyes bore directly into Winnie's. "What's going on with you? First you make a scene about Liza and Travis—then you start in on me and Mel and our jobs!"

Winnie glared at her.

"If you want a boyfriend or a job, Win," Lauren growled, "why don't you go out and find one, instead of blaming and ranting at us?"

Winnie flexed her calves and began rolling backward on her skates, her eyes stinging with tears. "I don't want a TV job—and I don't want a useless summer fling. I—I just want a little—*consideration*."

Lauren folded her arms across her chest while Mel looked on with an expression of fear. "How do you expect us to be *considerate* when all you've done this week is mope and then blow up at us?" Lauren fumed.

"Blow up?" Winnie shouted, tears streaming down her face. "Blow up? Do you remember how many times you blew up last year? Your middle name was *berserk*, Lauren Turnbell-Smythe, until you got back together with Dash. And you, Mel. You were the same way. And I put up with you! Why can't you do the same for me?"

Winnie turned and sped away as fast as she could down the path. Her roller blades bumped over pebbles. The sun blazed on her neck. But she couldn't stop. If she never saw Mel and Lauren again, she'd be very, very happy. Mel and Lauren were history. She didn't want their company, their friendship, or their constant chatter.

Good-bye forever, Winnie thought, angrily pumping her skates and wondering where the Santa Monica Greyhound bus station was.

After a while the path returned to Santa Monica's

commercial waterfront. Winnie rolled on, gazing at the chic cafés and dress shops. Everywhere there were people talking, moving, and eating. Everyone seemed to have some kind of purpose. Quietly, she skated on. She stared at the airy storefronts and lovely terrace restaurants. Beautiful people seemed to be everywhere.

It was amazing how being around so many people could make a person feel so lonely.

Seven

rab your beeper, Mel. It's pedal-pump time," Lauren announced, slipping the Jeep into its new space on the Television City lot.

"Oooooh," Melissa replied, rubbing her thighs as they walked into the *April Webster* staff entrance. "My achin' legs. Thank goodness it's Monday. Roller blading in Santa Monica's supposed to be recreation? If I were delivering messages on those things, I'd *really* be stiff at the end of the day."

Lauren's face dimmed. "Winnie's the one who should be stiff. She was skating like a madwoman on that Santa Monica boardwalk."

"Yeah," Melissa said casually, slipping on her

headband, "and she obviously didn't work a thing out of her system."

Lauren shook her head. "She won't even talk to me now."

"Melissa!" A woman from the promotion department came running up. "I need this on the north end of the lot in about two minutes. This on the south end in three minutes. And this two blocks down the boulevard in four."

Melissa calmly took the envelopes and gave her a brilliant smile. "Righteeo. Get your head chopped off if I don't, right?"

The woman made an exasperated face and put her hand on Mclissa's shoulder. "You are very fast, woman. And I bless you for it."

"Ciao," Lauren called out with a wistful look as Melissa rushed away. It was fun to see Melissa make such a success of her new job. Lauren only wished Winnie could find her niche like Mel. But so far Winnie's attitude was as black as the inside of a medieval dungeon. Was she having some sort of breakdown? Or were her friends actually doing something to make her feel like an outsider?

Her mind on Winnie, Lauren gazed intently at the floor as she headed for Elaine's office to get her first assignment. A second later she felt something smack into her.

"Agh!" a male voice cried out. She looked up and cringed. In her dazed rush she'd run right into Max Cantor, who must have been carrying a stack of files at least two feet high. Now they were scattered all over the hallway. Lauren felt her face go hot. She'd been dying to run into him for a week. Did she have to do it like this?

"Oh, Max. I'm so sorry."

"No problem," Max said quickly, stooping down to gather the mess. He looked up and flashed her a very white smile. "Look. Most of these files have these handy little ties."

Lauren dropped down slowly to help him retrieve the papers.

"Life in the fast lane, huh?" he said with a laugh, pushing up his glasses on his nose. "Hey, maybe we could write a screenplay together. This would make a great scene, don't you think?"

Lauren laughed out loud. She liked the long, lean lines of his clean-shaven face. His blazer was professional and new looking, but the faded T-shirt underneath read *"I'd rather be windsurfing."*

"The scene's been done before," Lauren replied, grinning, "in a million movies."

Max's smile widened as they stood up together. "So? We'll do a rewrite. Or maybe we could do an *April* show. 'People who meet through embarrassing accidents. Monday at four.'"

For a moment they just stood there, staring and smiling. Lauren felt her heart begin to climb into her throat. She coughed a little and wondered if she was blushing. She didn't expect to have this—this *reaction* to seeing Max again.

"We should get together," Max said suddenly as a guy with a sound boom hurried down the hall, squeezing them both against the wall. He cleared his throat and shifted a little. "I mean, you need to know a few things about Elaine—and about what they really need from you this summer. . . ."

Lauren made a face. "They need coffee. They definitely need coffee. Plain black. Espresso. Latte. Skinny latte. Cappuccino. You name it."

"Yeah." Max let out a short laugh, gathering his files under one arm and stepping near the wall. Lauren noticed that he'd moved a little closer to her and that he was taller than she'd remembered. His dark curls brushed the collar of his jacket, and she could barely make out the scent of his shaving cream. "They'll do that to the rookies. But believe me, if you get your face out there and pitch them some ideas, you'll be respected for it. Listen, why don't we get together and talk?" In one swift movement he slipped his free hand into his inside jacket pocket and pulled out his tape recorder. "Make a note. Get together with Lauren and talk. Any day will do. Today? Tomorrow? Wednesday?"

"Okay." Lauren looked down, trying to catch her breath. Max's rapid-fire conversation had thrown her a little. She hadn't realized it until now, but Max was definitely trying to ask her out.

Lauren tried to ignore the frantic footsteps and shouted orders surrounding them in the hallway. She didn't want to blow this moment. She'd seen

Max only once a week so far, and the summer ahead seemed suddenly very short. "Oh—I—uh, was just thinking about something . . . I—uh—sure, I'd like to talk to you about the dangerous pitfalls and ecstatic highs of this lowly job."

Max was smiling and not taking his eyes off her, even though people were stuffing pink telephone messages and manila envelopes into his hands as he stood there.

A sudden crash startled them both. Max turned around just as Elaine and April burst out of the conference room and into the hall. Lauren gaped as April's huge frame stomped past them, then stopped and whirled around. "Give this problem some serious thought, if you don't mind, Elaine," April boomed. A sheen of perspiration covered her forehead, and her huge silk scarf was starting to slip crazily off her shoulder.

Lauren and Max watched as Elaine followed her angrily down the hall, flipping back a square of her blond hair. "I *have* the ratings right here in my hand, April," Elaine shouted back, slapping a piece of paper with the back of her hand. "I spent the better part of last month reeling Walker Ingham into this studio, and the ratings were huge."

April stopped, turned, and narrowed her huge eyes. Her chest rose and fell. "The ratings—on average—stink, Elaine. They stink in middle America. They stink on the East Coast. And they stink just about everywhere but the old-age homes in Florida."

Elaine's mouth dropped open. "You're being completely . . ."

"Our twelve-to-nineteen-year-old demos look like someone stepped on the graph and squashed them, Elaine," April continued to rant, planting her fists on her military-tank hips. "Our eighteen-to-twenty-fours look even worse. The teens are watching cable. They're watching MTV. They're watching *I Love Lucy*."

Several curious staffers quietly poked their heads into the hall. "What's going on here?" April yelled. "We've got millions of teenagers who are out of school for the summer. Why are we doing shows on baldness and women who forgive their husbands' murderers? This is crap. This is complete and total madness."

April's head snapped around. Her black eyes blazed at Max. "And you, Mr. Underage Boy Wonder. You're incredibly, *obscenely* young. Why are you standing there? Why aren't you in your office coming up with brilliant ideas that teenagers will find fascinating? What *are* you people interested in besides sex, movie stars, and athletes who make huge amounts of money?"

Max stirred, then gave her a quick look. "Uh. We're interested in jobs. Getting them. Keeping them. Definitely keeping them. Stuff like that."

"April," Elaine tried to break in. Her voice was softer now. "Why don't we all just sit down and talk about it? You *know* Max has just what you're looking for. He always does. Come on. Let's give this conference another try."

April rolled her eyes and sucked in her cheeks. Then she put one foot dramatically forward and headed back to the conference room. "Let's go. Now! Max! Peter! Patricia! Constance! David! I want the entire staff in here pronto. We're going to finish talking about today's "Celebrity Pet Parade" show—and then we're going to *brainstorm*."

Max was suddenly grabbing Lauren's arm and pulling her aside. His face looked pale and excited, and his eyes were darting all over the room. "Look, are you free right now? I need your help."

Lauren gulped. Her brain was buzzing, as if she'd just climbed a mountain and she was dizzy in the high mountain air. "Sure, I—uh . . ."

"Okay, okay, okay," Max began talking so fast Lauren became convinced he'd had sixty cups of coffee for breakfast. "This is a really big break for me, because I've been researching the teen angle for a couple of weeks now and have a huge file on it. Look, in the top right-hand drawer of my desk is a big manila folder with a label on it that says 'Future Show Ideas.' Okay? It has about two dozen clips in it—all of them dealing with trends and current events that are likely to appeal to the fourteen-to-nineteen-year-old demographic group. . . ."

Lauren was breathing fast. Of course she knew what he was talking about. "Yeah, yeah."

"Make a dozen copies of each clip and bring

them to the conference room as soon as you possibly can," Max called out over his shoulder as he ran down the hall and bolted into the conference room.

Lauren turned and raced in the opposite direction, toward the huge staff room. She burst through the door, her head racing and her stomach churning. Hurriedly, she scanned the messy room. Max's office was a tiny compartment in the corner, partly hidden by two temporary partitions.

"'Future Show file,'" she murmured to herself. "'Future Show file.'" Suddenly she spotted a manila folder with that label on the top of his desk. "Bingo!" she muttered in victory, suddenly realizing that everything that day was destined to work out perfectly. It was luck. It was karma. It was L.A. She grinned to herself, then grabbed the folder and ran out, heading for the photocopy room.

"Dozen copies," Lauren murmured, punching directions into the machine and blindly tearing the news articles out of the folder.

Minutes later, her copies in hand, she rushed back through the busy hall. Before she could even catch her breath, she burst through the door of the conference room and slipped inside with confidence, pressing her back against the wall.

Her eyes met Max's, and he silently gave her the thumbs-up sign. The room was dead quiet.

"Yes?" April barked, staring directly at Lauren.

Lauren gathered her courage and took a breath. "Clippings. Show ideas to reach a younger audience this summer. Research asked me to deliver these."

April took one of the copies and passed the rest around the conference table. Narrowing her eyes, she began flipping through them. Then she pursed her lips and slapped the papers down.

Max suddenly gasped.

Confused, Lauren looked at Max, who was desperately flipping through his copy. Meanwhile Elaine had placed her elbows on the table and was covering her face with her hands. Some of the others were giggling softly.

"Planning for *retirement*? Displaced *homemakers*? Four Vietnam protesters talk about delayed-stress syndrome?" April shrieked, sticking her fingernails into her stiff hair. "Is this research's idea of grabbing a teenager's flea-sized attention span? *This is aging baby-boomer material, folks. I want young. I want infantile. I want something out of* Teen Flick *magazine!*"

Lauren felt her heart pounding in her ears. The file, she thought madly. She didn't get the file from the drawer. She took the one from the top of his desk. *The wrong one.*

"I'm sorry, I . . ." Lauren stammered, paralyzed by the sudden realization that all of her self-defense techniques would be useless against this gigantically powerful woman. "Max told me to copy the articles and drop them off here."

Max's face was turning beet-red. "April, Lauren brought the wrong . . ."

"Forget it, Max!" April shouted. "Just sit there and listen to us grown-ups, and go back to your office later and think about your mission in life."

Tears sprang to Lauren's eyes. She couldn't stand it a moment longer. Quickly, she turned and burst out of the room and into the hall. Everything was spinning and faded. She pushed one hand against the wall for balance and tried to breath. A wave of nausea swept over her, and her nose was running uncontrollably.

I'm a fool, Lauren thought miserably, staggering toward the bathroom. *I've ruined things for Max and for me. I thought I was going somewhere this summer, but I'm not. This is it. The end. For Max. For me. And definitely, positively, for Max and me.*

Eight

onk, honk, hoooooooooooonnnnnk.

Melissa shook her fist at the guy in the white Jaguar convertible. He'd nearly taken off the end of her bike as she'd begun to cross an intersection. She could have been seriously hurt, or even killed. But the guy just stared at her clinically through his dark sunglasses before stepping on the gas and continuing his right turn.

"Jerk," Melissa breathed, standing on her pedals, digging into her toe clips, and racing to beat the yellow light. Her legs were damp under her black racing shorts, and her silicon-padded leather gloves were pressed hard against the handlebars. Two blocks later she was diving into a narrow alleyway, shortcutting it to her destination, a famous agent's office in a Santa Monica high-rise.

Beep. Beep. Beep. Beep. Beep. Beep.

Melissa skidded to a stop in the cool alley. Whipping off her pager, she quickly checked the phone number. It was Elaine. Melissa readjusted her tool pack, checked her watch, and took a quick look in her helmet's rearview mirror before pushing off. Across the street from the alley's opening, she spotted a telephone booth.

"Elaine?" Melissa shouted, plugging one ear with her finger as morning traffic rushed by. "It's Mel."

"Wait!" Elaine shrieked. "Hold it. I've got calls on two and three. Let me get rid of them."

Two seconds later she was back on the line. "Okay, hon. Now. That packet for Walker Ingham that goes to the Sikes estate out on the coastal highway?"

"Yes, I've got it."

"Okay. It's got a handwritten thank you from April for appearing on the show. But it's also got a request for another appearance and a proposal for a collaboration on a book. Big. Big. Big. Very big. Millions. That is, if April can pull it off."

"Mmmm."

Elaine was getting excited. Melissa even thought she could detect her sneaking a puff from a cigarette. "Now. Your directions were to drop the envelope off at the gate? Forget it."

"Okay." Melissa took off one glove and began rubbing her sore palm.

"The problem is Ingham," Elaine went on. "I don't know if he's ever going to do another show. I mean, let's face facts. I had to practically stand on my head and do magic tricks to get him on just once. Who knows if he'll take the bait again? Why don't we try for Oliver Sikes too? You know. He's the big movie producer who's backing the whole meditate-and-love-yourself organization. He owns that big mansion Walker lives in out at the beach. So far he's never given an interview. But let's try to find his weak spot."

Melissa popped a Life Saver into her mouth. A guy in a white suit began pacing in front of the booth. "Weak spot?"

"Yeah," Elaine went on hurriedly, obviously relishing her idea. "Get inside his estate and snoop around a little, hon. Play it innocent, like you're trying to figure out where to leave the envelope. Find out if there's a girlfriend or a wife or *someone* you can butter up."

Melissa tensed. She was about as graceful as an elephant in social situations. She'd never lived anywhere but small-town Springfield, and she'd never known a single wealthy person in her life, except Lauren. How was she supposed to get anywhere on the Sikes estate? They'd see through her in a millisecond. "Okay," she replied instead, biting her lip. "I'll do my best."

"You're a doll," Elaine gushed. "Check your heartbeat when you get there. I want to see how low you keep it. Okay, hon?"

Melissa hung up, made her high-rise delivery, then took off like a shot toward the coast. Once she reached the end of Santa Monica Boulevard, she swung through a green park ringed with lush palms, then headed north up the coastal highway.

Maneuvering into the highway's bike lane, Melissa changed gears and grinned to herself. To her left the ocean stretched out blue and shining. To her right the cliffs were carpeted with a million nodding orange poppies. She breathed the salty air, feeling as free and strong as if she'd just beat her personal best in the four-hundred-meter.

A mile up the road the modest oceanfront homes gave way to the large estates, surrounded by acreage and wrought-iron gates that locked. Melissa began checking the addresses, then spotted a palatial stucco mansion rising from a border of nodding palms. She recognized it at once. It was the Sikes mansion she'd seen from the beach on Saturday. It looked even more imposing from the road.

Slowing, Melissa checked her pulse for Elaine, then crossed the highway. A black wrought-iron fence surrounded the estate, but she could see that it had been left open.

"Whew," Melissa breathed, unbuckling her helmet strap. She got off her bike and began walking it slowly down the gravel driveway, which had just been carefully raked.

For a moment Melissa just stood there, gaping. She'd never seen anything like it in her life. The blazing white home had at least three stories, which lowered themselves like huge steps down part of the ocean cliff. With its two towers, cement balconies, and fluttering blue-and-white-striped awnings, it almost looked like a huge cruising vessel headed out to sea. Melissa held her breath. In the center of the home's circular driveway was a huge magnolia tree, studded with white blossoms. The round garden at its base was planted with a perfectly green circle of clipped lawn, surrounded by a profusion of pink rosebushes. Blue, red, purple, and white bedding plants were everywhere, bordering the brick pathways that led down both sides of the house toward the ocean.

Keeping a sharp lookout for any well-dressed woman who might be Sikes's wife or girlfriend, Melissa continued nervously toward the far side of the house. A florist's delivery van and a silver Mercedes convertible were parked before the front door. Several gardeners were pruning a hedge around the four-car garage. A maid in a black-and-white uniform shook out a Persian rug over one of the balconies.

Slowly, Melissa crunched over the gravel until she reached a cascading brick staircase that spilled down to another vast, tiered garden, which surrounded a perfectly round swimming pool. It was here that Melissa's mouth dropped open completely. Like a vast Mediterranean playground, the hillside was covered with tall juniper trees, sculpted shrubs, and spikes of dense purple lavender. Next to the pool a half-moon of white patio extended over the cliff, bordered by a curved bench. The vast Pacific Ocean glistened beyond.

Mesmerized by the beauty, Melissa leaned her bike against a stone wall and stepped slowly down toward the pool. But a moment later she noticed something that made her heart stop.

"Oh my . . ." Melissa burst out, bolting down the steps. She stared at the blue water. Lying perfectly still at the bottom was someone's lifeless body.

"Hello? Hello!" Melissa called desperately toward the house as she scrambled down the steps toward the pool. In a flash she saw that it was a young man in swimming trunks, lying facedown. For a split second her eyes clung to the outline of his body, praying for movement. Then, when she realized he was completely limp, she flung her messenger pack to the side and instantly dived in.

Her arms dug desperately through the water. Her clothes dragged and her shoes weighed her down, but she was still fast. Quickly, she ran through her lifesaving techniques.

Prop the head back and plug the nose. Look for obstructions in the back of the mouth.

Once she reached the bottom, she saw that the swimmer was still motionless in the wavering blue light. A moment later she was grabbing him under the armpit and readying herself for a pull to the surface.

But something immediately jerked Melissa back.

She felt the guy's shoulder muscles flex beneath her hands. Her heart was beginning to thud wildly. He wasn't limp at all. In fact, he was flailing his arms crazily in front of her face. She tried to move back, but she felt his hands push against her shoulders. Then he kicked away; his knee shoved violently into her chest, forcing the last of the air out of her lungs.

Numb with terror, Melissa felt a searing pain in her chest. The warm water pressed around her. She tried to kick up, but when her head hit bottom, she realized she was disoriented. Desperately, she righted herself and struggled to the surface. Her heavy clothes dragged against the water.

"Nnnnnnnggggghhhhhaaahhhh!" Melissa gasped as her head finally broke through the water. She gulped for air, then coughed up against the horrible sting in her throat. Then, kicking away as fast as she could, she finally made it to the edge of the pool.

Melissa coughed again, realizing that she had swallowed water. Too exhausted to run away, she grasped the side of the pool, pushed the wet strands out of her face, and stared at the guy. He too was breathing hard, but Melissa wasn't taking any chances. He was shaking his head, as if he were still too starved for air to talk. Melissa stared at the rise and fall of his wide, muscular shoulders and bronze skin. His slightly scraggly hair was light blond, and it plastered the back of his neck. When he finally looked at her, still gasping, she could see that his face was all-American rugged, with high cheekbones that framed a pair of large brown eyes. Melissa couldn't stop staring. Still gasping, he glared back suspiciously, as if he didn't quite understand what she'd just done. A gold watch glinted on his wrist.

"Are—you okay?" Melissa finally said.

He coughed, then hoisted himself onto the deck of the pool. Beads of water slid down his wide, smooth chest. "Uh—yeah, I guess. Are you?"

Melissa nodded, still stunned. She wondered why he was looking at her as if she were some kind of intruder. After all, she'd just tried to save his life! She brushed away the water dripping over her face. Who was this guy?

He glanced at her, then looked away quickly. Then he lifted one leg out of the water and rested his elbow on his knee, staring intently into space. Then he breathed out a small, uncomfortable laugh. "Look—uh—did you just try to rescue me or something?"

Melissa looked at him, totally confused. He was giving her a funny, intense stare that scared her. Any ordinary person would have known exactly what she'd done, and thanked her. "Yes. Of course I did. I thought you were drowning."

Suddenly the guy broke into a huge grin. He bent his head back and let out a short, loud laugh, as if she'd told a joke.

Melissa sprang to her feet and began angrily dumping the water out of her biking shoes. Her eyes grew hot with humiliation. "Well, now that I know you're okay, I guess I'll be leaving," she snapped.

The guy's face dropped. His eyes lifted to hers, then darted out into the distance as if he were examining the outline of a distant mountain. She looked up and saw that his muscular arms were flexing as he gripped the side of the pool. "Hey. Wait a minute," he said loudly. Then he glanced up, a pleading look in his eyes. "Look. It's just that I work for Coastal Pools. You know. I'm the"—he spread his arms out over the pool—"pool man."

"The pool man?"

"Yeah." He nodded, laughing a little. "I was changing the filter."

Melissa's mouth dropped open. The pool man? She'd been trying to rescue the pool man? A smile spread slowly over her face, and she dropped back down to the side of the pool. "Oh," she said with a sheepish grin, dangling her legs back in the water.

He stood and walked over, smiling. Melissa shivered. He was very tall and well built. From the look of his deep tan, she could tell he spent a lot of time under the California sun. When he smiled, his white teeth flashed against the brown. It was a shy, I'm-not-sure-about-you smile. But it was more dangerous than anything Melissa had seen in a long time. And it pulled Melissa to him more than any bold show of confidence could have.

Danger. Danger. All persons must proceed immediately to nearest exit. Exit. Exit. Exit.

He sat down beside her, dangling his feet next to

hers. She stared at a single trickle of water making its way down the top of his brown, bulging arm. Then her eyes lifted to his intense stare. "You got your hair all wet," he said.

Melissa struggled desperately for her voice. "Sure I got my hair wet. What do you think?"

"Hey." He held up both hands to defend himself. Melissa stared boldly at his firm, muscular stomach. For a pool repairman he seemed to have lots of time to work out. "It's just that I've never been saved before."

"Really."

"Look." He struggled, trying not to smile, dug his fingers into his hair, and raked it back. "In this town this kind of thing doesn't happen very often."

Melissa crossed her arms over her chest. "I'm not from L.A. What kind of *thing*?"

He shrugged and seemed to search for an explanation, twisting his gold watchband. "You know. Someone going out of her way. I mean, it might be the politically correct thing to do, but I'll bet you fifty bucks nine out of ten people in this town would have split when they saw me at the bottom of the pool."

Melissa felt suddenly uncomfortable. She carefully wrung out the hem of her tank top.

"You don't look like you're worried about breaking a nail," he added, casting an admiring look down her body. His brown eyes held hers for a second longer than before. "In fact, you're an incredibly strong swimmer. Athlete?"

Melissa shrugged. "I run track. It'll keep you on your toes. And now I've got this bike-messenger job." Suddenly she remembered why she'd come. "Hey. I've got an envelope to deliver. Is there a Mrs. Sikes—uh—or some other woman of the house I can leave it with?"

The guy suddenly looked away. "Dunno."

"Oh. Okay."

"I guess I could put the envelope inside, if you want," the guy suddenly suggested, standing up and offering his hand. "I mean, there always seems to be some kind of maid floating around this place."

Melissa looked at him, then grasped his powerful hand, and he pulled her up. She felt a sudden bolt of electricity through his fingers so that when her feet found the ground, she momentarily lost her balance and fell against his chest. Standing there dripping on the wet cement, he lifted his brown eyes and gave her a long, curious stare that made her shiver. She wondered for an instant if she should ask him about any women in Oliver Sikes's life. But the moment lingered, and somehow Melissa didn't want to ruin it.

"Thanks," she finally said, stepping back and retrieving her pack. She pulled out the envelope for Walker Ingham. "I'd appreciate it."

"Yeah," the guy said with a serious look, taking the envelope, but not looking at it. He raked his hair back and glanced unsteadily at the big house. "Sure thing."

Melissa slipped on her shoes and tied the laces. Then she stood, trying to pry her eyes off his athletic-looking build and glowing suntan. "Well, bye then. Back to work and everything."

He nodded and shrugged. "Work."

Melissa hurried up the steps to her bicycle. Her eyes darted through the windows to the antique-filled mansion rooms. But she knew she didn't have it in her to snoop any further. Elaine would have to do it herself.

"My name is Evan," the guy suddenly called out from the pool.

Melissa turned around and saw that he was still standing there, looking at her, his arms crossed over his chest. "Look. I hang out at a place called Pirate Cove. Just a few miles up the beach from here—right down from Crescent, if you ever get over that way."

"Oh," Melissa called back lamely, her blood tingling. *Thank you, thank you, entire, wonderful, rich Turnbell-Smythe family.*

Evan's face looked earnest. "Lots of great swimming and diving if you like that sort of thing. Maybe I could give you the grand tour."

Suddenly Melissa couldn't breathe very well. Maybe it was the scare in the pool. Or having the wind knocked out of her. Or maybe it was just looking at this golden guy at the bottom of the steps, smiling at her as if he'd just given her the challenge of her life.

"Oh, and uh," he stammered, "sorry I got so rough in the pool and all."

"Yeah," she whispered with a smile, before turning and racing back to her bike.

Nine

wave crashed against a craggy boulder just off the Santa Monica beach, sending white spray into the sky.

Winnie dug her toes into the sand. All she wanted was to savor the thundering sounds of nature. Instead she had to listen to the thundering sounds of Liza Ruff.

"*Soooooooo,*" Liza continued to boom in her foghorn voice, which could much too easily be heard above the screams of sea gulls, the roar of the waves, and the yells of nearby Saturday volleyball players. "It's that way with the checkers in the grocery store, the waiters in every luncheonette, the bank tellers, and *every single person* at Sing It! They're all here in

L.A. because they *wanna be a star*!"

Somehow Winnie had managed to live in southern California for another week with her roommates. And today she had even decided to join Travis, Liza, Lauren, and Mel, who had driven down from Malibu to check out the crowds and have a pre-lunch sand-castle contest.

Readjusting her beach chair, Winnie glared at Lauren and Mel, who were working on their castles in the semiwet sand about ten feet in front of her. Meanwhile Liza and Travis had found a smooth patch of sand slightly farther down the beach. Those two couldn't keep their hands off each other. The whole situation was disgusting, Winnie thought with a scowl. The only reason she came was that she didn't want to be alone in the beach house for another day.

"Hey, Win," Mel called out, hunched over a tall castle she'd shaped, complete with moat and delicate towers. Mel's nose was covered with glaring white zinc oxide, but her shoulders were burned red. "Give me a hand. You're creative."

Winnie shrugged and pulled out a *Psychology Today* magazine from her beach bag. She shook the sand out of it and propped it up on her knees. "No, thanks. I'm going to read."

"Give it up, Win," Lauren said with an edge to her voice. Lauren was squirting a tube of cocoa butter onto her slightly generous thighs. In her wide straw hat and one-piece suit, Winnie decided she looked like a middle-aged matron watching her children at the beach. "You can read a magazine anywhere, but you're at the b—"

"Thanks anyway, Lauren," Winnie snapped, yanking the cover open. She turned up the volume on Melissa's radio and stared at the page. Why was everyone making such an obvious effort to include her? All last week Lauren and Melissa had been tiptoing around her as if she were some sort of mental patient. Pouring her coffee. Lending her perfumy shampoo. Why did they bother? She knew she was on the outside, and she wanted it to stay that way.

"Listen to this, Travis," Liza was bubbling, rolling over clumsily and running up the beach to her towel. She dug into her beach bag and pulled a big pink bow and an oversize lollipop out of her beach bag. Winnie stared in fascination as Liza tied the bow around her head, grabbed the lollipop, and sauntered back down the beach to sit on Travis's knee. "Happy birth-day to *you* . . ." she began in a simpering sugar-baby-doll-face voice.

Travis laughed. "You're sick."

Winnie closed her eyes. Why had she come to the beach with these clowns? Travis was the only sane person in the lot.

Mel stood up on her knees, brushing her hair away with her clean wrist. "Is that the singing telegram for the big movie director?"

Liza stood up, threw her head back, and posed.

"Yeeeeeeeees!" she belted out, as if she were singing scales.

Lauren and Travis clapped.

"This is big. Very big," Liza began chattering.

Winnie briefly considered putting her Walkman on to shut out Liza's ceaseless babble. But she couldn't resist watching Liza make a fool of herself.

"In less than four hours," Liza went on, pressing her palm to her chest dramatically, "I—Liza Ruff—will be traveling to Beverly Hills to deliver a birth-daygram to none other than *Mandy Shapiro.*"

"Who's he, Liza?" Winnie drawled, suddenly wondering if Liza's bathing suit had wire supports.

Liza jumped to her feet. "He's directed more than a dozen big, big films," she burst out. "Haven't you ever seen him at the Academy Awards? He's Mr. Huge! Mr. Power!"

Winnie closed her eyes in frustration as Liza continued to gush. Why had Lauren invited Liza to Malibu? How could she stand it?

"Anyway, a girlfriend of mine from Sing It!—Sandy Scott—she's the one who came out from Florida with about ten cents in her wallet—anyway, she says that Mandy Shapiro's right now casting a huge film about a gutsy girl from New York who comes to Hollywood to make her fortune, only to be stricken with a rare disease. It's got my name written all over it."

Travis moved away from his sand castle and draped his arm around Liza. "Not only that—the

Shapiro family wants Liza to stick around at his birthday, to help open presents and cut the cake."

Winnie smiled to herself. Liza was so uncoordinated, she'd probably end up dropping the cake on Shapiro's lap.

Liza suddenly covered her face with her hands and screamed loudly. "I can't wait, girls. Drive me back to Crescent. Help me get ready."

"We're ready when you are," Lauren said, sticking her foot cheerfully into her castle. "I'll help you get made up, then I'll drive you to Beverly Hills myself in the Jeep."

A moment later Liza was kissing Travis passionately on the lips and whispering good-bye. Winnie watched as the three walked off toward the Jeep.

For a moment Winnie studied the peaceful rise and fall of the waves. Then Travis sat down on his beach towel near hers. She realized then she was alone with him for the first time since last fall. Alone with Travis, she thought, her mind slipping back to the sweet way he used to kiss her. The funny songs he'd sing to cheer her up. The tender way he held her.

"I met you—on the highway—where the sun shone like honey," Travis began to sing to himself. Winnie watched, not breathing, as he unlatched his case and drew out his guitar. He positioned it on his crossed legs, picked out a few notes, then stared quietly into space. He strummed the guitar again, and its rich sound brought tears to her eyes. *"You*

saw me—you came with me—and . . ." He broke off, picking the strings in a sudden wild riff. He looked over at Winnie and grinned. "Oh, well, gotta start somewhere, huh?"

Winnie looked at Travis, suddenly unable to breathe. Her eyes traveled slowly down the length of his tanned, muscular body. Suddenly everything about the summer before in Paris came rushing back. Travis had been the very first boy she had ever loved. And her first lover. She needed him then. And in a rush of understanding, she realized that she needed him now, too.

"Yeah," Winnie said, leaning back on her elbows, "gotta start somewhere."

Travis smiled. "Nice break for Liza, huh?"

Winnie began slowly rubbing the bottom of her foot up and down her smooth calf. She wasn't paying attention to what Travis was saying. Instead she was thinking about what Lauren had said last weekend. Maybe she *did* need a summer romance. And Travis was the perfect man. Of course, if he really cared about Liza, then she wouldn't get in the way. That would be wrong.

But Travis was Travis. He was calm. He was sensitive and tender and intelligent. He was totally honest. He was the complete opposite of Liza. Wasn't he? Maybe—if she asked—he would tell her how he *really* felt about the redheaded blob from Brooklyn.

"Travis," Winnie said lightly, moving closer to him until she could see the individual twists on the rubber band of his dark ponytail. "Remember the Burger King in Paris?"

Travis let out a laugh. "Parisian hamburgers. I'll never forget it."

"Neither will I," Winnie whispered, reaching out and giving his ponytail a playful tug. She was only inches away from him now. "Do you remember the little pension I had with the funny water patterns on the ceiling? The smell of the bakery downstairs when Monsieur Monson was making baguettes?"

"Yep." Travis cleared his throat and looked at her.

Winnie looked back. His face looked uncomfortable, but she knew that he would be honest with her. That was the thing about Travis. If you wanted the truth, he'd never let you down. She just had to break the ice.

"Remember?" she breathed, slowly rising to her knees, reaching for his neck, and pulling his face gently to hers. She kissed him and felt her blood rushing through her veins like a locomotive.

Travis looked stunned. He pulled back a little, his blue eyes wet with confusion. Trying to collect himself, he put his guitar gently down in its case. Then he turned to her again and touched the side of her face. "Yeah, Win. I remember. Hey, man. I mean, look. You're throwing me this wild curve, and I—uh—didn't think you were still . . ."

"I am," Winnie replied. "Are you? Interested, I mean."

"Look, Win. Last summer was cool. And I'll

never forget it. But you can't just walk back through time and find that place again. It's gone, Win. It's gone forever."

Winnie gulped. She saw that look on Travis's face. It was the same look that Lauren had, and that Melissa had: It was pity. She was a fool and the whole world felt sorry for her. She was alone. Really alone now. And her heart felt as if it were falling through a deep, dark space.

"I loved you, Winnie," Travis admitted, biting his lip and looking back toward the water. "I loved you and I lost you in Europe, and then I went looking for you. But when I got there, you were already with someone else. With Josh."

"Josh," Winnie said softly, tears welling in her eyes. "Josh," she repeated, almost as if she thought he were actually sitting in front of her. What happened to Josh? They'd loved each other so much.

"It took me a long time to get you out of my head," Travis said softly, resting his elbow on his knee and the side of his face in his hand. "And when Liza came down to L.A. last spring, she helped me, Win. She really did. And now I can't let her down. I care too much about that crazy woman."

Winnie realized that she was clenching her teeth so hard, they hurt.

"There's more to Liza than you know," Travis tried to explain in a gentle voice. "She's out there, Win. She's got guts and hope and heart. And—and when I see you sitting here on the beach—so lonely, so afraid . . ."

Tears spilling down her cheeks, she stood up, feeling more like an idiot than ever before. Something deep inside her was falling apart. The pieces were swirling around, uncontrollable. She had to run. She had to get away somehow. "Forget it, Travis," she cut him off, sobbing. "I know you think I'm awful. Everyone does. So do me a favor and don't say anything. Okay?"

Travis stood up and put his arm around her shoulders tenderly. "Let me drive you back."

"No," Winnie snapped, grabbing her things and turning numbly away. Travis was the last person she wanted help from now. He was gone. Everyone was gone. Travis. Her marriage. Her baby. Her friends. She was going to have to start over.

"Good-bye, Travis. And thanks a lot." Digging her heels into the sand, Winnie marched forward, blinded by tears and the whiteness of the vast beach. She'd never felt so alone in her life. A wave could have swept her away, and no one would care. It just didn't matter anymore.

Eager to get away from the emptiness of the beach, Winnie turned numbly up the Santa Monica boardwalk, but she found herself glaring at the crowds of smiling people lazily taking in the boardwalk, licking ice-cream cones. Everyone belonged. Everyone was going somewhere. Everyone except her. She stumbled forward, threading her way through the crowd, wondering if she should scream or kill or cry or do all three at once.

Her eyes filled with tears again, but then she saw something that made her blink them back. To her left, just off the boardwalk, was a two-story Victorian home bordered by a tiny lawn. A broad porch wrapped around the front and sides, and hanging plants filled with blossoms swung gently in the sea breeze. She slowed. At that moment a group of smiling couples emerged, nodding and talking and wearing blissed-out looks. They looked so happy and fulfilled, Winnie couldn't decide whether to smile or to start crying again.

Moving closer, Winnie looked at the wooden sign swinging over the porch entrance. She drew in her breath as she recognized the name. *The Walker Ingham Institute*.

"'Join the Community of Man,'" Winnie read softly to herself, her lips beginning to tremble with emotion. "'Learn to Love Yourself. Believe in the Power of Your Potential.'"

Winnie didn't know how long she stood gazing at those words. Behind her she could hear the waves booming and shouts of laughter from the boardwalk. But she wasn't listening. She was thinking about the message on the Walker Ingham posters.

And she found herself memorizing the phone number to call for more information.

Ten
....

"o get 'em, babe," Travis called out of the van window. "Dish it out."

Liza flashed him a brilliant smile, then turned and faced the magnificent Shapiro home. In the last two hours she'd impulsively changed her baby-doll Ethel Merman act to 1940's Ginger Rogers. Her hair was perfect in its lavish wartime flip. Her lips glowed with fire-engine-red lipstick. And her matching red-satin shorts set off her legs and her bow-tied tap shoes.

Everything was ready. Her dance. Her song. Her entire self-promotion. She'd worked years for this. Singing lessons. Dance lessons. Comedy routines that fell flat one night and fizzed the next. One victory to every ten humiliations. But now, as the soft afternoon breeze lightly fanned her face, she felt her whole, fabulous show-business career about to begin.

"I'm gonna kill them with this act," Liza whispered to herself, gathering her courage. She could hear the sound of music and party laughter behind the polished-oak front door. "Now just let the maid open the door, so I can very, *very* politely and professionally ask for Mr. Shapiro. And then I'll . . ."

Suddenly the door swung open. A short, handsome man in his early fifties stood before her, wearing a pair of sloppy chinos, an untucked polo shirt, and a pair of deck shoes. Liza stared at the steely blue eyes, then the cigarette dangling between his fingers. She recognized him instantly as Mandy Shapiro.

The guy looked her up and down with a blank expression. "Uh—yes?"

Liza's eyes flapped open. "Oh. Yeah," she burst out with a brilliant smile. Then, taking a deep breath and placing her hands on her bent knees, she looked at him and began singing. "Happy birthday to *you*! Happy birthday to *you*!" Liza lifted her arms straight out from her body and began with an easy "Shuffle-off-to-Buffalo" step, grinning from ear to ear. "Happy *birth*-day, dear *Mandy*. Happy birthday to *you*!" Liza looked briefly and nervously at his distracted face, then launched into her second stanza of "Happy Birthday." She did a neat little tap across the porch, twirled several times, then completed the act by landing on one knee, with her arms stretched over her head. "Hi, I'm Liza Ruff, and I hope you have a wonderful day, Mr. Shapiro," she concluded in a sexy, breathless undertone.

For a moment Liza just stayed in her final position, staring at Mandy Shapiro's famous face and wobbling a little on her knee. She supposed she should stand up. But she was waiting for some kind of a response. Maybe even a little applause. But Mandy Shapiro's face remained blank.

Liza cleared her throat and stood, feeling the tiniest bit of doubt creeping into her head. "Well, then—happy birthday," she said lamely.

Mandy gave her a strange look, then took a drag off his cigarette. At that moment his face suddenly lit up, as if he'd remembered something. Glancing nervously over his shoulder, he put his hand on her arm and gently nudged her away from the door. "Look, doll. I forgot I ordered the singing telegram for my old man in there. . . ."

Liza's jaw dropped. "Your *old man*?"

He looked at her, unfazed. "Yeah. My dad. Mandy Shapiro, senior. He's ninety-five today."

Liza's lips were trembling with humiliation. What did he think she was? Some kind of windup doll with no heart?

"Look, hon," he drew closer, "I got this wild idea a couple of weeks ago to have a singing telegram, and my secretary arranged it. But if I sent you in there right now—the way you look—uh, well, the bottom line is, kid, he'd probably have a heart attack and it'd be on my hands."

Turning away from her, he took another puff of his cigarette and went inside. "Great song, sweetheart. A real original," he muttered before shutting the door in her face.

For a moment Liza just stared at the shiny door. Then she stomped her foot, burst into tears, and ran down the garden walk to the street. It was horrible. It was impossible. What was she doing in this business? It made her feel so cheap. People like Shapiro made her feel like garbage they could throw away!

She raced down the path, sobbing and wiping her cheeks with the back of her hand. Now she was stuck. Alone in Beverly Hills. The cruelest, coldest spot on earth. She stopped and stared down at the street. To her amazement Travis's van was still there.

"Why are you still here?" Liza sobbed, yanking open the van door and crawling onto the seat. She pulled off her tap shoes and threw them onto the floor along with the broken guitar strings, harmonicas, and scattered picks. Then she covered her face with her hands and wept.

"Hey," Travis said gently, slowly pulling her close. "I just wanted to wait until you were safely inside," he explained. "But . . ."

"But the party was for his practically dead father, and he didn't want me anyway," Liza wailed, tears streaming down her cheeks. She made two fists and slammed them against the dashboard. "I feel so *stupid*."

"Hey, lookit you." Travis pulled her over and murmured into her ear. "You're all frowned up."

"This is no time to tease me, Travis Bennett," Liza cried out, wiping a tear delicately off her face.

"You think *I* liked it when the Sing It! people told me to blow out of that audition room before I'd sung one bar of my new song?" Travis asked.

Liza looked over at his face. She loved his face so much. There were the blue eyes, a little too close together. There was the funky string of shells around his neck, and the red bandanna tied around his head. His lips had a fullness to them that always made her want to kiss him. He was tender and strong, all at the same time.

Travis tickled her under her chin. "I was *even* a little jealous."

Liza's eyes were hot. What had she done to deserve this wonderful, gentle man?

"But in the end none of it matters, Liza," Travis soothed, pulling her close and cradling her in his lap. "What matters is now. What matters is how we feel about each other. No one can take that away from us."

Liza flung her arms around his neck and kissed him on the mouth. For a moment everything she ever felt seemed to flood through her. Love. Hate. Sadness. Hope. Tenderness. Bravery. Bitterness. Self-pity. But most of all she felt love.

Love was definitely at the top of the pile.

Max Cantor.
Lauren slowly wiped the last pan from dinner and left it on the counter. She stared dully around the beach house.

Everything was beautiful, as always. But since her disastrous Monday news-clipping mix-up with Max, Lauren's perfect summer had come to an abrupt end.

Max Cantor.
Max Cantor had definitely come to an end, anyway, Lauren thought bitterly, looking down at her hands, which suddenly had nothing to do. She looked up at the ceiling, holding back the beginnings of tears. It was Saturday night, and she'd still barely talked to him. She'd tried to apologize on Tuesday in the lunchroom, but she could tell from his curt response that he was too angry to speak to her. She was convinced, in fact, that he'd been avoiding her all week. For days she'd been stuffing her feelings down inside, trying to forget the horrible incident, keeping her head focused on her work. The problem was with the quiet times like this empty Saturday night, when she had time to think about Max and what might have been. . . .

"Look at the sunset, you guys," Lauren called out across the living room, trying to distract herself from thoughts of Max. "It's incredible."

"Must have been a bad smog day," Winnie

drawled sarcastically from behind her "True Love" comic. Sprawled out on the floor, surrounded by junk-food wrappers and tapes, Winnie looked like a large cat who'd just had her way with a nearby garbage can.

Lauren had to bite her tongue to keep from lashing back at Winnie. She had enough trouble coping with pressures at work. The last thing she needed was another fight with Winnie in one of her inexplicable moods.

Melissa got up and walked to the window, sliding open the glass door to the deck. A warm, salty breeze fluttered in. "It is beautiful, Lauren."

Tears began to slide down Lauren's cheeks as she stared out the window. A few couples walked dreamily over the wet sand, enjoying the romantic light show. The sun was centimeters away from touching the ocean. Everything—water, sky, sun, and beach—had turned a brilliant, matching tangerine. Aside from Winnie's crackling candy wrappers, there was the sound of soft New Age music on the stereo, the snapping fire, and the distant boom of the waves in the distance.

Lauren stood perfectly still. People. Until the beginning of her freshman year in college, she hadn't really known how to go about connecting with them. She'd lived a pampered life with her parents. There was always a big room with a door that locked. There was always a big trip around the corner. A summer house. A good book. It was easy to avoid connecting with people. And so she spent most of her time alone.

Maybe it wasn't such a bad life, Lauren thought miserably. Relationships were such fragile, painful attempts at happiness. They were so easily broken. And when they failed, the costs were so high.

Shaking her head in frustration, Lauren leaped up and headed for the kitchen just as Melissa came in from the deck and headed down the hall.

"I'm going to make popcorn and stuff myself like a pig," Lauren announced, opening a cupboard. "Anyone interested?"

For some reason she couldn't shake the look of April Webster's coal-black eyes boring into her. She couldn't forget the horrible sound of her voice. The look of shock on Max's face as he sat at the conference table . . .

"There's someone at the door, Lauren," Melissa was calling out from the bedroom.

"I'm outta here," Winnie said grumpily, getting up from her pigpen pile. "It's probably Liza and Travis returning from another love fest in la-la land. As usual, she's forgotten her key," Winnie was muttering as she headed down the hall. *"Ahhhh. Let me in!"* she began impersonating Liza's screech. *"I forgot my key. I have to go to the bathroom. I'm gonna be a big star!"*

Lauren rolled her eyes, walked over to the door, and yanked it open.

It wasn't Liza and Travis at all. It was Max Cantor, standing in the half light of the evening, the sea breeze ruffling his hair.

"Nice place," Max said shortly, stuffing his hands into the pockets of his pants and hunching his shoulders. He rocked on his feet, restless and lost.

"Max," Lauren said, staring dumbly at his rumpled hair and faded jean jacket. His eyes looked at her darkly, and his lips seemed frozen in an expression that looked halfway between fury and confusion. "Did you—uh—want to come in?"

"Oh, sure," he replied, his voice soaked with sarcasm. He stepped inside, his eyes moving like a high-speed computer over the room. Lauren realized that he was taking in every detail, every cushion and every picture, and filing it away in his mind.

For a split second Lauren thought maybe he'd come to apologize for being so angry. For avoiding her. For making her feel so horrible . . .

"I figured you had a lot of money stashed away," Max suddenly tore into her. "Parents, huh? Must be tough. But, hey, you can afford to work as an unpaid intern all summer and mingle with the big shots. How'd you get the job, anyway? Parents, I suppose?"

Lauren's heart jumped. "What?" she whispered hoarsely.

"You've jeopardized my job and my future," Max lashed back at her. "And I'm not going to sit back and let you think it's okay."

"I—I'm sorry I delivered the wrong newspaper clips," Lauren began to stutter.

"It wasn't just that." Max looked over his shoulder, then returned his nervous stare to the ocean. He shifted uneasily, as if he didn't feel he belonged in the beautiful room and had forced himself to come. "You tried to blame the mistake on me."

"I just got flustered, Max. I—I didn't know what else to say, I—"

"You made me look like a fool," Max interrupted, swinging around to face her, his dark eyes flashing from behind his glasses. "This job may be a summer lark to you, but it's not to me. It's everything to me right now. I need the money. I need April. And pretty much everything that's important to me depends on this job."

"Look," Lauren retorted with gathering courage. She took a step toward him and narrowed her eyes. "I may not be getting paid for this job, but it is not a *lark*. And another thing. I'm not your slave or your secretary, unless I have the job description wrong."

Max planted one hand against the window frame and let his head sink. His face seemed to glow orange from the rays of the sunset. There was a long, tense moment as Max took in Lauren's reply. Then he straightened, pushed his glasses up on his nose, and crossed his arms over his chest. "I know you were just trying to help," he muttered, his voice softening. He gave her a quick look.

Lauren rubbed the back of her neck and switched off the stove burner.

Max was looking straight at her, tapping his fingers on his jacket, restless. It almost seemed as if there was something he wanted to say, but couldn't. Lauren's heart sped up. She wished she didn't like his face so much. The dark, wavy hair above the pale, slightly flushed skin. The clear glasses that didn't hide the quick expressions in his eyes. They were always changing. Always a little unfamiliar. She was starting to wonder why he'd gone to the trouble of driving all the way out here. If he wanted to tell her off, why hadn't he done it back at the studio? Why at sunset on a Saturday night?

"This job is all I have," Max said, suddenly serious. He took a step closer so there was just the kitchen counter between them. He let the tips of his fingers rest on its edge, and slid them back and forth in thought. "I just wanted to be clear on this, Lauren. It's not a game to me. It's something that I am determined to succeed in."

"Well," Lauren said weakly, trying to pry her eyes away, "I'm sure you will. . . ."

"I'm not going to screw it up, Lauren," he went on, suddenly making a fist and stepping back, "and I'm afraid I can't let anyone else do anything to screw it up either."

Lauren crossed her arms, unable to speak. She wanted to ask him to stay. She wanted to talk it out. But what he was saying hurt too much. Didn't he know how important work was to her, too? Or did she really seem like a silly, spoiled rich girl to him? "Fine, Max."

"Fine," he stammered, looking at her intently, then staring down at the toe of his running shoe.

Lauren began to glare at him, not knowing whether the guilt was worse, or the anger.

Max coughed. He lifted his shoulders and dropped them down again. "Uh. Fine, then. I'll leave. I'll see you Monday."

"Mmm-hmmm. Good," Lauren managed, not moving.

She sat back down at the window seat when she heard the front door click shut. Then she looked out at a dog running through the dim surf. And she burst into tears.

Eleven

ne breath in, two breaths out. Relax.

Melissa was running. Her feet made little pitter-patter splashing noises against the wet sand. Birds parted and flew away as she approached. And the Pacific Ocean waves continued to roar, sending swaths of foamy-white water over her feet.

Relax your shoulder muscles. Easy.

Melissa squinted ahead at the jumble of beautiful wooden beach homes that lined the Crescent Beach. She'd seen the people living in them, many of them as young as the executives on *The April Webster Show*. Young, like her, but fearless risk takers. That's what it took to succeed in a place like L.A., Melissa decided.

Play it safe. Don't take any risks. Just keep your head down and work hard. That's been my life, all right.

"That *was* my life, anyway." Melissa smiled again, thinking that anyone who passed her now would be convinced she was completely out there—not that it was so out there to be out there, in southern California.

She dodged a large jellyfish that had washed up on the sand, then waved to two joggers passing her on the beach. There was only one thing clouding her mind now. It had been a week since her daring "rescue" of the mysterious Evan at the Sikes pool. But she still couldn't shake the memory of him.

"Evan," she said his name out loud, slowing as she neared a rocky outcropping on the beach. An incoming wave splashed against the wet rocks, sending a spray over her body. Her skin tingled. And his face kept popping back into her brain. He'd had such a beautiful, golden face. His sad, sexy smile had touched her somewhere deep inside. She had no idea if she'd ever see him again. Or if she really wanted to. It was nice to think about him as an impossible fantasy, though.

After climbing over the rocks, Melissa found herself in a small, private beach, enclosed on the other side by another rock formation.

She sat down and braced her running shoes on a ledge of sharp rock. Melissa watched the seawater bursting through hidden spouts in the rocks. Delicate jellyfish quietly undulated, trapped in their temporary tide pools. Everything was rich with life and movement. Melissa was only barely aware of her broader surroundings or the passing of time as she scrambled ahead.

Two hours later Melissa realized she'd traveled much farther than planned—practically all the way to Santa Monica beach. The sun was still high in the sky. She felt as if she had enough energy to run to San Diego. But something began to nag at the back of her mind. Something told her to turn back.

A few minutes later Melissa was jogging back to Crescent, veering sharply to her right as a wave crashed unexpectedly in front of her. To her horror she realized that the advancing waters had squeezed her right next to the sheer cliffs. Since she'd left the house, she'd been blissfully unaware that a high tide was quickly overtaking every inch of sand. In a few moments the beach would be gone.

Melissa tried to think. Her eyes traveled desperately along the bare cliffs until her gaze rested on the last rocky outcropping she'd explored. From where the rocks met the base of the cliffs, there appeared to be a ledge leading to a path.

Just as the undertow began to surge back, Melissa took off toward the rocks, digging her toes into the wet sand. Reaching the rocks just as the wave crashed in, Melissa found a secure toehold and gripped the edge of a spout hole. Her stomach lurching, she carefully hoisted herself up. Then she saw it. A small grassy trail led up the cliff from the rock formation.

Melissa's heart was pumping. Taking the steep, gravelly trail at top speed, she headed up, hoping to hit the coastal highway and run home over that route. She slowed as the narrow path took her high over the crashing water. Tiny white flowers sprouted from the rocky ground. Flame-red poppies seemed to spring from every inch of soil.

As she ran higher, the path leveled and a stand of eucalypti shaded her from the hot sun. She took in their sharp, pungent smell and began to sit down just as her eye caught a small wooden sign ahead on the trail. She got up and strolled over.

" 'Pirate Cove'?" she whispered, reading the crudely carved letters on the sign. She looked ahead. A narrow, overgrown trail led steeply down. "*Evan's* Pirate Cove?"

Melissa stopped. She stared at the words, her mind slowly turning them over. Her thoughts returned to Evan, and she began to feel the old fear return. The gnawing, dizzying fear that used to grip her before a meet. Before a final. Before she visited her parents. She wanted it to go away. She didn't want it in her life anymore. But she couldn't help wondering about the handsome pool man.

Clenching her jaw, Melissa forced herself to check out the area. Lauren was always telling her to relax, and now she was going to take her advice. The rocky slope was dry and slippery under her running shoes. But fifty yards down she finally reached a wide solid-rock ledge. When she looked out at the view, she gasped.

The cove itself was almost perfectly round, and its opening to the sea was a narrow slit in the rock. Cliffs rose up steeply from the water, dotted occasionally with hard ledges like the one she stood on. Below, the blue water looked deep as it surged slightly with the movement of the waves outside the entrance. Sharp black rocks jutted from the surface. She felt as if she'd stumbled onto a secret, magical world.

There was a yell from above, and Melissa looked up over her right shoulder just in time to see a solo diver dropping from a ledge. She clamped her hand to her mouth in terror. His body was in control, and his arms were held out at his sides like two muscular wings. But Melissa realized that to make the water, his legs had to be incredibly powerful. The ledge was not directly over the water. What's more, the water below was filled with jagged rocks. Its depth was not clear.

Mel stared helplessly at his body soaring down toward the churning water. Then, just before he hit, he tucked his head and brought his hands together. There was a small splash, and she waited, her heart pounding, praying for his head to surface. Suddenly, after a long wait, a head emerged. He let out an exhilarated yell and shook his wet blond hair.

Her heart leaped to her throat. As impossible

as it seemed, the diver really was Evan.

"Hey," he called out from the water, immediately spotting her on the ledge. "You found it."

"Yes," Melissa stammered under her breath, watching him pull out of the water and scramble up the rocks to her perch. As he drew closer, she could feel her body go strangely limp. She sat down and dangled her legs casually over the edge, trying to hide her nervousness. He pulled himself up onto the ledge next to her, panting only slightly from the exertion, his wet swim trunks sticking to his thighs.

Melissa felt dizzy. The trouble with Evan was that he was almost *too* handsome. His body looked primitive and pure, like a bronze sculpture suddenly come to life. And his face looked as if someone had purposely chiseled it to exact proportions. She wondered if there was anything real under his unreal looks. But his eyes, they were dark and curious—and when she gazed into them, she knew right away that there was more.

Melissa cleared her throat and pried her eyes away from him. "It's beautiful." She glanced up at the ledge above them. "How many feet did you dive?"

He shrugged. "Dunno." He leaned forward. "Two hundred maybe," he whispered with mock seriousness, inches from her ear.

Mel shuddered. His daring and the closeness of his glistening brown shoulder were beginning to make her woozy. "Actually, I wasn't looking for this place," she admitted. "I got caught by a high tide and ran up here, looking for the highway. If I hadn't been on foot . . ."

"You wouldn't have found it," Evan finished her sentence. "That's why I like it. In California, places like this are unbelievably rare. It's completely hidden."

"But you can't get in at high tide?"

Evan pointed up the hill. "I drove, actually. There's a dirt road off the highway, but it's so overgrown, no one knows it's there anymore. I'm probably the only one who knows it." He looked at her. "Except you—now. And I don't even know your name."

"Melissa," she whispered, returning his gaze and feeling her mind go blank again. Beneath her feet the ocean water surged and splashed. The sun began to dip in the sky.

"Anyway, glad you like it, Melissa," Evan said quietly, gazing ahead, his face somber.

"Soooo," Melissa began, after a few moments of silence, "how's the pool business?"

"The pool bus—" Evan began, giving her a curious look. Then his eyes moved away, out over the view. "Oh, yeah. Pools. Pools are good. Pools are . . . great. Not exactly the most exciting business in the world, but it's—uh—a living."

Melissa hugged her knees and stared down at the churning water, remembering their last meeting at the Sikes mansion. She sighed. "But you must get to hang out at some beautiful estates."

"Uh, sure . . . "

"That place Oliver Sikes owns down the beach was so lovely," Melissa said, staring dreamily out over the water in the fading light. A warm breeze tickled her skin. "Did you check out the *gardens?* And the incredible *view?* I bet that it's bigger than the house I grew up in . . ."

"Where are you from?" Evan interrupted.

Melissa gave him a nervous look over her shoulder. "Up north in mountain country. Springfield, Oregon. It's where the University of Springfield is. I just finished my freshman year."

Evan nodded. "You said you did track, didn't you?"

"Yeah," Melissa said quickly. But she definitely didn't want to talk about faraway Springfield now. "Maybe you're used to places like that, but I couldn't believe the sheer size of the Sikes place." Melissa heard herself babbling, wishing she could stop. But she needed to talk, to escape the power of his penetrating stare. "I mean, I guess it's obvious I'm a small-town girl, but it was incredible. You must meet a lot of fascinating people in your line of work."

"Fascinating?"

Melissa looked at him. "Yeah. People like Oliver Sikes and Walker Ingham."

Evan's eyes seemed to turn inward. "Fascinating," he said with a hint of soft sarcasm. He tugged a blade of grass from the rocky ledge and looked at it, shifting with nervousness. "You could call them *that*, all right. Just fascinating."

Melissa's smile faltered. "What do you mean?"

Evan shrugged and shook his bangs out of his eyes. "Don't be fooled. I can tell you're smarter than that."

"Huh?"

He turned and briefly clamped his brown eyes on to hers. "The Sikes place has a very slick surface, Melissa. A glamorous, do-gooder surface. But that doesn't mean anything, does it? Plenty of things— plenty of *people* have secrets. Nasty ones."

Melissa frowned. "Nasty? What are you talking about? What secrets?"

Evan stood up and shrugged. He rocked back and forth on his feet, restless. "Forget it. I shouldn't have even . . ."

"You must do a lot of pool cleaning out there," Melissa started.

But Evan had disappeared. She looked around. He was already halfway up to the ledge where he'd dived off minutes before. "Come on up," he shouted over his shoulder, gracefully climbing the rock face.

"But . . ."

"Forget Sikes and Ingham," Evan shouted down. "They're not that interesting, Melissa. Trust me! Hey—I'll show you something interesting. Come on up."

Melissa gulped and began climbing toward him.

"Diving off and not knowing where you're going to land is interesting," Evan called down to her, stretching his hand down to pull her up to his perch.

Melissa tensed and turned around. The circle of surging water below her looked as far away as the moon. Seawater splashed hard against the jagged black rocks. Diving without knowing where she would land? She always wanted to know where she was going to land. "This is really dangerous," she said with a nervous smile.

"Yeah, it's dangerous," Evan shouted, throwing his head back and spreading his arms. "That's why it's so interesting. Danger is interesting. Don't you see, Melissa? Skydiving. Auto racing. Bungee jumping. It's all the same. You're out there. Will you be alive or dead in two minutes? You live for the thrill in your bones. You throw away the fear."

"Fear," Melissa repeated. She knew about fear. Fear pushed her through life. Fear decided practically everything for her. Fear of failing. Fear of having no money. Fear of being found out.

"Once you conquer the fear, Melissa, you can conquer anything."

Melissa's knees began to buckle. Her lips parted as she started to speak. But before anything came out, Evan was pulling away from her, spinning giddily on the edge of the cliff. A crazy, happy look spread over his face, and then, without warning, he suddenly threw himself off the edge into the thin air.

She held her breath as he landed like an arrow

into the bull's eye, barely making a splash.

"Come on down," he yelled, his head popping back up. "The water's fine."

Melissa stared at him, stunned and provoked at the same time.

The fear, she thought wildly. *Let go of the fear.*

The next moment, she was perched on the edge of the warm rock, stretching her arms out. She bent her knees and imagined her legs as two powerful springs that could take her anywhere. She closed her eyes and dived. The air rushed over her skin like a hurricane. Her body was straight and true. She was flying through space into the unknown, but somehow something told her that she was safe.

She hit the surface and felt the water close over her body. The smacking pain stung, but her mind was giddy with the power of what she'd just done. She kicked up and burst through the surface, gulping air.

"Aaaaaaaggggghhhhhhhh!" she heard herself scream. When she opened her eyes, Evan was swimming toward her, his smile breaking his whole face open.

"I didn't think you would do it," he yelled, grabbing her around the waist and dunking her.

"I let go," Melissa shouted, laughing so hard her stomach muscles were aching. "I let the fear go."

"You did!" Evan laughed back, circling her waist again. He started to dunk her, then caught her glance. Treading water, he slowly turned to face her.

His arm drew her against his body. Melissa's heart stopped. The surging ocean water swirled around them. But his face was so close now, she could feel the warmth of his breath. Gently, he bent forward and kissed her on the lips.

Let go of the fear, she thought again, kissing him back. She turned her whole body around to face him and felt his strong arms encircling her. She kissed his neck and she kissed the back of his ear. As they clung tightly together in the water, Melissa could feel the warm water enveloping them. She could feel the fear falling away like dragon scales. She didn't want it anymore.

For a moment she felt as if she would never be afraid again.

Twelve

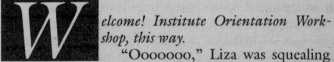

Welcome! Institute Orientation Workshop, this way.

"Ooooooo," Liza was squealing softly. "The Walker Ingham Institute. I never thought that finding yourself could be so chic."

"*Ssshhhhhhhh,*" Winnie hissed over her shoulder. She clenched her jaw and followed the signs along the side of the elegant Victorian bungalow.

Each day since she'd arrived in L.A. had been an acute reminder of how disconnected and lonely her life had become. Now she felt she was on the verge of a profound change. Her only problem was Mel, Liza, and Lauren. Feeling a momentary rush of generosity, wanting to share such an important discovery, she'd invited them to join her this morning. And now she was beginning to regret it.

"Inner peace, here I come," Lauren was muttering in a sarcastic voice.

Winnie pushed open a beautiful wrought-iron garden gate, gritting her teeth. *That's right, inner peace,* she thought grimly. *What have you guys got against it? Inner peace is exactly what I'm looking for. Inner peace through the act of giving. Connection with others. Purpose. These people know what it's all about, and I'm going to let them help me.*

When they reached the Institute's back garden, Winnie took a deep breath. It was the most beautiful, romantic place she'd ever seen. Teak benches were arranged on its wide brick terrace, shaded by blossoming trees. A tiny babbling stream ran through the garden, spanned by a lovely Japanese-style wooden bridge. Chimes and tiny crystals rustled softly on tree branches, and a large antique cage near the garden's far corner held two gray doves.

"I think I'm gonna pass out," Liza giggled behind her. "I'm overdosing on serenity and tastefulness."

Winnie stepped forward, barely hearing her. Of course Liza didn't understand. Her mind was too obsessed with power and noise. Walker Ingham's Institute was all about selfless giving as a way to self-fulfillment. Liza couldn't possibly understand something like that.

Winnie took in the beautiful garden. Already a good-sized group of people had assembled, talking quietly among themselves. A few were strolling through a carefully tended herb plot that ran along the south-facing stone wall. She stared intently at one beautiful woman in a flowing crepe dress, who was clinging to the arm of a tall man with jeans and brand-new sandals. It took all of her self-control to keep from walking up to her and saying, "I'm like you. I want to know you."

"This is great stuff," Lauren said into her ear. "If April does another show with Ingham, I'll need to know everything about the guru-guy."

Sure, Lauren, Winnie thought, irritated, *go ahead and look at Walker Ingham as a potential* April Webster *story idea. Look at the cold, hard facts the way you always do. Don't try to go any deeper. Don't feel. Don't listen to your heart.*

"Did you know that Kim Flora *herself* took one of Walker Ingham's seminars just before she landed that starring role in *Deadly Palace*?" Liza gushed, grabbing a lumpy brown cookie from the woman's tray. "I read it in *People* this morning. Elizabeth Mc-Narry went too. Then she got that big part in *Tie My Shoes* and won a Tony."

"Here's your big chance to tap into their secret, huh?" Lauren drawled.

"Why not?" Liza giggled. "Hey, check out this hunky."

Winnie glared at Liza, then looked up. A slender, square-jawed man in his late twenties was standing expectantly on the deck, smiling at the group. He wore a faded polo shirt, pressed jeans, and leather mocs. Winnie thought he was good-looking in a quiet, precise way. His curly brown hair and dark eyebrows made his dark eyes look intelligent and penetrating. "Hope you enjoyed the refreshments, everyone," he called out. "Please join me in the great room, and we'll get started."

"Get his phone number, Win," Liza whispered loudly.

Winnie glared at Liza over her shoulder again, shaking her head at Liza's beehive hairdo and out-of-place shiny polyester jumpsuit. She kept trying to remember why she was supposed to be Liza's friend.

Inside the building tastefully framed posters of Walker Ingham covered the walls. Winnie's eyes teared up at one picture of Walker kneeling beside a ragged, big-eyed girl in a devastated third-world-country slum. There was something in his eyes that pulled her. Something calm. Something powerful. Whatever it was, Winnie thought with growing hope, she wanted some of it.

"Please make yourselves comfortable," the guy was saying, ushering the group into a large room with rows of comfortable-looking chairs. "My name is Randall Stuart."

"Mmmmmm," Liza was murmuring next to Winnie. "Nice."

"Stop it, Liza," Winnie whispered, feeling her eyes burn with anger. "Why don't you just leave if you're not interested?"

"Let's get started," Randall began energetically, pacing before a wall-sized close-up of Walker hugging a woman with a tearfully ecstatic expression. The room suddenly hushed. "Now." He clapped his hands together. "How many people in this room are truly happy with the way their lives are going? Come on. Don't be shy. Let's have a show of hands."

Winnie kept her hand firmly down, then sneaked a glance around the packed room. To her left a blue-eyed woman wiped a tear off her cheek. Several men were looking downcast into their laps. She watched with growing amazement as the entire room fell creepily silent.

"Hey!" Winnie looked over in horror as Liza's squawk filled the room and she waggled her hand in the air. "Wait a minute. I'm pretty happy. What's the matter with you people? *Life's candy and the sun's a ball a butter,*" she sang out.

Winnie covered her face with her hands. Mel and Lauren giggled softly. Why had she invited them? Why did she have anything to do with them? In a flash of realization she saw how disconnected she'd become. She didn't have friends she could really share her life with. She was always moving around the outside of things. Different. Alone. The wacky, odd one out. Now, as she looked around the room, she realized all that could change. There was a chance now that she could be in the center of the circle, with people who really interested and moved her.

Randall turned and gave Liza a polite look. Then

he looked up at the group, making a thoughtful steeple with his hands. "But what about everyone else? Happiness! We all grow up thinking that somehow we will find it. So . . . what has happened? Why does life's precious gift elude us—elude so many?

"We are not happy because we do not *allow* ourselves to be," Randall said in a firm voice, making two fists and holding them out in front of his chest.

There was a murmur of understanding through the room.

"Blocks to happiness are *self-created*," Randall said forcefully. He let his fists spring open. "But we can *break* the invisible bonds that imprison us. You all have incredible power within you. You are the only one responsible for your happiness. All you need are the tools to *unlock it*."

Winnie could barely breathe. Every word was like a ray of golden light. It was true. She did have power. She did know she was responsible for her own happiness. All she needed was a way to get there.

When Randall was nearly done, the audience was buzzing with excitement.

"Finally, folks"—Randall held his hands up for attention—"about the workshop. The cost is five hundred dollars and lasts for one week. We meet here each day at ten, break for lunch in the garden, and resume work until four P.M. Mr. Ingham conducts all workshops personally, and enrollment is limited to twenty-five individuals per session. The fee also includes a private consultation with Mr. Ingham himself."

A man near Winnie raised his hand. "That's a lot of money. How do you set your fees?"

Randall placed his palms together in front of him and gave the man a look of complete understanding. "It *is* a serious investment. I can't argue with that. But I *can* say that it probably will be the most important investment you've ever made. You're not investing in stocks or bonds here, ladies and gentlemen. You are investing in *yourself*. You are investing in your *life*. And the payback will be immense. Beyond your wildest dreams."

Winnie felt her heart rise into her throat.

"Please remember also that your tuition fee is not just benefitting you," Randall said in a solemn voice. "It's going to help thousands of impoverished people around the world."

Winnie nodded and caught the eye of several others who obviously liked what Randall was saying.

"Before we conclude, please join me for a brief meditation exercise," Randall continued, stepping toward the group and taking the hand of a pretty young woman on the aisle. "I want you all to join hands, close your eyes, and quiet your inner space."

Winnie reached for Liza's hand, and the hand of the man sitting next to her. She could hear Lauren begin to giggle again, but tuned her out.

"I want you to seep yourself in the joyous feeling that is rooted in the core of your being," Randall

chanted softly. "Imagine yourself reaching down inside yourself. Grab the joy. Grab the love. Take
them and bring them up into the light."

Winnie's eyes were wet. She could feel something hidden deep inside wanting to come out. She
knew it was there.

"Now hold it up to the sun," Randall continued.
"Hold the love and the joy in its golden light. It is
yours to cherish. Feel the light pour through your
body. Feel its warmth. Thank you, everyone. Thank
you for coming."

Winnie let out her breath and opened her eyes,
just as the guy next to her reached over and hugged
her tearfully. She sat, her body feeling strangely
light, her mind oddly at peace. She could see Lauren, Melissa, and Liza hurrying for the door, but she
was almost afraid to move and break the beautiful
spell Randall had put her under. For the first time
since she'd arrived in L.A., she felt as if she really
and truly belonged.

Glowing with newfound energy, Winnie floated
up to the front of the room, where Randall was saying good-bye to the last of the guests.

"Hello," Randall said, turning and giving her a
friendly smile.

"Hello," Winnie said quietly. "Your message
was—powerful."

Randall looked at her intently, his body perfectly
still. "We find many people are hungry for peace—
ready to break down the walls."

"I'd like to take the workshop," Winnie said, suddenly shy. She fidgeted with her star-shaped earrings. "But I don't—well, I'll have to figure how—I mean, my finances and everything."

"Yes," Randall said simply, staring at her. There was a long pause as he seemed to look deep into her eyes. "I can tell that you are a searcher and an explorer. Perhaps exceptionally so. So please let me suggest something. Walker has set up a scholarship program for young people like yourself. In exchange for tuition you could work for the Institute. Would you be interested?"

Winnie's heart was beating wildly. "Yes. Yes, I would be."

"Check back on Monday at ten A.M. We'll see what we can work out."

A few moments later Winnie found herself floating joyfully out of the Institute's front door, filled with hope. Across the boardwalk she spotted Melissa, Lauren, and Liza, looking bored. She strolled ahead, suddenly unafraid of what they might say. "What did you think?" she asked boldly.

Lauren put her hand on her chest and crossed her eyes. *"Hold the love and the joy in its golden light,"* she chanted before bursting into laughter. "Hey, look, Win. I don't need some cult to show me how to get what I want."

Winnie stared at her, suddenly filled with loathing.

"Yeah, give it up, Win," Liza agreed. She pulled a compact out of her bag and dabbed her nose.

Then she whipped out a tube of lipstick and began coating her lips. "I mean, I can take charge of my life and my career. What's the big secret?"

Winnie's face was hot with rage. "You guys are being completely unfair. These workshops are probably helpful to a lot of people."

Lauren snorted, starting to walk toward the Jeep. "Yeah. Helpful for the *helpless*."

Winnie's entire body was shaking with anger. "You are a spoiled, insensitive brat, Lauren Turnbell-Smythe," she shouted. "You hide your insecurities under a mask of self-confidence. But let me tell you something. You're completely *transparent*. And you are fooling yourself if you think you're something special."

Turning away, Winnie marched away from the group toward the beach.

"Winnie," Melissa shouted. "Don't you want a ride home?"

"I'm walking," Winnie screamed back, nearly tripping on an uneven board. Dodging a beautiful couple licking matching ice-cream cones, she ducked down a stairway to the beach and ran down to the sand. Taking off her sandals, she thrust them into her bag and headed angrily down to the water.

A small wave rolled in, and a sheet of warm water swirled around her ankles. Above, the sea gulls screamed and dived. Ahead, the blue Pacific stretched out smooth and perfect. She breathed in deeply, remembering Randall's words.

We can break the invisible bonds that imprison us. You all have incredible power within you. All you need are the tools to unlock it. . . .

Winnie felt something stir within her. She looked back across the sand at the Ingham Institute's white Victorian house. Then she looked out at the serene Pacific. Life didn't have to be so hard, did it? There *had* to be a way to disconnect herself from selfish, negative people like Lauren. There *had* to be a way to find serenity—even after a lifetime of chaos and pain.

She would stay right here in southern California and find the truth with Walter Ingham. She'd show *them*.

Thirteen

"aisin, onion, plain, and sesame," Lauren announced heavily, dumping a bag of fresh bagels onto the table of the studio's lunchroom. "Let's eat them all and see what happens, Melissa."

"Yeah," Melissa agreed, slicing open a sesame and reaching into the grocery bag for a square of cream cheese. "We explode and lose our jobs."

Lauren let out a stifled laugh.

"Actually," Melissa bent forward, confessional, "Monday-morning breakfast at the studio beats breakfast at the beach house in the shadow of Winnie's dark stares."

Lauren swallowed and fidgeted with the edge of

the bagel bag. She didn't really want to talk about Winnie. Lauren had been cruel to Winnie after the Ingham orientation on Saturday. Every time she thought about it, the knot of guilt in her stomach got tighter.

She gritted her teeth and shook her head. Little bagel crumbs spilled down the front of her khaki jacket. She hated the bratty, know-it-all feeling she got when things were going her way. Maybe she wasn't used to success. Maybe she just wasn't grown-up enough. But she'd been a brat after she became a successful investigative reporter at the U of S *Weekly Journal*. And she got bratty again when she started interning at *The April Webster Show*.

Now, Lauren thought miserably, she'd hurt Winnie. Winnie Gottlieb, who along with her best friends Faith and KC, had been her anchor of support at the beginning of their freshman year. They didn't have to accept her when she'd arrived on campus in her frumpy clothes, paralyzed with shyness and cowed by her dominating mother. They didn't have to encourage her in her writing. Or welcome her to their parties. But they did. And now look at the thanks she had given Winnie.

Lauren put down her bagel and wiped her hands on a napkin. "Winnie won't even accept my apology. She just looks away as if I'm not there. I hate it. There doesn't seem to be anything I can do."

Melissa munched and nodded. "I can almost see the frost forming on her when you come near."

Lauren crossed her arms over her chest. "And on Max, too," she burst out. "He's apparently still fuming over the mixed-up photocopies. Don't you think I've apologized to *him* enough too?"

Melissa tossed her hair out of her eyes and let out a heavy sigh. Her freckled face was glowing from the sun and exercise, but something suddenly clouded her green eyes. "I still don't understand why he had to drive all the way out to Malibu to let you know what a terrible person you were. Men are weird."

"Men are malfunctioning, semievolved babies from Mars," Lauren finally announced, burying her face in her hands.

Melissa propped her chin up and gazed dreamily into space. "At least I had one wonderful, magical encounter with a member of the inferior sex."

"Evan," Lauren reminded her. "Evan, the pool guy from heaven."

"We met, we dived, we kissed . . ." Melissa whispered.

"Look out, Mel," Lauren interrupted, "your head's wobbling from excess fantasizing."

"But he didn't even . . ."

"Get your phone number," Lauren said impatiently. "I know. I know. What do you expect? He's a guy."

Her expression softened. She reached over and patted Melissa's hand. "You'll see him again." Her eyes lit up. "Plus, you *have* to run into him. He said some pretty intriguing things about Oliver Sikes and Walker Ingham."

"Maybe."

Lauren paused and looked thoughtfully at the soda machine humming in the corner of the room. "Actually, I have a funny feeling about the whole Ingham thing."

"Thing?"

Lauren nibbled on her thumbnail, remembering the Saturday seminar. She thought about the Ingham Institute's expensive building and garden. She thought about the carefully photographed pictures of Walker Ingham. And she thought about the strange effect Randall's message had on Winnie. She was so vulnerable. Anyone could . . .

"Lauren?"

"I don't know." Lauren tried to focus on her bagel. "It's just a feeling. Call it my suspicious nature. Call it my journalistic instinct. But something's very strange in the Ingham kingdom. There's a story there. I know it."

"Mmmmm." Melissa looked only mildly convinced. "I suppose. I don't know how you'd ever figure anything like that out, but . . ."

Lauren looked up and narrowed her eyes at Melissa, who was suddenly making funny faces and jerking her head strangely. She looked over and felt her stomach do a flip-flop. Max Cantor had just walked into the lunchroom for coffee. Now he was leaning uncertainly against the candy machine, sipping and staring at her. Lauren stiffened. Hadn't he already stalked her out at the beach house? Hadn't he already told her how spoiled and childish she was? What did he want now?

Melissa checked her watch and grabbed a bagel to go. "Big day for me, Lauren," she said in a rush. "I saw about a thousand delivery requests in my box on the way in."

"Bye," Lauren said with a nervous nod, glancing briefly at Max, then looking down at her own coffee.

Abruptly gathering her things, she stood and walked boldly up to Max. "Hi."

Max coughed a little as he took a sip from his paper cup. His eyes widened, and an embarrassed smile flickered across his face. "Uh, hi, Lauren."

Lauren reminded herself not to keep apologizing. She'd apologized, hadn't she? And her life as a professional apologizer and guilt monger had ended months ago. "Hi," she came back quickly with a challenging look. "Still mad? Or do you want to talk about something important? Like an idea for a show I have?"

Max's face reddened slightly, then recovered. He pushed his glasses up on his nose and threw the empty coffee cup in the garbage can. Then, with an apologetic look, he pulled out a chair from the nearest table. "Sit."

Lauren sat down, and Max sat down next to her, his hands folded in front of him on the table. He looked down and let out a small sigh. "Look. I'm sorry."

Biting her lip, Lauren looked over at his ear and the clean line of his jaw. His dark hair curled a little down his neck, below the fold of his denim shirt. He turned to give her a brief look, and she could see that his eyes were slightly red. She even detected dark circles under them, as if he'd been working too long with too little sleep. "I'm sorry too," Lauren said, leaning back and stuffing her hands into the pockets of her skirt.

"I feel like a fool—charging over to your place that night," he stammered, "saying all those things. . . . It was . . . crazy."

Lauren fell silent, not knowing what to say.

Max shook his head. "April's still crazy over the ratings," he said rapidly. "She's got me running around like a cocker spaniel, digging up teen angles." He shoved his elbow out on the table and dragged his fingers through his hair. "And now they've got Walker Ingham coming back for a second show."

Lauren raised her eyebrows. "April talked him into it?"

"Sure she did," Max said with a smile. "She can sweet-talk anyone into anything."

Lauren felt her old energy return. Just talking to Max did it. It was amazing.

"So, anyway, I'm working with promotion on the show," Max explained. "A couple of weeks ago I told April she should think about writing one of those self-help books with Walker."

"Oh, yeah, right," Lauren laughed back. "Sell

them on TV, why not sell them in the bookstore, too? It's brilliant."

Max nodded, sliding his elbow out on the table. "Yeah. They're both into the "You have the inner power to achieve anything" syndrome. It's perfect. And if it's done right, it'll mean a lot of money for both, as long as it's promoted right."

"Ah, the power of promotion," Lauren cracked. "The perfect spin. The image that's worth a thousand lousy words."

Max grinned, loosening and pushing out his chair a little. "Get this. A beach party. A very fancy beach party. Out at the Sikes mansion. April, Walker, and Oliver are there, along with about five hundred of their closest friends with about a hundred Academy Awards and Grammys between them."

"Oh, wow. Photo opportunities galore," Lauren replied. She loved the way Max's mind worked. It was so free. So fun. So smart.

"You got it," Max cried out, making a fist in the air. "The press will descend on us in droves. There'll be more reporters and photographers than real people." In a flash he withdrew his tiny tape recorder and held it in front of his lips, pretending to interview himself.

"Hello, Mr. Ingham. Does eating broccoli result in inner peace?"

Max held the tape machine a few inches away and deepened his voice with mock drama. "No, actually, Tom, it results in world peace. That is, if the entire world ate it. The karma would change the position of the planets, and millions would rejoice."

"Thank you, Mr. Ingham."

"Thank you, Tom."

Lauren laughed out loud as he put away the machine. Then she saw that he was laughing too, not taking his eyes off her. There was a pause and she felt suddenly shy. The women at the next table burst into laughter, and a can rolled loudly out of the machine behind them.

"Scored big points for the party idea, I guess." Max turned serious again. "But that doesn't take care of April's problem with the falling teen ratings. The advertisers are breathing down her neck. And since April's smart enough to know she's not hip to teenagers, that puts all the pressure on me, resident teen and indentured servant."

Lauren shook her head and felt a twinkle in her eye. She recognized the feeling she had about Max. It was like the feeling she had about Dash when they were working on a story together. It was friendship, but it was more than that. There was electricity. There were sparks flying. "Because you know what speaks to those acne-lotion users and soda-pop drinkers."

Max nodded. "You bet. And those sponsors will dump their advertising dollars elsewhere if I don't prove it—and soon."

Lauren leaned forward, slipping a stray lock of hair behind her ear. "Look. This is what I'm hearing. It might help."

"What?" Max rested his chin in his hands and looked at her seriously.

"I've heard that there's something on Walker Ingham," Lauren said in a low voice. "Something nasty."

Max's eyes widened. He pulled a small notepad out of his jacket and sat up with interest. A pencil appeared and he poised it over the pad. "What source? Where'd you get that? Walker's never had anything on him."

"Melissa delivered something to the Sikes mansion last week," Lauren explained, "and she talked to the pool man."

Max's face fell. The pencil sagged a little. "The pool man?"

"Yeah." Lauren's voice dropped, taking in Max's doubtful look. She couldn't suppress her smile. "But he appeared to be a particularly well-informed pool man."

Max shrugged. His pencil perked up again and he scribbled something. "It's thin. But who cares? We're desperate. And desperate times . . ."

". . . call for desperate measures," Lauren finished his sentence with a broad grin.

"So put your journalistic instincts to work on the teen angle, Lauren," Max urged her, softly kicking the side of her shoe under the table as he continued to scribble. He pushed his glasses up on his nose and stared into space. "Walker Ingham, April Webster, and twenty million teens. How do we put them all together in one package with one big, beautiful bow?"

Lauren nibbled a hangnail and thought. Her mind drifted back to the orientation at the Institute. There hadn't been any teenagers there. . . . She jerked her head up with a start. *They* had been there. *Liza* had been there.

"Young hopefuls in Hollywood," Lauren said suddenly, staring into space.

"Huh?"

Lauren's head was spinning, remembering Liza's brazen suggestion to have April do a show on teens who come to Hollywood seeking their fame and fortune. She turned to Max, her face beaming. "Young hopefuls in Hollywood," she repeated. "Forget Ingham for a minute. Look, thousands of teenagers flock to Hollywood every month, looking for their big break. . . ."

Max's face was deadly serious. "The classic American story . . ."

"The one-in-a-million chance." Lauren was nodding with excitement. Max knew what she was talking about. She didn't have to explain. He was reading her thoughts.

"And it happens every day in L.A. . . ."

Lauren twisted around in her seat to face him. "The big talent comes to town. Will she make it, or pack her bags and take the bus back to Kansas? We dig these kids up. April puts them on the show so they can talk about their dreams."

"The crazy day jobs they take while they wait for an agent to call about a one-liner on a TV show. . . ."

"Yeah." Lauren was buzzing, propelled by the flash in Max's eyes. "And then April gets a hot teen director to appear on the show with them."

"Yeah!" Max was jumping up and rubbing his hands.

"And she pumps up the audience with 'Which one of these Hollywood hopefuls will get a big break today from Mr. Big Director sitting right here before our studio audience?'"

Max clapped his hand to his forehead. "Yes!"

Lauren's head was flooding with ideas. "Jack up the tension even more with publicity, Max. You pick the Hollywood hopefuls. You invite them to the Sikes beach party and tell them to hang around April. Then you steer the photographers over. April's picture suddenly appears everywhere, hanging out with hip, up-and-coming teen stars!"

"Staff meeting in one minute, Max," someone called into the room.

Max grabbed his notepad again and scribbled furiously. Then he jumped up, barely able to contain his joy. "I love it." His face turned serious. "Look, Lauren. Would you let me propose it in the meeting?"

Lauren's face turned somber too. "Yes, but I have only one request."

"Say it, say it," Max said excitedly.

Lauren rose from her chair and gathered her things. She'd burned Winnie, but she wasn't going to do the same thing to Liza. "If you do the show, my friend Liza Ruff—she gets an audition for the show. She really *is* a Hollywood hopeful. And she really *is* a big talent badly in need of a break."

"Of course," Max said, looking at her with a huge, grateful smile. Suddenly he stepped forward and wrapped his arms around her. "Thank you, Lauren. Thank you so much."

Lauren stood still, then gradually lifted her arms slightly to return his embrace. Her cheek pressed briefly against his shirt. His body was so close. She could smell the shampoo scent of his hair. She could feel his hands move slowly up her back as he stepped away. Then he turned abruptly and rushed out of the room.

She stared at the door, barely breathing. Then, hiking up her shoulder bag, she walked out, took off down the hall, and burst out into the parking lot for air. She didn't know what Max's hug had meant. It had been so close. And it had lasted so long. Longer, Lauren thought, her heart in her throat, than any ordinary hug.

Bending her head happily back, she looked up at the sky, brown and fuzzy with smog. Suddenly it was the most beautiful sky she'd ever seen.

Fourteen

Winnie sat up and stared out over the crowded Santa Monica beach. The Ingham Institute was definitely her starting point on the road to sanity. All week long she'd been volunteering at their headquarters. The tapes, the laid-back atmosphere, and even Randall's soothing breathing exercises were really helping. She *did* have power. She *was* beginning to take responsibility for her life.

Jealousy. Loneliness. Pain. They were intruders and destroyers, Winnie reminded herself. With the right training she'd be able to sweep them out of her mind in an instant—leaving her to bask in the serenity of the moment.

Right?

"I'll march my band out. I'll beeeeat myyy drum!"
Liza suddenly burst into song, drowning out
Travis's gentle song. Liza stopped, stared briefly into
the waves, then threw her head back and shouted,
"Thank you, Lauren!"

Winnie felt her control starting to fall apart. "So,
great," she said to Liza. "You have an audition and
your comedy routine is bound to crack everybody
up. You got what you came down to L.A. for."

Liza opened her eyes so wide, Winnie thought
they were going to pop out. Then she shook her
head and made little exasperated, blubbering noises
with her mouth. "I'll never understand you, Winnie
Gottlieb. Don't you realize what's at stake? When
I'm chosen to appear on national television with
April Webster, I will be meeting *Geoff Hansen.*"

"Mmmmm."

Travis stopping tuning and heaved a huge sigh.
"Come on, you two. Look, Liza. Winnie's not into
it, okay? And, Win—give Liza a break, it's a really
important day. . . ."

"Geoff Hansen!" Liza shouted over Travis's gentle peacemaking. "As in the most important director
of teen flicks, Winnie. I'm there. Face-to-face.
Cheek to cheek. *And,* since my audition is bound to
be a big success, I'll actually get to be on her show.
And I'll get one of those gilt-edged invitations to
the big beach party at the Sikes mansion."

Whoop-dee-do, Winnie thought to herself, reaching for a tube of suntan oil and checking her watch.

"It's been fascinating, but I'm outta here."

"More hours at the Ingham Institute?" Travis wanted to know. He was standing too, putting his guitar back in the case and stuffing sheets of music into his small pack. "It seems like you're always there, Win."

Winnie straightened her sunglasses and tried not to make the painful eye contact. "I know. My hours are stacking up, but it's going to take forever to earn enough to pay for the workshop. Oh, well."

She watched, nervous, as Travis hiked his knapsack on his shoulder, picked up his guitar case, and looked down gently at Liza. "I'm jettin' too, babe. Got some stuff to take care of."

"'Kay," Liza replied with a distracted smile, giving her hair an extra coating of spray. She wiggled five orange nails at him.

"I'll walk up the beach with you," Winnie heard Travis call out behind her as she picked her way through clusters of beach towels, stray pop cans, and half-collapsed sand castles.

Winnie hurried up the beach, trying to ignore Travis. "Yeah, sure." When they reached the boardwalk, the lunch crowd had already packed the shops and restaurants. Couples gazed into the windows of high-priced art galleries and boutiques. Sea gulls screamed. Children in bathing suits laughed. And Travis persisted, deliberately matching Winnie step for furious step, even though she was clearly trying to lose him, clearing ignoring the fact that his usual stride was more of a meander.

"Look, Travis," Winnie finally said. "Forget about that crazy move I made on you. I've forgotten all about it. And I'm sorry I can't relate to Liza. I know she's harmless, it's just that . . ."

"It's cool, Win," Travis broke in. "Actually I've—I've got something else on my mind lately." He shook his head. "But talking about it will just get me all wigged out."

Winnie nodded quietly and slowed down a little. Maybe she was getting just a little paranoid lately. Travis didn't seem interested in hassling her, after all. Still, Winnie was relieved a few moments later to wave good-bye and hurry through the Institute's Dutch-door entrance. She could almost feel her muscles relaxing when she reached the mail room, where a large stack of pamphlets waited for address labels. Through the piped-in stereo system she could hear a soothing soprano singing over the sound of rushing water. The spicy smells of the Institute's all-organic bakery drifted through. In the front waiting room a bearded man wearing silk pants read a magazine. And she could hear Randall's deep voice on the phone in the office next door.

Winnie grabbed a stack of Walker Ingham's new fund-raising mailing and carried it over to a worktable. A black-and-white photo close-up of a small boy with rumpled hair covered the front panel of the brochure. In green letters at the bottom, she read the words "You have the power to heal." Inside she stared at several new pictures of Walker hoeing a muddy field, surrounded by a group of smiling African women. Her eyes welled up looking at a photograph of Walker wearing traditional Indian dress, spooning food from a wooden bowl to a group of children in a Calcutta orphanage.

She closed her eyes and rested her hands, palms-up, on the table. Tears spilled down her cheeks. She needed something. She needed the peace now. Lauren. Liza. Travis. She couldn't cope with them. She couldn't cope with anything. Then, in a brief moment of calm, she visualized Walker Ingham's face as Randall had taught her. Mentally, she imagined his gentle spirit seeping into her soul. She pictured the vastness of the ocean, and then she turned the image into her own life. Limitless, with no boundaries. It would have beauty and purpose.

Slowly, she opened her eyes, feeling refreshed and energized. But when she glanced at the door, she felt a twinge of embarrassment. Randall Stuart was leaning quietly against the doorjamb, staring at her. Wearing jeans and a loose-fitting tunic, he had the same look of self-control and peace that she'd noticed at the first orientation. It made her feel protected and wanted.

"Oh." Winnie cleared her throat. She shrank in her seat a little and hoped he hadn't noticed her tears. "I was just labeling Walker's new mailer."

"Hello," he said softly, walking in and sliding his

hip onto the edge of the table. He looked down at her and smiled. Then he pushed up his sleeves, revealing his tanned forearms. "We encourage our staff members to meditate, Winnie. It refreshes the spirit, especially when you're doing paperwork," he added with an understanding smile.

"Yes." Winnie sighed and leaned back in her chair. "It really helps. I wished I'd learned how to do this a long time ago."

Randall smiled and looked shyly down at his leather watchband. "You're doing really well here, Winnie. All of us here at the Institute recognize your commitment."

"I feel at home here," Winnie said simply, peeling a white address label off the sheet and sticking it onto the mailer. "And I believe in what you are doing."

"Been on the beach today?" Randall asked casually, picking up a pencil and rolling it thoughtfully between his thumb and forefinger.

Winnie nodded. "Nice day. Every day's a nice day down here, though. It's not like being in the mountains, where everything is always changing. Heat, snow, wind, rain—you name it."

"Winnie?"

Winnie slid a nail under a label and gazed at the crystal paperweight on the table in front of her. "Uh-huh?"

"Would you like to meet Walker?"

Winnie froze. Then her breathing came faster,

and she felt a flush creeping up her neck. Actually meet with the man whose taped voice had been in her head for a week? Pushing her pile of brochures away, she twisted in her seat and looked up at Randall's smiling face. "What? Are you kidding?"

Randall shrugged. "Walker wants to know everyone on staff. Besides, I was given two tickets to the party April Webster and Walker are having at the Sikes estate this weekend. Why don't you come with me? It would be a good chance for you and Walker to share some time."

Winnie's mouth went dry. Meet Walker Ingham face-to-face?

"Look." Randall let out a short laugh. "The whole thing's just a big publicity stunt to sell books. Walker understands that, and he's willing to play along. But he's got his eye on the goal. He wants to reach the *real* people out there."

Winnie studied Randall as she tried to calm her growing excitement. Right then she knew that Randall wasn't coming on to her. He was conveying a much more important message. She was being accepted into the Institute's inner circle. He could tell she belonged, just as she knew it in the very center of her heart.

And now she was going to meet her spiritual leader—in the flesh.

"Yes, Randall," Winnie said, her eyes burning with feeling. "Of course I'll go with you.

* * *

Liza's leotard was wet with perspiration. And though she'd finally arrived at *The April Webster Show* studio, she was now late. She'd twisted her ankle running across the Television City parking lot. And she was shaky with hunger. In her rush she'd forgotten to eat.

Six other teen hopefuls were scattered around the hallway outside the audition room. Liza found a chair and pulled out her makeup bag, her eyes darting across the room as she checked out the other contestants. As she reapplied a coating of Wet Raspberry lipstick, she tried desperately to remember her jokes. Across from her a blond girl with an upturned nose stared, bored, at the ceiling. A guy with wiry hair wrung his hands and shook his head.

"The last guy who went inside for an audition," the wiry-haired guy said, jerking his thumb to the door, "is taking forever. Most of these clowns are shuttled in and out in the space of five minutes."

Suddenly the door to the audition room clicked, and Liza could hear laughter. Her stomach tightened. Clicking her lipstick tube shut, she straightened in her chair and looked up. Then she felt a bolt of shock run through her body. *It was Travis.*

For a split second their eyes met. Travis, looking flushed and wearing a half embarrassed smile, moved forward into the hallway, grasping the hand of none other than Geoff Hansen himself. Travis had changed out of the tank top and cutoff jeans he'd been wearing only two hours ago. Now he looked almost professional in his pressed jeans and tucked-in sports shirt. The director, wearing his trademark aviator glasses and two-day stubble, slung his arm around Travis's shoulders. "You've got something there, pal," Geoff Hansen was saying. "It's fresh. It's simple. And frankly—I like the romance of it. It's something the young girls don't find in the macho-metal bands. I see things happening for you, man. With your looks and presence, you'll transition right into film. No problem."

"Thanks," Travis said simply, gripping the handle of his guitar case and casting Liza a nervous look.

"Elaine," the director called into the audition room. "Can we set him up?"

Liza's blood was pounding in her neck. Travis? What was he doing there? When he'd left the beach, he'd simply said he had some "stuff to take care of." This was the "stuff"? Travis being courted as a possible teen idol by one of the hottest directors in Hollywood? Her brain couldn't process this new information. She watched numbly as an older woman with sleek blond hair rushed out, carrying a clipboard and pen. "You're on for the show, Travis. And if it's convenient, we'd also like you to be our guest at a book party April's having out at the Oliver Sikes estate this weekend. Are you free?" she asked hurriedly. "Okay. Please come this way. We have a few simple contracts to sign."

Liza's mouth dropped open as Travis turned to give her a secret thumbs-up sign. She watched the back of his faded T-shirt disappear down the hall. Tears flooded her eyes. Had he asked Lauren to get him an appointment? If so, why hadn't he told her?

Her feelings swirling, Liza gripped her bag and sat on the edge of her seat. *Travis,* she thought, her mind suddenly racing. *Travis is finally getting his big break*. His secret had hurt her, sure. But Travis was finally on his way to stardom, she knew it. She slumped in her seat, taking in the new situation. All she had to do was breeze through this audition and they'd *both* be huge stars—sharing their success together in wild and wonderful L.A. . . .

"Ms. Ruff?" a woman's sharp voice interrupted her thoughts. "I'm Elaine, the show's producer. Please come this way."

Liza jumped to her feet, her feelings swinging wildly back and forth between elation and frustation over Travis. She followed the producer into the audition room, her heart about to explode. Then she glanced briefly around. A long table was set up, behind which Geoff Hansen was flipping through papers, a telephone crammed into the crook of his neck. Elaine sat down and bit into a sandwich.

"You can do your routine," she said distractedly, "then we'd like to ask you a few questions about yourself."

"Okay," Liza said, suddenly afraid. "Um. Yeah," she launched into an old routine she'd done about a Beverly Hills matron and her poodle. The skit involved a funny story, peppered with several funny dance routines performed by the poodle's snob groomer. "Okay," she began, struggling for light-hearted gusto. "How many of you have dogs out there?"

Liza looked at Elaine, who had a blank look on her face. Then she looked at Geoff Hansen and felt her heart sink into her tap shoes.

"Get that shot, Danny," Geoff Hansen was saying loudly over his portable phone. "I don't care about the light. What kinda picture you think we're doing here, pal?"

Liza looked desperately over at Elaine, who had looked away to take another large bite out of her sandwich. Her mouth was full, so she nodded wordlessly and gave Liza a speed-it-up gesture.

"I've got this fabulous friend who grooms doggies," Liza continued, plastering on a brave face. "In Beverly Hills, if you can imagine. Yeah. Makes a ton of money. Actually, he does the women in the morning and the canines in the afternoons. Says he gets his ideas interchanging techniques." Liza let out a laugh and tap-danced over to an imaginary dog, which she pretended to clip.

She heard clapping behind her, and Liza turned around. Elaine had just swallowed and now had a big smile on her face. "Thanks, Liza. Great. We'll call you if we can work something out."

Liza opened her mouth to explain that she wasn't done, then closed it, giving Geoff Hansen one final, longing look. Her heart sank. He was still talking on the phone. Slowly, Liza picked up her bag. It was clear he hadn't paid any attention to her routine. Struggling desperately to keep from crying, Liza walked carefully down the hall and out into the parking lot.

She stopped and closed her eyes against the painfully bright sun. Then she opened them and felt her heart break in two. Leaning against a studio cart, his guitar case slung over his shoulder, was Travis. For a moment she just looked at him. He looked so expectant. So excited. So full of hope.

"How did it go, babe?" he yelled with an ecstatic grin. Whooping, he ran toward her, lifted her up, and twirled her in the air. "We're gonna make it. We're gonna hit the front pages of *Variety*. We're *there*, Liza."

Liza wrenched herself angrily away, stomping off. He wasn't excited for her. He was excited for himself because he'd just made it big with Geoff Hansen.

"Liza," Travis called out, running behind. "What happened?"

Her eyes storming, Liza whirled around to face him. "Who invited you to this audition?"

Travis's blue eyes looked wounded. "I decided to talk my way in, Liza. I didn't want to tell you. If they'd kicked me out, I wouldn't have been able to face you."

Liza shoved her hands on her hips, blood rushing wildly into her face. Suddenly she didn't know if she trusted Travis anymore. If she *loved* him anymore. He'd gone behind her back.

"*Don't you understand?*" she screamed. "*You're going to be on TV with Geoff Hansen. You're going to the Sikes party to meet everyone in Hollywood. And I'm not!*"

She watched numbly as Travis opened his mouth to say something, then closed it. He turned and slowly walked away. Liza sank down onto the edge of a planter box in the sweltering parking lot, choked with tears. But the next moment she felt him next to her again. His arm slipped around her shoulders. Then he took her chin in his hand and turned her wet face to his, softly kissing her.

"It hurts," Travis said, his eyes full of tenderness, "I know."

Liza looked away, drained. Her thoughts kept flipping back to the Ingham Institute meeting. They were right, weren't they? Each person has the power to take charge of his life. And that's what Travis did when he talked his way into the audition. He was barging his way into stardom, just as she would when *her* moment finally came. Quickly she wiped away the tears with the back of her hand. Then she sniffed and looked steadily ahead.

"I'm okay, Travis," she whispered. "I'm okay."

Fifteen

"Wicked cool." Lauren mocked her reflection in the mirror, fluffing her frizzed-out hair and dabbing her lips with gloss. She jutted her hip out and posed in her white jeans and sleeveless turtleneck.

Suddenly she dropped her pose and turned away from the mirror. She looked down at her hands, which were trembling slightly. The Sikes party was less than an hour away. She, Mel, and Winnie had planned to drive there together. But that afternoon everything had changed. Max had called. Would she go with him?

Now Lauren's head was fizzing like a lit firecracker. She'd been to plenty of fancy parties before.

But not with Hollywood celebrities. And definitely not with Max. It was a date. An actual date with Max Cantor.

"Ready to dialogue with the hunks and scope out the hardbodies, Lauren?" Winnie nudged her out of the mirror, her voice dripping with sarcasm.

"Oh, give it up, Win," Liza complained, stretched out on Lauren's bed in her bathrobe, hugging an open carton of ice cream to her chest and pouting. "Don't you get it, hon? You're going to groove on the hottest party in L.A. tonight."

"And you're not," Winnie said lightly, spiking her hair out and clipping on a pair of tiny crystal earrings.

Liza swallowed a mouthful of ice cream before she spoke. Lauren noticed that her hair was set up in purple rollers the size of frozen-orange-juice cans. Was Liza planning to go out too? "Okay, I'm cuh-razy with jealousy. I admit it. But, I mean, even *Winnie* is going to this party. And she doesn't even *care* about making a big impression on the Hollywood scene. It's not fair."

Winnie turned around and gave Liza an innocent look. "Oh, but Liza"—she glanced menacingly over her shoulder at Lauren—"you're right. I don't care about the trendy, materialistic Hollywood scene. I'm going for an uplifting spiritual experience with Walker Ingham. I'm going to stare into his deep blue eyes and get in touch with my inner, childlike being. I'm going to groove on being a New Age Airhead—right, Lauren?"

Lauren clenched her teeth and said nothing. Lauren promised herself she wouldn't react to Winnie's taunts. Lauren knew she'd been cruel to Winnie, and she was willing to accept the consequences. Someday Winnie would forgive her.

"New Age or not," Liza blared, jamming the cover on her ice cream and heaving herself up from the bed, "I'd crash the party if I could."

"You can't." Melissa looked up, shocked. "You can't crash the party. *It would be totally embarassing!*"

Liza threw her feather boa over her shoulder and gave Mel an outraged look. "I know I can't, doll face. The damn invitations are specially embossed to keep out undesirable babes like me. Lauren has explained."

Ding-dong.

Lauren's heart jumped into her throat, nearly choking her. Quickly, she hurried down the hall and opened the front door.

"Hi," Lauren said, drawing in her breath, then letting it out with a nervous laugh. "Come in."

"Hi," Max replied, looking slightly shy. Dressed in khaki pants and a yellow sport shirt, he looked completely unlike his usual, harried self at the office. His face was relaxed, handsome, and slightly flushed. The contrast almost took Lauren's breath away. She could still see the wetness in his hair from a recent shower. His dark eyes looked darker and more mysterious than ever. And the smell of spicy cologne wafted in through the doorway. "I return." He cleared his throat and pushed up his glasses. Then he gave her a curious look. "Um, are you going to let me in, Lauren?"

Lauren's eyes opened wide, realizing she'd forgotten herself. She'd spent the whole afternoon thinking about this moment. Somehow she wanted to put on a casual front. She couldn't let him know how strongly she felt, yet. She was falling for him. She knew it now. And now that everything was happening too fast, she could barely find a single word to say. "Oh. Yeah. Yeah, come in. I just have to . . ."

"Ah, what a place," Max was saying happily, following her into the living room. "One day I'm going to have a place like this to come home to. The big, beautiful Pacific staring at me in the morning. A roaring fire at night." He stuffed his hands into his pockets and stared out at the beach. Then he turned abruptly and looked at her, his eyes shining. "You look—wonderful."

Lauren sucked in her breath. "Thank you."

Max bit his lip and looked down, rubbing the back of his neck. "Look, I've got a twenty-year-old Toyota that needs carburetor work sitting out there in the driveway. It's been stalling all day. . . ."

"We can take my car."

"Why don't we just stroll down the beach?" Max suggested, taking a step toward her. "It's not very far. And the tide's out. Look."

Lauren stopped breathing. She kept forgetting

how tall Max was, and how her heart always skipped a beat when he smiled like that. It wasn't a wide, obvious smile. It was an "Are you thinking the same thing I am?" smile. It was a smile between people who understood one another. A smile between people who shared something secret. "Okay," she said finally, glancing toward the beach. "Mel and Winnie can take the Jeep and we can all meet there."

Max opened the sliding glass door to the beach and grinned. "Ready to get your toes wet?"

"Mmmmm," she managed. Together they started down the soft, breezy beach.

"I love the beach too," Lauren finally said, trying to keep up with Max's long strides. She smiled, remembering he was from New York. People from New York always walked as if they were chasing down cabs. "But I don't know if I could live down here for long," she admitted, feeling the breeze blow through her hair. "There's something about this huge ocean that makes me wonder why I take it all so seriously."

Max tilted his head back, laughing as they headed toward the waves. "But you still come to work each morning . . ."

". . . taking it oooooooh so seriously," Lauren finished his sentence, smiling and shaking her head. The sand felt warm beneath her bare feet. "I can't help it. I turned into an overachiever my freshman year. It's an addiction, I guess."

Max looked at her. His dark eyes were warm with

understanding. "I would have pegged you as a born workaholic. What were you like before?"

Lauren felt suddenly shy. The sand turned wet and Lauren rolled up her pants bottoms. She let a line of foamy water wash over her toes. "I was like—a shadow."

Max frowned, looking concerned. "Whose shadow?"

Lauren shrugged. "My overachiever parents' shadow, of course."

"Of course."

"Shy, oversensitive Lauren. The more they pushed, the more I retreated. Until college. And I got as faaaaaaar away as possible."

Max picked up a stone and threw it into the ocean. "You could breathe. You figured out what you wanted."

Lauren stopped and looked over at him, stunned. "What are you? Some kind of a mind reader? Yeah. As a matter of fact, I did figure it out. I figured out that I liked to write. And I liked to find out how things worked and what people thought. Journalism was a natural for me."

"Me too," Max said softly, looking at her with serious eyes.

Lauren waited for him to explain, but instead he took a step forward, stuffing his hands into his pockets again, thoughtful. For a few moments they walked in silence, tossing stones into the water and dragging sticks in the fine, wet sand. Lauren let her eyes drift toward Max, taking in his graceful, lanky body and his thoughtful face. It felt so natural to be walking down a deserted, sun-soaked beach with him, as if they'd done it a million times before. And yet it was so different from anything she'd ever done before.

"Thanks again for the idea, by the way." Max bent his head toward her and whispered over the sound of the waves. Her skin tingled where his lips lightly brushed her ear. "April's totally jazzed about the show. So now I've stopped walking around with my tail between my legs, wondering when I'll get my impersonal pink slip."

"Now she's convinced you're a bottomless bucket of great ideas, huh?" Lauren teased, climbing onto a black rock formation at the end of the beach.

"Hey," Max protested, scrambling toward her across the rock, "I told her it was your idea."

Lauren stopped, bracing her toes on the edge of a tiny tide pool on the other side of the craggy formation. She looked up at Max, who was climbing toward her, looking down for footholds. "You told her? You didn't take credit for the idea?"

Max stopped and let out a short laugh. "You're kidding! You thought I'd . . ."

"I didn't know. I just . . ."

"It was your idea, and it was great. What kind of a person do you think . . ."

"I think you're an amazing person—one of the best," Lauren blurted, unable to stop herself once the words began to tumble out. She bit her lip and turned away, embarrassed. Not knowing what else to do, she knelt down and stared into the sloshing tide pool. A pink starfish clung to the rock. A moment later she felt Max kneel down next to her.

"Thanks."

Lauren flushed. His face was so near. Didn't he know that she was falling for him? It was impossible to hide. What was happening to her? It was impossible to speak.

"Look." Max picked up a smooth white shellfish from the bottom of the pool, delicately changing the subject. "Beautiful, isn't it?"

Lauren relaxed and listened as a wave roared in, spilling inches away from where they were perched. "Beautiful."

"Look again," Max said, prying the shellfish off the rock and turning it over. An ugly sluggish animal appeared on its underside, slick with brown slime.

"Ugh," Lauren replied. "Its true nature revealed," she said with mock seriousness. "Oh, how hard it is to see beneath the surface of things."

"Especially in L.A.," Max said with a sigh, placing the animal back into the tide pool and standing up, stretching. "The place will drive you crazy. People you think are friends turn out to be your worst nightmares. People you think are totally crazy turn out to be your salvation. Bike messengers end up becoming starlets. Rock stars burn out and get jobs in the post office. You can't peg anyone in this town."

Lauren picked her way along a series of gentle tide pools, letting the salt spray hit her face. "And you? Can you be pegged? Who *is* Max Cantor?" she challenged him with a playful look.

"Me?"

Lauren planted a hand on her hip. "Yeah. First I thought you were a car thief. Then you became my co-worker. Then a bully. And now—well, now you're my friend."

"I know you don't understand—yet, anyway," Max said quietly. "But just try to imagine my parents. They're both painters, living in the same cheap city apartment they've had for the last twenty years in Manhattan. They struggle. They get excited about a show, then the show falls flat. They work so hard—and they have nothing."

"They have their art."

Max shook his head violently. "Their art has worn thin. They have *nothing*. They struggle to make the rent and utilities the same way they did in 1974. That's not going to happen to me, Lauren. I want a future. I want hope. And I'm going to stick with April until I put together the greatest show she's ever done. The one show that will make my career."

Lauren's eyes were burning with excitement. A wave drew back, and she ran splashing through the soaked sand. Max ran too, following her closely. "I know exactly what you mean, Max," she finally replied when he drew up next to her. She panted a little. "I mean, my parents weren't poor, of course. But they were controlling, Max. You come to a point where you've just *got* to carve out something for your very own—or you'll be sucked into someone else's void."

"I figured that." Max bumped against her softly, then slowly took her hand in his.

Lauren shivered, then turned away, unprepared for him. If just looking at Max made her dizzy, kissing would definitely make her pass out. "I can see the party from here," she quickly changed the subject, squeezing his hand and pulling him along. "Look at the striped tents set up on the beach."

Max squeezed her hand back. "Black-tie waiters right on the beach. Mmmm. Classy."

"Walker Ingham," Lauren said thoughtfully, breathing in the faraway scent of wonderful food. "A sumptuous place for Mr. Spare and Spiritual to hang out in. What do you think of my hot tip? Think there's dirt beneath the beautiful surface?"

"Ah, the pool man," Max teased. "Actually, I doubt it. Someone would have dug up the story by now if he's not clean. We need something more concrete to investigate."

"Yeah," Lauren agreed softly, padding closer to

the crowd of beautiful people descending the steps of the Oliver Sikes estate. The sun was lower in the sky now—a burning orange and gold. Laughter tinkled through the air. And Lauren felt something rising inside her, as if something important were sure to happen soon.

Sixteen

By the time Melissa and Winnie arrived at the Oliver Sikes estate, the coastal highway looked like a Beverly Hills car dealership without the tacky balloons. BMWs, Mercedeses, Jaguars, and Range Rovers jammed both sides of the road. They parked as close as they could get and began walking.

"Whew," Mel muttered under her breath, as they approached a reception area set up in the circular driveway. Streams of guests in sleek beach outfits and elegant silk were casually pouring in through the wrought-iron gate. Melissa looked down at her leggings and simple flats, a wave of panic flooding through her. Swiftly, she clutched the silk gardenia

Liza had playfully tucked behind her ear. Squishing it in her hand, she slid it slowly down the side of her head, stuffing it into her tiny belt pack.

Up ahead on the driveway three big men in tuxedos were checking invitations and press passes. Two others were scanning the shrubbery for intruders.

"Check this out," Winnie whispered, motioning toward a special parking area inside the gate, where several stretch limos waited, their drivers lounging inside. And closer to the house four television news vans had set up camp, complete with remote-broadcast dishes and scurrying camera operators.

"Winnie," Mel heard a male voice call out. She looked through the throng and recognized the guy named Randall from the Institute's orientation. Though he wore only a denim shirt and pressed jeans, he looked more like an insider than the hundreds of expensively dressed guests milling about the garden.

"Hi," Winnie called out, breathless. Mel glanced at her face, which suddenly seemed bathed in happiness.

Randall waved her through. "She's with me," he said to one of the burly bouncers. "Come on. I want you to meet some of our own. We're inside."

Mel watched helplessly as Winnie was rushed away without a word through the huge front door of the mansion. A moment later her invitation was carefully inspected, and she was crunching nervously across the gravel toward the music.

Mel bit the inside of her lip and wandered toward the pool area. At the top of the stairs that spilled down to the beach, she finally spotted April, a white silk pajama outfit swathing her huge frame. Mel smiled to herself. April was laughing and posing with Walker, but Elaine was nearby, conversing with a stunning teenage girl in a halter top. She frantically motioned for the girl to join April. Soon photographers were clustered around the two, snapping their picture.

"Ah hah hah hah hah!" there was a screech of hysterical laughter. Mel jumped, then realized it was all part of the normal party scene. Screeching. Kissing. Posing. Conducting business.

She drifted on, spotting Travis with several young girls. She saw huge guys who had to be basketball players, clustered around a beautiful but plastic-looking tall, thin woman, and one celebrity she did recognize—an Olympic ice-skater who now promoted breakfast cereals and athletic wear.

"Thanks," Mel said tersely, taking a stuffed mushroom from a silver tray. She popped it into her mouth, trying to act casual, even though she was clearly the only person for miles who knew absolutely no one.

She turned and pretended to gaze cheerfully out at the shining Pacific, when she suddenly saw something out of the corner of her eye. Turning slightly, she narrowed her eyes and heard her pulse begin to beat behind her eardrums. "Evan?" she whispered to herself, spotting a familiar profile in the throng next to the pool. She glanced momentarily at the light blond hair and tawny skin. She took in the elegant linen blazer and silk tie, then shook her head. The guy looked like Evan, but guys who work for pool-maintenance companies definitely didn't dress like that. And she was pretty sure they never got invited to parties like this one, either.

I've got Evan on the brain, Melissa thought dejectedly, turning away and taking a mineral water and lemon slice off a tray. *Now I'm hallucinating.*

"Melissa?" she heard someone call out.

Melissa looked around, then felt her knees buckle. It was no hallucination. She braced herself against the edge of the terrace railing. The guy walking toward her in the jacket and tie really was Evan the pool guy. Evan the high diver. Evan the risk taker. Evan the boy who had kissed her in the ocean.

"Evan?"

"Melissa?" Evan said, edging toward her through a crowd of Hollywood hopefuls. "What are you— doing here?" he stammered, a slow smile spreading across his face. "I mean, I'm glad and . . . ."

"I work for *The April Webster Show*," Melissa explained with a nervous smile. Her head felt strangely light.

Evan's gaze traveled the length of her body. He took a step closer. Melissa could barely breathe. "I thought you worked for some kind of delivery service. . . ."

"What about you?" she blurted in confusion. "I mean, since when does the guy who cleans the . . ."

"Evan," someone boomed loudly over the crowd. Melissa glanced up and recognized the balding head and red nose belonging to the voice. Lauren had shown her his picture. It was Oliver Sikes himself. *"Come on over here. There's someone I want you to meet."*

Melissa stepped back a little as Evan turned. She clutched her drink and watched in amazement as Evan was dragged over to Oliver Sikes's side.

"This is my son, Evan Sikes, everyone," Oliver Sikes boomed, patting Evan heartily on the back as flashbulbs popped and several people clapped gaily. Oliver was much shorter than Evan, so he had to reach up when he hugged him around the waist for the photos. His loud Hawaiian shirt contrasted with Evan's sleek outfit. "And as you can tell, he definitely takes after his beautiful mother."

Evan *Sikes?* Evan was Oliver Sikes's *son?* This fabulous mansion was his *home?*

Melissa gasped. The crowd laughed. She stood, paralyzed with shock, as Evan's embarrassed look caught hers over the milling crowd. Finally Evan broke away from his father's grasp and hurried back toward her. Melissa stared, her thoughts seesawing between amazement and fear. Evan had lied to her. Why?

"Look," Evan said tensely, slipping his hand around her arm and pulling her away from the crowd. "I . . ."

"Why did you tell me you were the *pool man*?" Melissa confronted him.

Evan's expression dropped. "What does it matter who I am?"

"What about the truth?" Melissa was surprised to feel a surge of hot anger. "Don't you care whether you're telling the truth—or lying? I thought there was something between us—that day—at Pirate Cove. Now I have no idea whether you're someone I should have trusted."

Melissa watched as Evan's father began to glare at her. Evan glanced over his shoulder, then turned toward her again, looking helpless and desperate. Just then a waiter carrying a tray full of wineglasses passed. Her heart in her throat, Melissa watched as Evan grabbed a glass with each hand and drank both as fast as he could. Then, staggering back a little, he reached through a group of partygoers and pulled another glass off the server's tray. He took it too, dropping his head back and closing his eyes as he gulped.

Casting one last, longing look at Melissa, Evan turned on his heel and strolled unsteadily toward his father.

Liza stared defiantly at the blue sky as she marched down the coastal highway. Dressed in her red tap outfit and wartime flip, she was ready. Completely ready. She patted the tap shoes in her backpack, her thoughts bubbling with anticipation.

An hour ago. That was when it had hit her. She didn't have an invitation to Oliver Sikes's fabulous party. But she did remember Randall's stories about Leona Cartell barging into the producer's office. Then she knew what she had to do. She would snake her way into this party and deliver a singing telegram to Geoff Hansen himself.

"You don't realize it yet, Mr. Hansen"—Liza wiggled her shiny nails in the air—"but tonight you're gonna get a surprise singing telegram like you've never heard before. You've got your next film's casting problems taken care of. *Because I'm gonna blow you away, big guy.*"

Liza's hopes soared as she walked down the beach. Already she could see the line of shiny cars and hear the jazzy music echoing off the beach cliffs. As she passed the main gate, she spotted the party bouncers positioned in the front driveway. There was no way she was going to get through the gate without an embossed invitation.

Undeterred, Liza put her head down and kept walking. Soon a thick hedge was the only thing separating her from the estate. Wide openings were visible at its base. It would be a tight squeeze, but she would manage. A moment later she ducked her head and plowed her way through the hedge.

She reached the other side quickly and triumphantly scrambled to her feet. After straightening her hairdo and dusting off her shoes, she proceeded to take mincing steps across the lawn. Up ahead she could see the north wall of the vast Sikes mansion, bordered on one side by a deck that led around to the ocean side, where the party was taking place. Liza picked her target and moved quickly, her smile brightening by the millisecond. A moment later she was on the view deck, tapping politely on the huge French doors that led into the living room.

She waited nervously, spying the party below, not exactly sure what she was going to do next. If she'd brought a climbing rope, she could have scaled the wall down to where the action was. But she wasn't Batman. If she was going to avoid the bouncers, the only access was through the house. She glanced down at the party again, suddenly noticing Geoff Hansen himself down by the pool, shaking the hand of a pretty "Young hopeful" type.

"Yes?" A young woman in a black skirt opened the door. "May I help you?"

Beginning with a few snazzy dance steps, her taps clicking pleasantly against the concrete deck, Liza spread her arms wide. *"I'm heeeeeeere,"* Liza sang. *"And it's cleeeeeeear. You're gonna cheeeeeer!"*

The woman bit her lip and looked over her shoulder. "Um. Excuse me. But I'm Fawn, the caterer. Is there something I can help you with?"

Liza didn't waver. All she could do was pray the girl would get her inside. Liza got down on one knee and posed. "I'm Liza. The singing-telegram girl."

Fawn looked confused, then suddenly brightened. She wiped her hands on her white apron and nodded. "Oh yes. I know all about you. I met Mrs. Hansen a minute ago. Wow. Married all those years and still making your anniversary such a major event. And in Hollywood, too. They are so lucky to have each other." Liza's entire being shuddered with relief and joy. She had no idea why this airhead was babbling to her, but she was getting some very useful information.

"Yes, yes they are," Liza said cheerfully. Her brain was buzzing steadily. This was her moment. It had come. She knew it. She'd taken a big risk, but now every muscle and nerve in her body knew exactly what to do. "Mrs. Hansen wanted me to make a big splash—sort of surpriselike," Liza lied. "She said Mr. Hansen really likes surprises."

Fawn waved her hand and shook her head. "I bet he does. I just met him, too. What a character, that guy. Come on. I'll show you the way."

"Thanks," Liza said politely.

"It's kind of a maze down here," Fawn apologized. "There's a door that opens out onto the pool area from the wine cellar."

"Oh, good," Liza said. "I'll be able to make a quick entrance and do my gig."

The door opened and Liza had to squint against the bright sunlight. Once her eyes adjusted, however, she could barely contain her joy. Standing right next to the pool were Oliver Sikes and Geoff Hansen. Through the crowd she could see that the two were surrounded by a group of young wanna-bes. Steadying herself, she moved briskly through the fluttering silk and tanned shoulders. When she'd finally found a spot directly in front of Oliver Sikes, she made eye contact with Geoff Hansen and gave him a huge wink.

"Happy anniversary to *you*," Liza began with gusto, twirling and stomping her tap shoes. Out of the corner of her eye, she saw Geoff Hansen break his handshake and conversation with a young man. In one brief panic of a moment, she realized it was Travis—and that her sudden appearance probably had broken his big chance to yuk it up with the director.

Liza couldn't think. In a split second she had to decide. "Happy Anniversary to *YOU*," she continued without missing a beat. Travis would understand. She focused and broke into a rapid-fire tap dance that took her to the edge of the pool. The crowd parted and watched in obvious admiration. A quick glance revealed she had both Sikes's and Hansen's complete attention. Travis, in the meantime, also had stepped back to make room for her act. But the move had distanced him from the famous director. Now he was standing off to the side, unable to maneuver his way back.

"Happy anniversary, dear *Geoff*," Liza sang out, planting her feet and raising her hands above her head. She bent her knees and knocked them together, dropping her voice in a whisper to the amused crowd. "He loves this kind of wacko stuff—

don't you know it, folks. He's my kind of *man*!" Liza paused and the crowd remained silent and breathless. "*Happy anniversary* (his wife made me do it) *to* (I *love* this guy—he's got a cute butt) *Yoooooouuuuuuuuu*!" Liza finished to a roar of laughter and applause.

Liza stood breathless and teary before the huge crowd of wildly clapping celebrities. Oliver Sikes was doubled over with laughter. Travis was now leaning against a pool chair, alone, fiddling with his drink and glaring at her. And Geoff Hansen was approaching, holding out the most precious prize of all—his business card.

"Call my office," Geoff Hansen said over the din. "I'm developing a new film. Think I could use you."

Liza bit her lip. The blood pounding in her ears was deafening. Could he hear it? She mouthed a silent thanks to the director, then turned to leave, dizzy with pure joy.

"Liza!" she heard Travis shout angrily. Though they were surrounded by exuberant partygoers, she could tell that they were both near the end of the pool, just before the garden rose up toward the front entrance. She turned and stared. He was standing in front of her, his face red with anger. "How could you do this?"

Liza spread out her arms, helpless, stung and confused. "I'm only trying to . . ." she began. But as her arms went out, she felt something whack hard against her elbow. She gasped. She'd hit an entire tray of stuffed, curried eggs, which flipped over her arm and slammed straight into Travis's front. "Travis!" Liza gasped, as a lumpy mass of wet egg began dripping down the front of his only decent pair of pants.

"You," Travis said low, his voice dripping with rage, barely looking at the mess.

Liza gasped in horror. "Travis . . ."

He stepped back, his eyes, once blue and gentle, now narrowed into two furious slits. His flushed face was beginning to pale to chalky white. "Don't come near me," he breathed, stepping backward. Liza stared helplessly, her heart breaking. Laughing, screaming, eating guests swirled around them. "You could do this," Travis growled. "You could walk in here without an invitation and spoil this big chance I have. . . ."

Liza's eyes suddenly flapped open wide. She watched, helpless, as Travis's foot stepped back to the edge of the pool. "Travis. Look out!"

Travis froze, but as he looked over his shoulder, he began to lose his balance. His body began to tilt slowly backward, over the water. Desperately, he flailed his arms to right himself, but it was too late. A moment later he fell back and hit the water with a huge splash. Travis's head surfaced among the bobbing water lilies. Hard-boiled egg floated everywhere. The entire crowd gasped in horror, then broke into hysterical laughter.

"How could you do this, Liza?" Travis screamed over the din.

Liza clutched Hansen's business card, then turned away, unable to face Travis's terrible humiliation. She ran, her heart plummeting, her eyes filled with tears, up toward the highway. And then she kept on running. Faster than she'd ever run in her life.

Seventeen

innie stepped into a large room banked on one side by windows overlooking the Pacific. The floor, an expanse of polished wood, was dotted with small straw mats, on which several simply dressed men and women were sitting quietly. Winnie suddenly felt weightless and shivery. Sitting cross-legged in front of a tiny table in the middle of the room was Walker Ingham himself.

"Go right in, Winnie," Randall was saying quietly behind her. "It's okay."

Winnie moved forward, her eyes fixed on Walker, who had just finished speaking. The sparsely furnished room was so unlike the rest of the opulent

Sikes mansion, she felt as if she'd been transported into another universe. A small ceramic incense holder had been placed on the table before Walker, from which rose a thin column of smoke. In the corner, near the windows, a white futon was rolled out, surrounded by several neat stacks of books.

"Hello," Walker said quietly, looking up at Winnie and Randall. Winnie took in his intense blue eyes and lean jawline. In his loose muslin pants and tunic, he looked smaller than he appeared in photographs, but just as powerful.

Rising from his mat, Walker strolled quietly over to the west-facing windows. As he cracked open a window, Winnie suddenly heard music and laughter floating up from the party. Walker smiled down. "Looks like April's book-promotion idea's working as planned. I see many faces down there. Mmmmm. Lots to eat. Lots of alcohol. Aha. And here's the obligatory guest falling into Oliver's lovely pool."

There was a murmur of amusement among his disciples in the room. Winnie shared a smile with a serene-looking blond woman holding a single lily.

"I think it's time for me to meet a few of the guests," Walker said with a rueful smile. "April tells me I must have my picture taken. Please join the party—and enjoy yourselves."

Winnie bit her lip, not knowing what to do. The Institute staffers were rising slowly, some of them doing meditative stretches while looking thoughtfully into space. She stood and looked expectantly at

Randall, who was exchanging a few words with Walker by the window. Deciding to wait for Randall, she sat down again, staring quietly at a simple metal sculpture on the far side of the room.

"Welcome," she heard a voice murmur above her after a few moments had passed. Winnie looked up, shaking herself out of her reverie. Then her eyes widened in amazement. It was Walker Ingham. "Thank you for coming today. Your name is Winnie . . ."

"Gottlieb," Winnie finished, standing up and glancing briefly at Randall, who was slipping out the door, leaving her alone in the room with Walker. "I'm an intern at your Santa Monica office."

"Yes," he said simply. "I know."

Winnie looked into his eyes, blue and deep. His slightly lined face was so wise. So understanding. She had the distinct feeling that he knew everything about her. And that he knew the answer to each and every one of her difficulties. "I—I believe in what you're doing," Winnie stammered, her lips trembling. "And I just want to tell you that you've changed my life."

"We share the same wavelength," Walker said, moving his head slightly to the side, as if he were listening for something. He touched the side of her arm. "I can feel it. I'd like to meet with you alone. We'll talk then. I'll be in touch."

"Okay," Winnie murmured as he walked calmly past her, out through the door. "Thank you," she whispered to herself, covering her face with her hands. Tears dripped through her fingers. All of her fears seemed to lift and fly away into space. She felt as if she were standing several inches off the ground, overwhelmed by the joy. Transported by the feeling of finally coming home.

"The pool man is Oliver Sikes's *son?*" Lauren was murmuring. Max was trying a small door on the bottom floor of the Sikes mansion. Though it was just off the pool area, dark had fallen, and April's book party was going full blast. It was the perfect time to slip into the house unnoticed.

Max pushed the door open into a small hallway. He nodded. "If Melissa's friend is actually Sikes's son, then his tip about Walker's nasty secrets is hot, Lauren. Very hot."

Lauren bit her lip. "Melissa seemed so upset when we found her by the pool. I guess she was mad at Evan for not telling her the truth."

Max moved forward, and Lauren followed him inside into a dark hallway. They'd been at the party for only a few minutes before they'd run into an irate Melissa. Since then Mel had run to the beach to calm down. But Lauren and Max had decided to stick around, suddenly eager to do some investigating of their own. There they were—right on the Sikes estate. What better time to do a little journalistic snooping? If they could uncover the terrible secret that lay behind Walker Ingham's Institute, they'd have a national story on their hands. And their careers would zoom.

"Shhhh." Max stopped suddenly, halfway down the hall. "Someone's coming." Quickly, he reached back and took Lauren's hand.

The sensation of Max's hand sent a thrill through Lauren, but she was quickly distracted. In the distance she could hear male voices in the middle of a violent argument. At the end of the hall, a door opened. Like a flash, Max tightened his grip on Lauren and hurried back down the hall, ducking into a small room at the end, near the door.

"Hey," Max whispered, looking around, "it's a wine cellar."

"Shhhhhhhhhh," Lauren warned, stepping back and pulling him with her. Her eyes adjusted to the dim light. The large room was lined with wall-to-wall wine bottles, many of them old and dusty. But at the back of the room she could see that there was a closet with louvered doors. Quickly, she opened the doors and slipped inside, grabbing Max.

Once inside the closet, Lauren realized that they were standing chest-to-chest with absolutely no room to move. Wine bottles were perched on the ledge above them, as well as on shorter shelves at elbow height. If they moved an inch, they were sure to knock one over.

"Yeah, yeah, yeah yeah," an older man with a booming voice was yelling angrily in the hall.

Lauren carefully slipped a finger onto an inside

latch and managed to shut the closet door all the way. She could feel Max's warm breath. Her cheek rested on his firm chest. Slowly, as if to make more room for himself, he wrapped his long arms around her. Lauren drew in her breath. She'd never been this close to Max.

"Hey, *Dad*," the second, younger man was yelling in a sarcastic voice, staggering and slurring his words. "Whatsamatter? Didn't you like what I said to all the nice reporters?"

Lauren peered through the slats in the closet door. *Evan Sikes,* she thought, lifting her chin to make eye contact with Max. In the dim light she could see his eyes answer back. He gave a slight nod.

"You worthless piece of garbage," Sikes roared back, lunging for his son. "You lousy, good-for-nothing drunk. Do you realize what you just did out there?"

Lauren stared as Evan staggered back, a silly, drunk grin plastering his face. It was clear he'd had way too much to drink. But she still liked his sensitive face. She noticed that he seemed strangely overpowered by his father.

"No, Dad," Evan came back, "what did I do? Wreck everything for you again? Spoil the party? Change all the pretty headlines you were yearning for?"

Oliver Sikes grabbed his son's arm and wrenched it around behind him. Then he held his taller son tightly in his powerful grip. Lauren stared through the slats, shocked. "You're a loser, is what you are,

Evan. Always have been, and always will be."

"Gee, thanks, Dad," Evan grunted in pain, as his father gripped him tighter. "I didn't know you cared."

"Don't you have any self-control?" Oliver said in a menacing tone. "How about decency? Is that a word you're familiar with, young man?"

Evan finally shoved his way out of the armlock, pushing his father backward toward a bank of wine bottles. Lauren winced, trembling in Max's arms. She watched in horror as Evan grabbed the front of Oliver's shirt, twisted the cloth in his fist, and pulled his father's face to his. "Decency is it? Is that the subject we're on? Well, let me tell you something. I've had it up to here with you and your Mr. Spiritual Guru. I'm sick of your lies and I'm sick of your false decency."

"Shut up!"

"How long do you think I'm going to stay quiet, *Dad*?" Evan began to rave. He let go of his father's shirt and looked at him with contempt. "No wonder I have a few drinks now and then. I need a little help keeping it all in *because I don't have the guts to come out with it*."

Lauren bit her lip. She could feel Max jerk his head up. *Come out with what?* Lauren thought with growing excitement. What did Evan know that he was hiding?

"If I had any *guts*," Evan continued to rant, "I'd kill myself instead of just wishing for it when I'm diving off cliffs or throwing myself out of airplanes."

"You crazy, lying, ungrateful drunk . . ." Oliver approached him, his fist balled up.

Lauren watched in horror as Evan lashed out with his fist, nearly hitting his father in the face. Oliver staggered back to avoid him. His body teetered for a few seconds in front of the closet door before it hit. Lauren's heart stopped. She didn't know if the impact was going to spring open the door. For a second she relaxed when it didn't; but Max's body had flinched.

Her cheek still pressed hard against Max's beating heart, she stared over his shoulder at a dark bottle of wine that Max's sudden movement had jiggled to the very edge of the shelf. Her eyes were now glued to its outline in the semidarkness. It rocked slowly back and forth. Lauren could barely breathe through the torture of its slow-motion dance. Oliver and Evan were just standing on the other side of the thin closet door, panting and staring at one another. The wine room was dead silent. If they heard the sudden crash of a falling bottle, they would surely open the closet.

Desperately, Lauren slid her hand up the warm front of Max's shirt. If she could reach the bottle in time, without knocking over any other bottle, she could keep it from dropping. Her fingers stretched. Her body pressed even closer to Max's.

CRASH!

The wine cellar was dead quiet. Terrified, Lauren

looked down at the shattered glass beneath their feet. Red wine soaked into her sandals. Max motioned his head at the stream of wine headed out under the closet door. Her head pounding with confusion, Lauren peered quickly through the slats. Oliver and Evan were staring at the closet door. Then Evan turned and started toward the door.

Lauren thought she would pass out from fright. But another sensation took over. Slowly, deliberately, Max began slipping his hands up her body. When he reached her shoulders, he encircled her with his arms and bent his face down to hers. Suddenly, unbelievably, Lauren felt her lips pressing against his. His arms held her tighter, and she lifted her arms to embrace him back.

She closed her eyes against the light as Evan flung open the door. She could feel Max gripping her even more tightly, as if he were signaling her to play along.

Brilliant, Lauren thought, her blood pounding in her ears, her kiss deepening. *Max has devised the perfect cover-up. The passionate couple looking for privacy.*

"What the hell are you doing?" Evan barked.

Max clung to Lauren's lips for a final moment. Then, her heart rising and her knees buckling, Lauren felt him pull away. She couldn't breathe. The kiss may have been a cover-up, but she also knew it was more than that.

"Oh." Max pretended to be embarrassed. While Evan and Oliver stared, he reached back for Lau-

ren's hand. "We—uh—we're sorry. Got—uh—a little carried away, I guess."

Lauren giggled as Max dragged her out of the
room, into the hall, and out into the pool area. By
this time Max was laughing too. Together they
raced down the stairs to the beach, nearly knocking
over a caterer's tray.

"Let's get outta here," Lauren yelled gaily, still
holding Max's hand. Up ahead the party was in full
swing. A second, livelier dance band had been set up
in a huge striped tent on the beach. Tiki torches
blazed. Couples boogied. April Webster danced
wildly with a basketball star.

Lauren felt Max squeeze her hand and pull back.
Then, with one swift movement, he was pulling her
close again. His face neared in the moonlight, his
lips touched hers, and Lauren felt the kiss begin all
over again.

"Close call, huh?" Max whispered, lifting up and
kissing her neck.

Lauren's knees buckled. The warm wind was slipping through her hair and tickling her skin. "Close
call." She stared out at the ocean, then squinted
when she saw two familiar figures in the dim light
near the water's edge. They were arguing loudly,
and Lauren, in a split second, recognized them as
Liza and Travis.

"I'm glad I did it," the girl shrieked over the
crash of the waves. Taking off one chunky shoe, she
threw it at the long-haired guy she was screaming at.

"Liza?" Lauren called out, staring at the profile of the girl's huge 1940's flip hairstyle. No one else in southern California wore her hair like that. She was sure of it. "What are you doing here?"

"You're crazy and selfish, man," Travis shouted at her, throwing the shoe back. All of his clothes were completely soaked, and a huge, crumbly yellow mess covered the front of his shirt.

"I detest you, Travis Bennett," Liza screamed wildly, jumping up and down in the sand.

"Great," Travis shouted back. *"Then maybe you'll stay out of my life."*

"Fine."

"Great," Travis said, turning and marching up the stairs to the house.

For a moment Lauren and Max just stood there, helplessly watching. Travis soon disappeared into the darkness, and Liza was left sobbing in the sand, waving them away.

"This is too crazy," Lauren finally said, turning to face the ocean crashing and pouring up the beach. The foamy tips of the breakers shone white against the darkness. The stars were brilliant and sharp in the sky. Everything was happening too fast, she thought wildly. The horrible, cruel exchange between Travis and Liza. The discovery that the pool man was really Oliver Sikes's son. And most important, the deep, longing kiss Max had given her just moments ago. The kiss had been real. It *wasn't* just an act.

Lauren turned to Max, who'd slipped his arm around her waist. Music blasted in the distance. And suddenly she felt as if everything around her were completely crazy, except for Max. She held on to him like an anchor in the night. "I don't know why, Max," Lauren called over the pounding waves. "But I'm scared. I'm scared, Max."

Max turned to face her, holding her tight as the wind began to whip at her hair. "Don't be." He bent his head down and kissed her again, long and deep. Lauren felt her knees weaken. She dropped slowly down to the soft sand, and Max lowered himself down with her, still kissing. A moment later she was on her back, her legs entwined in Max's, kissing him and never wanting to stop. The waves rolled in, and the warm water rushed up over their legs.

Eighteen

"It's not like I actually give a flying flip," Liza was complaining, switching on the TV and tuning into *The April Webster Show*.

It was four o'clock Friday afternoon. Lauren and Melissa were at work, and Winnie was sitting cross-legged in a corner of the living room, meditating.

"You're eighteen. You're broke. And you have a dream in your heart that won't let go," April Webster was saying into her mike, staring into the camera. "The dream? To make it big—really big—in the dog-eat-dog world of the entertainment industry. Thousands of kids like this arrive in Hollywood every day. Musicians, actresses, dancers and comedians—all searching for their big break. What's it like? How do they survive? And how do they feel when they finally get their first big break? We've scoured Hollywood for the best of the Hollywood hopefuls. And they're with us today to share their stories—after this message."

It was impossible to believe how angry Travis had been with her for crashing the Sikes party. After all, *he'd* crashed the Hansen audition for the *April* show. And he'd completely upstaged her, distracting Hansen from even giving her a chance. It was a selfish, secretive move.

"We're back!" April murmured excitedly into her microphone. "Ladies and gentlemen, Mr. Travis Bennett!"

Liza stiffened. There on her TV screen was Travis's sweet, soulful face. His blue eyes. His head of shaggy hair. A wave of fury swept through her like a raging fire. Travis was perched on a stool, strumming his guitar. Then he launched into a slow tune he'd composed only two weeks before on the beach.

She tore at her hair and screamed at the screen. "I practically *wrote* the lyrics to that song, and now you're ripping me off."

After only one bar Travis stopped singing, strummed his guitar with a flourish, and bowed. Instantly the entire studio audience burst into wild applause. April Webster's ecstatic face appeared. "Okay, everyone," she said, clapping along with the audience and smiling as if she were about to stun the world with a huge surprise. "If you're crazy about Travis Bennett, let's see what one of Hollywood's hottest teen-film directors thinks. Please give a warm welcome to Mr. Geoff Hansen."

"Get outta here, you cheap, slimy know-it-all," Liza ranted, throwing the entire bag of caramel corn at the TV screen. She watched, her head on fire, as Geoff Hansen leaped energetically onto the set, shook April's hand, and slapped Travis on the back.

"What I like about this act, April," Hansen was explaining, punching Travis playfully in the shoulder, "is that Travis is a born romantic. Actually, he's appealing to me as a potential major motion-picture star. He's very fresh. Very real. Very believable."

Angry tears poured down Liza's cheeks. She rose from the couch and jumped up and down angrily on a pillow. "He's unbelievable, is what he is. He's a lying, two-faced creep."

Liza switched off the television, nearly breaking the knob. Then she threw herself down and pounded the floor with her fists. "It should have been me. It should have been me. If it weren't for Travis, it *would* have been me. *Wiiiinnnnnnnnnnie.*"

Winnie remained silent, meditating, in the corner of the room, her eyes fixed on a photograph of Walker Ingham.

"Why do I even bother to talk to you, hon?" Liza fumed, waving her hands in front of Winnie's glassy eyes. "Okay. Right. No one home. Everyone gone bye-bye. Great. That's all I need. A brainwashed roommate."

RRRRRIIIIIINNNNNGGGGG!

Liza lunged for the phone across the room. "Hansen. I know it's him. I can feel it. Come on, baby. *Come ooooon.* Hello?" she said calmly.

"Hello," a polite voice on the other line replied. "This is Randall Stuart. Is Winnie Gottlieb available?"

Liza dashed the telephone to the ground. "Wwwiiiinnnnnie!" she bellowed. "Are you theeeer-rrre? It's Randall-Wandall."

She watched Winnie rise as if in a trance, then, walking with her back straight and her face calm as a statue, she stooped slightly to pick up the phone from the floor. "Hello?" Winnie said quietly.

Liza flung herself down on the couch, bitter and frustrated.

"Yes," Winnie said in an eerie voice, her eyes fixed on a single, distant point. "I would very much like to meet personally with Walker. It would be an honor."

"Get your butts in here, you crazy, adolescent know-it-alls," April bellowed at Lauren and Max from the other end of her sleek office. She grinned at them and walked over to her small conference table. Then she shoved a sheet of paper at them. "Take a look at the overnights, kiddleewinks. Our Friday ratings went through the roof with our Hollywood-hopefuls show."

Lauren stepped across the plush carpet, then sat

down next to Max, her eyes fixed on April. Over the weekend she'd read a long article about April Webster. Born in the poorest section of L.A., April had to fight prejudice, ridicule, and poverty to get to the top. And now she was there. She'd believed in herself. She'd had ideas and imagination. And out of thin air she'd carved something big for herself.

April saluted Lauren, her huge smile hovering like a hundred-watt lightbulb. "Jump up to the ozone layer and back, thanks to our friend Lauren here."

Lauren smiled. "Thank you."

Max punched her playfully in the shoulder.

"Whew, we needed that ratings boost," April said, rolling her eyes and shaking the top of her enormous silk blouse for ventilation. "Generation X: This could be the beginning of a beautiful friendship."

Lauren lifted her coffee cup to her lips, but she was too keyed up even to take a sip.

"Okay," April suddenly boomed, her face dropping into intense seriousness. "What have you folks got for me? Make it quick. I've got a meeting with the bean counters in ten minutes."

Max took a deep breath and began. "We're planning another show on Walker Ingham sometime in the next two weeks."

April sat back and winced. "Yeah. And now I've got to write a friggin' self-help book with the guy—thanks to you, Max, baby. There's no turning back now. Not after the Sikes' blowout last Saturday."

Max drummed his pencil on the table. "Actually, April, you might not want to, after what we're about to tell you."

Storm clouds gathered in April's massive brown eyes. She pursed her lips and leaned forward over the table, clasping her hands together. *"What?"*

"Here's what's happened," Max went on matter-of-factly. He pushed his glasses up on his nose and leaned back in his chair. "A couple of weeks ago Lauren received a tip that connected Walker and Oliver Sikes to some kind of big cover-up involving the Institute."

"Really?" April looked interested, her eyes darting between Lauren and Max.

Lauren cleared her throat. "The tip came from a friend of mine. She knows Oliver Sikes's son, Evan, and he's been hinting strongly that Walker and his dad are being dishonest in some way."

"Meanwhile," Max continued, "at the beach party, Lauren and I overheard a pretty wild argument between Oliver and Evan. Lauren's friend was right. Evan's accusing the whole Institute of dishonesty. We think it's worth checking out."

"We'd like to spend some time on research," Lauren broke in, realizing that April's presence was actually making her feel bolder than ever. "I'd like to place a few long-distance phone calls to his international food centers and orphanages. Then I think it would be worthwhile to track down some of the Institute's former members. Oliver Sikes himself might be worth checking out too."

"Oliver Sikes," April muttered, heaving herself up from the table and walking over to a bank of files. She yanked open a file drawer and whipped out a manila folder. Flipping it open, her eyes scanned the papers like a powerful computer synthesizing data. "Oliver Sikes. Oliver Sikes. Produced *King of Champions* in 1975. Oscar for best picture. Produced a string of big box-office hits through the mid-1980's. A couple of duds after that. In 1990 he became Walker Ingham's first major Hollywood follower. And later that year he gave up his successful career to produce Walker's inspirational videos and documentary films."

"Walker won him over big," Max remarked.

"Yeah, but Sikes must be getting something out of the deal," Lauren theorized.

April's eyes narrowed sharply as she glanced up at Lauren. "You haven't been here long, gal. But you've done your homework. In this business—*nobody* does *anything* for free."

"What about Evan Sikes, April?" Max was asking, rubbing the back of his neck. "Got anything in there on him?"

April flipped rapidly through a sheaf of news clips. "Plenty." She pursed her lips and shifted her balance to another hip. "He's adopted. Uh-huh. Look at these headlines. 'Coast Guard Picks up Evan Sikes for Surfing in Illegal Waters Near Santa Monica.' 'Producer's Son Arrested After High-

Speed Chase on Coastal Highway.' 'Santa Monica Skydivers' Association Cites Producer's Son for Reckless Endangerment in Annual Drop-from-Heaven Event.'"

"Whew," Max whistled.

April shook her head in disbelief. "You're really sure about this, aren't you?"

Lauren nodded. Her mind felt sure and firm and cool. "I have a feeling about this. Call it good old journalistic instinct, or sheer craziness. I don't know. All I know is that I can smell a great scoop out there. There's foul play in the Ingham Empire. And it's just waiting for someone to look beneath the slick surface."

"I agree," Max backed her up, rubbing a spot between his eyes. "I'd like to take a crack at this story with Lauren. And, April, you know what this would do to the ratings. They'd zoom."

April sat down, her eyes burning with thought. "And you know I don't want to get involved with the book if he's some kind of crook."

There was a long pause. Lauren sucked in her breath, praying that April would make the right decision.

"Evan Sikes," she muttered, staring at the ceiling while rolling her pencil between her thumb and forefinger. "Who do we know that can get close to him? We need to draw him out. Maybe even bring him on the show." April looked sharply at Max and Lauren. "What about one of you?"

Lauren bit her lip. She was hesitant to blab about Melissa's friendship with him. But Mel was her only way into the scoop. And she *had* to get the story. Suddenly nothing else mattered. "Um—my roommate—Melissa McDormand. The one who's become friends with Evan. Actually, she's the show's summer bike messenger. The girl with the red hair?"

April's eyes popped out. "That one." Jumping up from her chair, she hurried to her desk and flicked the studio intercom. *"Melissa McDormand. Please report to April Webster's office immediately."*

A moment later the door opened, and Lauren watched as Melissa peered in through a crack. "Um. I'm Melissa McDormand," Mel said with a nervous smile. "Did you need a package delivered?"

April sprang from her chair, ushering Melissa in and pointing to a chair. "Come on in and plant your bod right there. We need you, gal."

Melissa bit the outside of her lip and gave Lauren a pinched look. Wearing her biking shorts, helmet, and flapping poncho, she looked as if she were ready for a rainy ride.

"I understand you are close to Evan Sikes," April demanded, clasping her hands in front of her on the table.

Melissa paled. She gave Lauren a quick, terrified look.

Lauren reached over and touched her hand. "Mel. Please."

April bored her gaze into Melissa's eyes. "We need information about the Walker Institute. Oliver Sikes. The whole ball of wax. Your relationship with Evan Sikes is the key. Find him. Ask him about the secrets he's been hinting around about. Tell him we'll put him in front of the cameras if he needs to get the problem off his chest. Just get him."

"W-well," Melissa stammered, her eyes like two pinpoints of fear, "I don't know if I want to—see him again. I mean, I suppose I could go look for him at the beach. . . ."

April's eyes darted down to the news clips. "Or at the Santa Monica airfield." Her eyes quickly scanned them. "Yeah. Here it is. He belongs to the skydiving association, if they haven't kicked him out yet. And the association meets every Monday at the airfield to experiment with new techniques. It says here right in the *L.A. Times,* date May eighteenth."

Lauren gave Mel a pleading look.

Melissa looked uncertain, but then stood up and adjusted her belt pack, clenching her jaw. "Okay." She nodded. "I'll do it.

Nineteen

wo hours later Melissa was roaring into the parking lot of the Santa Monica airfield, her eyes scanning the broad tarmac for Evan. Dark clouds hovered over the low hangars in the distance. The air smelled damp and salty. The rising wind whipped her hair about her face.

Melissa zipped her windbreaker to her chin and jumped out of the Jeep. Then she strode ahead to a beat-up terminal, trying to sort out her feelings. When April had first called her into the office that morning, it was clear Lauren had blabbed about her friendship with Evan to get a scoop. She'd been angry at first, but now she felt she was on the right track. It wasn't that she cared about an Ingham Institute scandal. She cared about Evan. She suddenly wanted to find him. She knew why he was scared. She'd been through it. The self-hate. The feeling that nothing mattered and no one cared. Somehow she'd survived it. Was it possible for her to help him survive it too?

"Hello?" Melissa knocked on the terminal office door. She tried the knob and found that it was locked.

Stuffing her hands into her pockets, she hurried around the building. An hour before, she'd been climbing the rocks at Pirate Cove, looking for Evan with no luck. Now, however, as she stood gazing across the vast airfield, she could see a familiar form in a white jumping suit stowing gear into a small prop plane.

"Evan," Melissa whispered, stopping in the middle of the breezy field. She stared as he turned sideways to talk to the pilot coming around from the other side of the plane. The wind flattened his blond hair on one side of his head. His expression was intense, but the reckless glint in his eye was still there, as if he didn't know whether to laugh or to spit. Dancing a little on his feet, he took a few playful boxing jabs at the pilot. Then he scooped a duffel off the tarmac and threw it energetically into the plane. The pilot jumped inside, and a few moments later the props began to roar.

"Evan," Melissa shouted, jogging forward.

She watched as he spun around and looked at

her. His face—one moment cocky and careless—suddenly turned serious. For a split second he stared straight into her eyes, his eyes full of pain and longing. Then he looked down abruptly and finished tying a knot on his parachuting gear.

Melissa hurried closer, desperate to talk, even if for only a second. Now empty-handed and ready to jump into the revved-up plane, Evan grabbed the railing of the plane's stepladder, took the first step, then hesitated.

"Evan!" Melissa shouted again.

Dropping one foot to the ground, Evan turned to look at her.

Melissa rushed forward and grabbed the railing, pulling herself close to his body. "Why didn't you tell me?"

Evan narrowed his eyes in anger. "Tell you what?"

"Tell me that you were Oliver Sikes's son?" Melissa pleaded, her eyes hot with tears. "Why did you lie to me about being the pool man?"

Evan looked down at the toe of his shoe, his jaw clenched.

"What were you doing at the bottom of the pool?" Melissa yelled over the scream of the engine. The wind and propellers were whipping her hair wildly, so that she could barely see.

Evan turned away and started to climb into the cockpit.

Melissa reached out and grabbed Evan's sleeve.

"Tell me, Evan! You've got to tell me. *What are you afraid of?*"

Evan turned around, stunned, as if she'd just sunk an arrow into his heart. *"Afraid?"* he shouted back. "Okay, Melissa. I'll tell you what I was doing. I wanted to see how long I could stay under the water."

"What?" Melissa screamed.

Evan's eyes took on a crazy shine. He cocked his head a little. "Some people say you just pass out and drown. I wanted to see if it was true. Hey, then I'd know what it was like to drown at the bottom of my dad's pool. Maybe I should have stayed down there," Evan shouted. "But then you rescued me, didn't you?"

Melissa's eyes grew round. She took a deep, shuddering breath. "Please tell me about it, Evan. I care. I really do."

A look of panic flickered briefly in Evan's brown eyes. Then, with a toss of his head, he recovered. "If you want to know so much about me, Melissa—get in the plane with me."

Melissa felt a bolt of dread shoot through her body. Her gaze traveled the length of the tiny plane, its flimsy wings shuddering in the rising wind. "What? Why would I do that?" she replied, her blood throbbing in her ears.

Evan gazed at her, his look challenging and hard. He jerked his thumb back toward the door of the plane. "I brought an extra parachute. What's the matter? Are you afraid?"

"Of course not," Melissa said instantly, biting the inside of her lip as she met Evan's level stare. "Take me with you."

At first Evan didn't seem to believe her. But once the shocked look wore off his face, he reached out his hand and Melissa grabbed it, warm and strong. Though she had never been on a plane before—any plane, including a jet—something told her she was ready. Ready for life. Ready for death. Ready for Evan. Ready for anything.

"Okay, Larry," Evan shouted above the whining engines.

Melissa climbed into the cockpit and stared at the complicated array of dials and switches. The pilot, wearing dark glasses and a leather jacket, gave Evan the thumbs-up sign. Melissa crawled through a small space into the back of the plane, and she heard the plane's passenger door slam shut.

The engines screamed higher and higher until Melissa thought her eardrums would burst. Still crouched and unsteadily holding a canvas loop hanging from the ceiling, she felt the plane begin to turn and lumber down the tarmac. The wind whistled menacingly and rocked the wings. Something inside her tensed up, then slowly released itself. Climbing onto this plane seemed to be something she had to do. And it had much more to do with Evan than with her promise to Lauren.

Pushing her gently into a seat, Evan strapped a seat belt over her head, then sat down opposite her, leaving his own unbuckled. The plane, now barreling down the runway, was shaking violently. She felt the wheels lift off the ground, then the wings dipping wildly back and forth in the violent wind. She shut her eyes, her heart in her throat. Then she pushed the fear down and stared straight ahead into Evan's gaze.

"What happened at the party?" Melissa shouted. "Why did you drink so much? Why were you fighting with your dad, Evan? Lauren and Max said . . ."

"What were those friends of yours doing down there in the wine cellar, Melissa?" Evan shot back, gripping a loop on the plane's ceiling and swinging himself up. "Those *were* your friends, weren't they? What did you do? Send them into the house to spy on us? They tried to pretend they needed the cellar to climb all over each other in private. What a joke."

"Evan!" Melissa screamed as the plane dipped and swooped up again. "Listen to me!"

But Evan had already turned around and unhooked his parachute pack. He yanked it over his shoulders, his eyes burning with fury. Looking up at her for a second, he reached over and pulled another pack out for her. Then he threw it at her chest. "Put it on," he ordered, unlocking the plane's side door and sliding it open with a shove.

A hurricane-force wind nearly knocked Melissa out of her seat. Wrapping her ankles around the bolted-down seat legs, she slowly pulled on the heavy parachute pack. Her body sagged from the weight.

The straps dug into her shoulders. But she began buckling it in front just as Evan was doing.

"Come on!" Evan screamed. "We're going to do a beach landing."

Melissa looked at him, terrified. His face was so wild and desperate, for an instant she thought he was about to grab her around the waist and hurl her from the plane. He pointed to a small cord on the vest. "This is the rip cord," he shrieked, grabbing the edge of the open door for balance. "Pull it five seconds after your jump. Then watch my movements. We'll head for the beach."

"What do I do when I hit ground?" Melissa shouted back.

"Loosen up," Evan replied with a smile. Suddenly he looked relaxed and happy, as if life on the edge of a deadly cliff was where he belonged. "Bend your knees. Let your body relax. It's easier on your body."

Melissa took two steps toward the gaping, howling opening in the side of the plane's fuselage. She clutched the side of the door and peered down. Suddenly she felt dizzy. Between them and the rolling brown California hills was nothing but empty space.

"Watch me," Evan shouted. "Then jump. I dare you, Melissa."

"Wait!" Melissa shrieked, just as Evan grinned at her, spread his arms wide, and jumped off the plane into space.

For a split second Melissa stepped back, horrified. Then, a moment later, she felt mysterious, reckless energy turn loose inside her. The wind raced over her body, and for once she wasn't thinking about tomorrow or yesterday or anything but the moment before her. Her adrenaline raced. She clenched her fists. And then she jumped out of the plane into pure, empty space.

One.

At first Melissa closed her eyes and felt the wind press powerfully against her face, as if she were lying on a clear pane of glass. The wind howled horribly in her ears. She struggled mightily to keep her arms and legs out in a perfect star.

Two.

Hurtling through space, Melissa could feel the wind drafts pushing her body up, then shoving it down. Her body began to spin. The soaring free fall gave her the overwhelming sensation of being completely powerless against the forces of nature—of life. Her thoughts began to flash crazily between everything good that had ever happened to her: Crossing the finish line and hearing the thunderous cheers from the stands. The day she won her U of S premed scholarship. The day she fell in love with Denny . . .

Three, four . . .

"*Pull the rip cord!*" she heard Evan scream.

Her eyes flapped open. Evan had dropped near her and was pointing wildly at his rip cord. She clutched her chest and fingered the vest until the rip cord was in hand. Then she pulled it in a single jerk.

WHOOOOOOOOOSH. Melissa felt the parachute open far above her head. Her body pulled up as if she'd been suspended by a huge rubber band. The damp sea air softened. The shining blue Pacific curved endlessly to the west. Suddenly she could feel and hear and smell again. She was back from somewhere deep inside herself.

Below, the wide yellow-gray line of deserted beach loomed. She glanced briefly to the right for Evan, then gasped in horror. Inside of pulling his own rip cord, he was still hurtling to earth. In a split second she realized that what he was doing now was no different from what he'd been doing in the pool, or at Pirate Cove. Whether it was nearly drowning himself—or nearly killing himself by diving into rocks—he was living on the very edge of his life. Maybe that was the only thing that gave it meaning. Maybe he really wanted to die. She didn't know for sure. All she knew was that if he didn't pull his cord in the next few seconds, Evan's body would smash into the earth.

"Evan!" Melissa screamed into nothingness. She shifted her weight and the beach drew closer. Below, Evan's body plummeted. For a few brief seconds Melissa prepared herself for the worst. Then, incredibly, Evan's chute opened and whipped up like a flame above his head, filling with air moments before he crashed into the sand.

Melissa clung to the straps above her, watching his body below, rolling over and over until he lay motionless near the edge of the water. Meanwhile the sandy beach was rushing up under her own feet. She held her breath, praying the gusty winds wouldn't push her out over the water or crush her against the rocky cliffs. Then, just before she landed, she let her body go limp. Her feet hit the sand, sending a searing pain up into her bones. The parachute collapsed above her, but a moment later she was crawling out from under it and racing toward Evan's crumpled body.

"*Evan,*" Melissa called out, diving next to him and burying her face in his outstretched arm. Huge sobs began to emerge from somewhere deep inside. "*Evan. Are you okay?*"

She felt a stirring next to her. Evan rolled over and clamped his hand to his forehead. He groaned softly and turned his head. Then, as he opened his eyes and looked up at Mel, his face suddenly froze. Slowly, he lifted his hand and touched the side of her face. "You jumped," he said softly, his face full of wonder, the hard line of his lips quivering. He winced and clutched his side, shivering.

Melissa's throat was choked with feeling. Tears trickled down her cheeks. Taking her hand, she brushed the sand off the side of his face. "Of course I jumped. You needed me to."

Evan's lips parted. He struggled to lift himself on his elbow, not taking his eyes off her. "You must be as crazy as I am, Melissa. Like that day we met at Pirate Cove. You dived in after me like . . ."

"I know what it's like, Evan," Melissa sobbed, holding him.

Evan's eyes narrowed. "How could you know . . ."

"I do," Melissa shouted over the roar of the waves soaking their feet. "I know the fear. I know what it's like to hate yourself so much you want to wipe out everything. You don't want to think. You don't want anything real."

Evan's face suddenly softened. His arms encircled her. Tears began to well up in his eyes. Melissa nestled her cheek in his warm neck, the sand soft and wet beneath her body. "I'm scared, Melissa," Evan finally said. "I want to run—and make a life for myself—but, I'm just a—a shell—a ghost, Melissa."

Melissa looked at him, stroking his forehead.

Evan let out a long sigh. "Everything about my life is a lie."

Melissa bit her lip, her vision fuzzy from tears. "What do you mean, Evan?"

"*It's a lie, that's all,*" Evan screamed, sobbing against her shoulder. "My father," he said with disgust, "adopted me to show how *big* and *magnanimous* he was. Mr. Humanitarian who loves children. Mr. Big Shot Do-Gooder. He knew his Hollywood crowd would fall for it. They always do."

"It's all a lie?"

"Melissa," Evan said, half crying, half laughing, "I'm just a Hollywood prop. Don't you see? I'm just like everything else that surrounds my father and Walker Ingham. I'm just there to help sell the package."

"Listen, Evan," Melissa said quietly. "Whatever lies you're talking about . . . I mean, if you think you need to expose them, Lauren can help. She can."

Evan shook his head and leaned into her shoulder. "I don't know anymore. All I know is that you're here. It's all that matters to me right now, Melissa."

Melissa wrapped her arms across his strong back. "You've got to trust yourself."

"I've got to trust you," Evan murmured into her ear. "And I do. You're the first person I've trusted in a long time."

Melissa clung to him, her heart aching.

"I'll get Lauren and Max into the house," Evan suddenly spoke, taking her hand and pressing it. to his chest. "They can look around. And maybe they'll find what they're looking for."

Twenty

ack at the beach house, Lauren and Max were warming cups of hot cocoa. Fifteen minutes earlier, Melissa and Evan had stumbled through the front door, windblown and limping. Melissa had briefly mentioned something about a rough parachute jump. But just looking at their pale faces, Lauren knew instantly something was up.

"Here," she told Evan, who was huddled on the living-room couch before a roaring fire. Melissa had wrapped a blanket around his shoulders and was kneeling next to him on the couch.

"Thanks," Evan said with an unsure smile, still shivering. He took the cup of cocoa, and Lauren saw his muscular forearm, broad enough to belong to a champion windsurfer or tennis player. A brand-new gold watch gleamed on his wrist.

Lauren smiled back. The last time she'd seen Evan, he'd been totally different. Drunk. Rude. Rough. But this was not the same Evan. He was nice. He was gentle with Melissa. And he had a funny kind of intense sadness to his eyes that made her want to protect him. She wondered which Evan was real. But whoever he was, she wanted desperately to use every last bit of information stored in his brain about his dad and Walker Ingham.

Max, who'd followed Lauren home after work, had settled on the floor by the fire. Though he pretended to scan the morning papers, Lauren could tell that he was like a coiled spring, waiting for the perfect moment to begin asking questions. "Bad jump, huh?" Max began carefully.

Evan's mouth tightened. "Yeah. I . . ."

"Lauren!" Liza suddenly burst into the room, wrapped in a robe covered with hot-pink flamingos. "You still got that funny-smelling perfume that costs a fortune?" She stopped, realizing that Max and Evan were there. *"Hi, guys!"*

Lauren cringed. "It's in my top drawer," she said shortly.

Liza slunk slowly into the room, her eyes fixed on Max, then on Evan's craggy profile against the fire. She rested her hip against the end of the couch. "Just getting ready for a callback from Geoff Hansen," she confessed to Evan in a casual tone. She tossed her head and stared up at the ceiling. "You probably saw me with him at the Oliver Sikes party."

"Liza . . ." Lauren tried to break in, noticing the tense lines in Evan's face.

"Yeah," Liza continued to blab, twisting a string of fake pearls around her neck. "Well, I've got a big callback tomorrow morning for the part of my life, complete with a fabulously wet and wild love scene that will make my ex-boyfriend go nuts."

A blast of wind shuddered the house. The fire flickered.

"Bye, guys." Liza turned on her heel with a sexy flounce. "Gotta hit this fabulous script and get my beauty rest too. Oh, and in case you hadn't noticed, Winnie's still back there, putting mascara on while chanting Walker Ingham's name to the beat of her crystal chimes. She's going out tonight with that fun-lovin' Institute gang."

A peaceful silence settled briefly over the living room the instant Liza closed her bedroom door. But a moment later she'd punched the button on her tape deck. A brassy Broadway tune boomed through the walls.

"Let's watch the storm from the deck," Lauren suggested, grabbing a stack of old blankets from the storage beneath the window seat.

Evan and Melissa looked at each other and stood up. A few minutes later they were settled with Max and Lauren on the deck chairs. A stormy sky hovered over the ocean, and the waves crashed in, gray and cold. The wind picked up, sending lashing rain toward the house, but the four were dry under the eaves.

Lauren tried to relax, but her insides were bubbling with impatience. After her meeting that morning with April, she'd made a decision. There was definitely something rotten at the core of the Ingham Empire. And she was the one who was going to expose it for what it really was.

Max was pacing the deck, his fists punched into his pockets, staring intently down at his feet.

"Evan?" Lauren finally spoke up. She sat up on her deck chair and twisted around, the wind swirling her hair. Then she looked straight into Evan's eyes. "Can you tell us what's wrong?"

After a long silence Evan finally spoke. "Okay," he said quietly. "This is what I can do. If you need to know more about the Ingham Institute, you can go look for yourselves."

Lauren sat up and planted her feet on the deck. "Then there *is* something illegal going on. . . ."

"Lauren," Max said sharply, putting his hand on her shoulder.

Slowly, Evan pulled a key from the pocket of his pants. He took Lauren's wrist and pressed the key into her palm, closing her fingers over it. "Here's the key to the basement of my dad's house."

Lauren looked up slowly into his eyes. She knew how much hatred there was between Evan and his father. Was he using them for some purpose they didn't know about?

"Go now," Evan said in a half trance. "Enter through the bushes just south of the main gate. Then head for the west entrance under the main deck. The alarm-system switch is behind the water meter to the right of the door. Press the red button to disconnect it."

Lauren nodded. She knew she had to do it, even if she wasn't completely sure about Evan. "Okay," she whispered.

"There's an editing studio near the wine cellar," Evan went on in a tired monotone. "Videotapes are stored everywhere, you'll see. Check out any unmarked ones you can find. Dad's people always forget to throw them away."

Lauren and Max stood. She felt Evan suddenly grip her wrist. "Be careful," he warned, looking up at her, serious. "Walker's a dangerous guy. And so is my dad. Just don't let anyone see you."

Lauren gulped as he released her. A moment later she and Max were running hand in hand through the pouring rain to the Jeep. Lauren started the engine and flicked on the windshield wipers. She backed out just as a pair of headlights swung into the driveway and a slim figure emerged from a shiny BMW sedan. "It's Randall," Lauren said in a hushed voice. "I guess he's picking up Winnie."

"Yeah," Max said thoughtfully as Lauren roared up the road to the coastal highway. "Randall arrives the moment Evan sends us off to check out an Institute scandal. Hope it's just a coincidence."

Lauren looked at him in horror. Rain pelted the Jeep, and a gust of wind nearly knocked her into the opposite lane. "Would Evan set us up? Is he capable of that?"

Max shook his head, serious. Then he pulled a pad from the inside of his jacket and made a small note to himself. "I hope not, Lauren," he said softly. "I just hope not."

Lauren flicked the wipers on full speed as they approached the darkened Sikes mansion. Peering into the black night, she could barely make out the locked front gate. She slowed, switched off the headlights, and let the Jeep slowly rumble onto the gravel at the side of the road. Rain pelted the windows. Quickly, she turned off the engine, then reached into her glove box for a flashlight. "Let's go," she murmured, swallowing the fear that was beginning to clutch at her throat. She'd covered dangerous stories before. But there was something different about this one. It wasn't just all the money involved. It was people like Winnie. People who actually entrusted their hearts and minds to the Institute.

"Come on," Max whispered, parting the hedge along the side of the road. "Be careful." Lauren followed, shivering against the bone-chilling rain and fog. Wet leaves slapped against her face. Her running shoes squished with water.

Lauren ran across the side lawn toward the lower

part of the house. She shone her flashlight behind the meter. As Evan had promised, the alarm-disconnect button was there. Quickly, Max pushed it. Then she turned and slipped the key into the small wooden door to the basement.

Creeeeeeeeeeeeeak.

Lauren froze. She prayed the alarm wouldn't go off as they opened it. Max placed a reassuring hand on her shoulder. Slowly, they moved ahead into a cramped hallway. It was paneled in dark wood. Spiderwebs clung to the ceilings, and a damp, musty smell filled Lauren's nose. Max shut the door quietly behind them, muffling the roar of the ocean storm. Lauren shuffled ahead, shivering with cold and fear. The hallway turned abruptly. When she ran her flashlight up ahead, she saw a line of doors, a cobwebby ceiling hung with pipes, then another hallway that turned off to the left.

"Whew," Max breathed, touching her back. "Some kind of underground labyrinth. Maybe Sikes and Ingham bury their nonbelievers down here, huh?"

Lauren glared back over her shoulder.

After several twists and turns through the maze of hallways and doors, Lauren finally recognized a door at the end of a passageway. "The door to the pool area," Lauren whispered. "It's right next to the wine cellar. And Evan said the wine cellar was right next to the editing room."

Max nodded grimly; he reached ahead to slip his

hand into hers. "Please be careful, okay?" he whispered, drawing her near to his face. "I can't let anything happen to you." Lauren saw his face contort in the dim light. "I—just can't."

Lauren put a hand on his soft mouth. "I'm okay. We'll *be* okay, Max. This is it. Don't you see? This is the story of our lives. We're going to get it—together." She felt him pull her close. Their lips brushed briefly. Then his eyes swept to the side.

"Look," he breathed, pushing open a small door.

Lauren shone her light inside and let out a tiny gasp. Along the walls of the narrow room were rows of tapes and glossy, high-tech video-editing equipment. Without a word they stepped inside and shut the door.

"Look." Max pointed. He sat down at a wheeled chair in front of a monitor positioned in the middle of a long counter. Feeling along the back of the screen, he found a switch and clicked it. Then he reached up to the shelf and grabbed a random tape. "'Salvation Farm and Orphanage,'" he read the label. His hands flying as if he'd edited tapes thousands of times before, he slipped it into the editing machine.

Lauren kneeled down next to him, a clutch at her throat as he began punching buttons. She bit her lip and looked nervously toward the door.

"Okay, here we go," Max said tersely. "Just watch that door. And if it's a choice between your safety and getting the tape, just forget the tape, okay?"

Lauren nodded and stared at the screen, first a grainy black and white, then suddenly green with tropical colors. "Walker," she breathed, staring at his lean body clad in worn jeans, bent over a row of vegetables. "Hoeing a field with farmers in—maybe Central America." The tape stopped, and Lauren was suddenly gazing at Walker playing on his hands and knees with children in a ramshackle room. Smiling and touching, he passed out boxes filled with books, toys, and nutritious food.

"Makes him look like a damn hero," Max muttered, shoving his hair off his forehead. A sheen of sweat covered his upper lip. "Still—these takes are really short. It's almost like . . ."

Lauren frowned and moved closer until her cheek was touching the damp shoulder of his sweater. His wet curls clung to his neck, and in the close darkness she could feel the rise and fall of his breath. Lauren suddenly felt dizzy. She drew her breath in and stood. "Evan said to look for unmarked tapes." Sweeping her flashlight around the room, she finally let the beam rest on an old cardboard box in the far corner. "Look."

"What's that?" Max murmured, his eyes glued to the fast-forwarding images on the screen.

Lauren yanked the box toward her, sending up a cloud of dust. Then she shone her light and rummaged inside. It was full of dirty, unmarked tapes, just as Evan had told them. "Take out that tape, Max, and try this one," she ordered, hurrying over to the editing machine, nearly tripping on a loose cord.

Max took the tape from her hand and flipped it over once or twice in the dim light. "Unmarked tape, huh? That was easy enough. Just like Evan described." He punched the stop button, then ejected the first video. "Okay," he whispered, a suspicious look on his face. "Let's see what old Evan left for us."

Lauren held her breath as Max shoved the tape in and it disappeared inside the machine. Instantly another picture appeared of Walker and film-crew members working in an impoverished, dusty village. "Looks like Africa," Lauren whispered, biting her thumbnail. "The kids look really dirty, but not all that thin, huh?"

Max was staring straight ahead in the bluish light, his eyes slowly narrowing. He bent forward until his nose was nearly touching the screen. A second later he froze the frame and pointed to a corner of the fuzzed picture. "Look. There's Evan. Looks like he's in on this whole deal."

Lauren leaned over Max's shoulder and crouched. Evan's blond hair and familiar movie-star-handsome face could be seen clearly in the background. Wearing a tank top and a pair of sunglasses, he was carrying a large piece of lighting equipment on one shoulder.

Max flopped back in the seat and repunched the play button. "Just a bunch of outtakes, I guess."

The camera jerked awkwardly, as if the camera-man had been bumped. Suddenly the scene swung around to a small black child on the dusty road, running with arms outstretched to a serene, smiling Walker. To the right Lauren could see another camera taping the scene. She frowned and instinctively gripped Max's shoulder. "This is strange. . . ."

While the tape continued, Walker suddenly thrust the child away. His face took on an impatient expression, and he began shouting angrily to someone off camera. "Angie—get your butt over here, and *now*," he yelled. "These kids are supposed to be dirty, okay? We're supposed to feel *sorry* for the poor, downtrodden kids of the world. Get it? Now get your makeup case over here before I kick the goddamn set in."

Lauren's hand rose to her face in horror. She muffled a scream.

"That lowlife," Max breathed in the flickering light. "The whole thing's a setup. Evan must know it. He was there."

"It's all fake," Lauren whispered, suddenly terrified. "It's pure fiction. The documentaries. The photos. Probably all of his programs."

Max nodded, his fingers drumming on the top of the editing machine. "He and Oliver Sikes must rake in the donations and dump them into their own bank accounts. Hence, this gorgeous mansion. Los Angeles, California—what a place."

Max stopped, looking over his shoulder. Then they both stood, hearing noise at the end of the hallway. "Someone's coming, Max," she said, her

heart suddenly thumping with terror. Max punched
the tape out of the machine and stuffed it into his
jacket. Then he lunged for the box and grabbed as
many as he could.

"Someone's broken in," a deep voice boomed on
the other side of the door. "The editing room."
Lauren heard the sound of pounding footsteps, then
reached over and locked the door. "Just shoot 'em
first. Then we can figure out what they're doing."

Lauren's head spun. Leaving through the hall
door was impossible. Then, in a split second, she
spotted a small door high on the wall—apparently
leading to a crawl space or storage compartment.
"Quick, Max," Lauren whispered, grabbing his
hand. Together they climbed onto an editing table
and opened the small door. "Look, it's some kind of
entrance." She lifted one knee, then crawled forward, with Max close behind her.

Shots were fired, and she could hear the sound of
the editing-room door being broken down, just as
Max managed to get the small door shut.

"Max!" Lauren whispered harshly, suddenly finding herself in a plywood-lined compartment.

"It's okay, Lauren," Max said. "I'm right behind
you. Just move as fast as you can. We're going to get
out of this together. We have to."

Please don't let them find us, Lauren silently
prayed, her hands and knees suddenly falling onto
bare earth. The compartment had opened into the
home's underground crawl space. A cool, salty

breeze fanned her face, and in the distance she could hear the sound of the ocean crashing against the cliffs below. "Max! It's a way out!"

Lauren stood up. The storm lashed in from the ocean. She looked around and saw that they had crawled out of the mansion's basement and were now standing on the edge of a cliff. The top of a staircase was only a few feet away. "Come on!" Lauren shouted over the howling wind.

"Be careful!" Max shouted back, squeezing out of the crawl space and running for her.

Lauren headed down the slippery staircase, rickety with age. It dropped about twenty feet onto a beach, but the beach was quickly filling with water as the high tide rushed in.

"Jump in," Max hollered over the roar of the storm and crashing waves. "We'll have to swim. It's the only way, Lauren. These guys are on their way, and they would not hestitate to put bullets in our heads."

Lauren nodded. It wasn't until that moment that she realized just how far Ingham, Sikes, and his guru goons were willing to go. But how had they known she and Max were down in the editing room? Had someone warned them? Taking a deep breath, she jumped into the freezing-cold, shallow water and, with Max close behind, let the waves tumble her roughly down the beach.

"The tape!" she screamed over the crashing sea and pelting rain.

"We've got to stay together!" Max yelled, his head bobbing behind her in the water. A wall of water swept over her head, but she kicked violently forward, keeping her eye on the rocks looming to her left. After a few moments she realized that she had lost sight of Max in the raging waters.

"Maaaaaaaaaax!" Lauren screamed into the darkness, treading water as she looked in every direction for his dark head in the moonlight. She couldn't lose Max. Not now.

With rocks looming ahead of her, Lauren had to kick away from the beach. She swam with every ounce of strength in her body. And after what seemed like an hour, a smooth, wide beach appeared. Her face and hands were numb. Her lungs sucked for air. Her legs were barely able to pull her frozen body onto the sand before she collapsed.

"Max," she moaned, lifting her head to check the waves rolling in behind her. A dark head appeared, and her body sagged with relief when she saw that it was Max, swimming valiantly through the blowing, whitecapped water.

"Lauren!" he screamed over the roar of the waves, which washed him up on the sand. "Lauren! You're okay! You're okay!" His feet hit the sand. He staggered up the beach and collapsed next to her, wrapping his wet arms around her with joy. His eyes were filled with tears of relief. "I thought I'd lost you," he called out. "But you're here. We did it, Lauren. We did it together."

Lauren embraced him back. Their legs tangled on the wet sand. The rain poured down on them. They were blue with cold. But they were alive.

Max unzipped his jacket a little and pulled out the tape victoriously.

"You still have the tape," Lauren gasped.

Max nodded. "If we move fast and get it to a lab, we can reverse a lot of water damage."

Lauren stumbled to her feet, her eyes darting up toward the cliffs. "If we run up the beach, we should find the Jeep just north of here."

Hand in hand, Lauren and Max ran up the beach, stumbled through the side yard of a fancy beach house, and finally made it to the highway. There, just a hundred yards up the road, was the Jeep.

Max slammed the passenger door shut as Lauren collapsed with her forehead against the steering wheel. Sobs welled up from deep within her. She felt the warmth of Max's arms around her, and she nestled softly against his chest. "For a minute there," she wept, "I didn't think we'd make it."

"Yeah," Max murmured back, stroking her cheek. "I was beginning to wonder too. You—you have a lot of courage, Lauren. I never thought I'd meet someone like you. Maybe I thought finding you was impossible."

Lauren looked at him closely and saw something she'd never seen in Max's face. Maybe it was trust. Maybe it was something more. Whatever it was, it was stirring something powerful in her. She wasn't sure whether she reached for Max first, or the other way around. But the next moment his lips were on hers.

"I'll drop you off," Max finally spoke, pulling away and looking at her softly. "Then I'll take this tape to the lab in your Jeep, if that's okay."

"Take the Jeep," Lauren insisted.

Max nodded, serious, and Lauren started the Jeep, suddenly thinking about the end of summer and wondering if she would have to choose. But the next moment Max was pulling her into his arms again, his soft lips pressed to hers. And all her thoughts and worries flew away like the snowy white gulls on the wind.

Twenty-one

"**H**ello, Winnie," Walker was saying softly, his blue eyes luminous and direct. He gestured for her to come into his room, the large, spare quarters in the Sikes mansion that looked out over the ocean. Walker then smiled briefly at Randall. "Thank you, Randall."

Winnie nodded, moving ahead easily, as if her feet were two inches from the ground. She reached for her cat's eye and held it briefly for reassurance.

"Walker?" Randall's sharp voice suddenly intruded behind them. "Oliver's sent a security guard down to the basement. Apparently there's some kind of disturbance near the wine cellar or editing room."

"Take care of it," Walker said sharply, looking over his shoulder. An instant later he was looking warmly into Winnie's eyes, touching her elbow slightly as he guided her into a second sitting room overlooking the ocean. Unlike his sparsely furnished front room, Walker's inner retreat was a lavishly decorated living space, complete with leather sofas, Persian rugs, crystal lamps, and a fancy stereo system whispering soft jazz. A crackling fire burned in the manteled fireplace, as the storm lashed against the windows.

"It—it's nice," Winnie stammered, confused. She'd believed that Walker lived in an ascetic room with few comforts. From his teachings she'd learned to spurn material things, which distracted from the development of a meaningful spiritual life. Frowning briefly in confusion, Winnie sat down on the buttery leather couch.

"I see you've found the most comfortable space in the room," Walker said gently above her.

Winnie smiled as Walker sat down next to her. "Yes," she replied in a tiny voice, drawing her head back a little. Instead of sitting at the end of the couch, Walker had chosen an awkward position on the middle cushion, next to hers.

"Now," he murmured, staring at her, "where were we?"

Winnie cleared her throat and nervously touched one of her earrings. "Um. I'd like to talk a little bit about the universality of selflessness. In your tape

Self Versus World, you talk about survival—and how it isn't really survival of the fittest. It's survival of the willing. . . ."

"Yes," Walker said distractedly, leaning into the sofa and extending his arm over the top. He ran his eyes down the length of her leg.

RRIIIIIIIING.

Winnie jumped.

Walker's lips tensed as he reached behind them to pick up the phone. There was a moment of silence as he listened to the message. "*How? How* did you lose them?" he snapped. His eyes traveled back to hers, and she could see him deliberately softening his expression. Then, without a word, he hung up. He readjusted his slender body on the couch, moving a few inches closer to Winnie.

"Um," Winnie began again, trying not to focus too much on Walker's closeness. After all, Walker was an unusual man. A giving person. He probably didn't require as much personal space as most people did. "I guess I wanted to talk about that a little. I mean, isn't selfishness the driving force in society . . ."

Walker reached out and playfully touched the side of her bare arm. "Winnie. Relax."

Winnie stirred uncomfortably, inching away until her back was jammed against the armrest. She took in Walker's tanned, crepe-paper throat. The deep lines that surrounded the blue eyes. The chunky gold ring on the little finger. Then she looked at his distant expression and realized, in a flash of pain, that Walker wasn't listening to her at all.

He shook his head with understanding as he reached his arm around her waist and pulled her to him. "Survival is about giving oneself," he murmured. "It's about people reaching out to one another, Winnie."

"But I . . ."

He put his foot down and gave her a serious, pleading look, touching the side of her face. "When two people connect, there is joy, Winnie. Let down the walls. Take responsibility for the moment. It's spread out before us like a rich kingdom. Enjoy it."

Winnie's mouth fell open. She understood what Walker was saying, but his closeness was suddenly unbearable. She gazed into his eyes, trying to think—trying to make him understand.

"Live each moment to the fullest," Walker whispered, nudging toward her and slowly reaching for the top botton of her blouse. Like silk, he undid the first one.

Tears began to form in Winnie's eyes. Then, as her second button fell away, something inside of her went dead. In an instant the face of the man she'd worshiped turned into the face of an oversexed, middle-aged manipulator. Moaning softly, Walker pushed himself on top of her, burying his face in her neck. Winnie sat paralyzed, her mind suddenly panicked, her thoughts racing.

Walker's just a lecherous creep who uses Randall to keep him supplied with young girls, Winnie thought, horrified, her eyes darting toward the closed door. She knew she could try to run out, but wondered about the other men in the house. Would they force her to stay?

"Come," Walker urged, clasping her hand and leading her to a far door, through which she could see the corner of a large bed.

Suddenly Winnie's panic turned to anger, and her anger cleared her mind like a cold wind. Standing with Walker, she leaned seductively into his side and winked. "I've got something to show you," she lied in a throaty voice.

"Mmmmmm," Walker replied, nuzzling her until Winnie thought she'd be sick.

"I left it with my things downstairs," Winnie whispered, winking again. "Something really wicked."

Walker's blue eyes glittered with excitement. But they quickly dimmed when someone began knocking violently at the door. He opened it a crack, and Winnie saw that it was Randall. "What?"

"They were in the editing room," she could hear Randall's muffled voice. "But they're long gone. We have descriptions, though—and we think we know who they are."

Walker pounded a fist into the doorjamb.

Winnie quickly saw her opportunity. Rushing past him and Randall, she blew a kiss. "Be right back."

A moment later she was fleeing down the mansion's main staircase, her hand clutched over her mouth, praying Walker wouldn't follow. Flinging open the front door, she ran through sheets of rain into the circular driveway. She stopped, and for a moment she just stood there, wringing her hands as the swelling summer storm pounded her head with rain.

She had no car. She couldn't go back inside the mansion. The only thing she could do was run home.

Winnie felt a swell of grief deep inside her. Walker Ingham. She'd believed him. She'd trusted him with her thoughts. Her life. Her whole soul. But he was only a hollow image, just as Lauren had said.

Lauren, Winnie thought bitterly, turning and running out the front gate. *Why did Lauren have to be right? And why did Winnie always have to play the fool?*

Twenty-two

"I never thought I'd feel this way about anyone, David." Liza muttered her memorized lines the next morning as she hurried through the huge outdoor movie lot.

She checked her watch, her head light with excitement. This was it. It wasn't a stupid singing telegram. It wasn't a stupid talk-show appearance. This was a callback for an actual movie role. Geoff Hansen *had* loved her at the Sikes party. She had almost given up hope when, finally, his casting director had called her to read.

Her eyes scanned the lot. The casting director had told her to look for the Megastar studio sign, located just past a huge 1940's city-street backdrop.

Last night's storm had blown the sky clean, and the sun shone down bright.

"Megastar. Megastar," Liza sang softly to herself. "They're gonna make me a megastar."

Liza raced through the bustling morning activity. Two women in turn-of-the-century costumes walked by, smoking cigarettes and looking bored. Another guy, dressed in a futuristic warrior suit, passed her, biting into a doughnut. There were bloodied cowboys. Nineteen-fifties housewives. Nurses. Charred firefighters.

She struggled to hide the excitement bursting inside her. Just walking through the lot was like being in a movie. It was the most exciting, wonderful place she'd ever been. Costumes. Fantasy. Music. Storytelling. She'd spent a lifetime being an oddball because she loved these things so much. And now she was in the middle of it. Here, where she really, finally belonged.

After wandering for several minutes, she finally spotted the Megastar studio, a large warehouselike building toward the end of the lot. Liza rushed inside the front entrance. There was an empty lobby, and the smell of coffee and sugary doughnuts wafted through. Liza followed a series of signs to the casting office. Finally she reached a glass door that read Auditions.

Liza paused to neaten her lipstick. Then she snapped her purse shut and walked in. It was a large, carpeted waiting room, filled with at least two dozen other teenage hopefuls just like her, flipping through magazines, or mouthing their lines into space.

Liza marched in, flouncing her hair with her hand and looking for the nearest seat. Her nerves were steeled. Her mood was confident. She was practically whistling with happiness. But then, just as she turned to sit down, she saw him sitting against the far wall.

Travis, Liza thought, staring helplessly at his familiar shaggy mane and blue eyes, which had just made contact with hers. A split second of surprise flickered across his face, but quickly fizzled. He looked down sadly, crossed a foot onto his knee, and began bouncing it up and down with obvious nervousness.

Liza looked away and bit her lip, suddenly overcome with regret. A minute ago she'd been on top of the world. Now she felt empty and lost inside. Their horrible fight at the Sikes party seemed so long ago. And though she hadn't admitted it to anyone, she'd been thinking about him constantly. She'd been angry. She'd been insulted. And she'd been hurt deeply. But now, she realized in a flash—Travis wasn't someone she could just forget about. He was someone she loved. Someone she missed terribly.

"Liza Ruff?" a woman with frizzy hair called out through a door, as a guy with an Elvis 'do strolled out. The woman looked down at her clipboard thoughtfully.

Liza stood up.

"Your scene calls for a male partner, Liza." She called into the room, "Any one of you guys want to volunteer to read with Ms. Ruff?"

Liza watched in amazement as Travis instantly rose and walked up to her, carrying his guitar case. Wearing a red bandanna around his head, blue jeans, and his plain white T-shirt, he looked like his usual self. Except when Liza looked closer, she could see that his face was a little pale, and dark rings had appeared under his eyes.

"I'll do it," he said simply, casting a longing, sideways glance at Liza that made her heart turn over.

Liza just stood there, unable to move. She would have thrown her arms around his neck if she could. But nothing could change the horrible words they'd shouted at each other Saturday night. Everything was different now, as if someone had dug a deep canyon between them—a canyon so wide Liza didn't know if they would ever be able to bridge it.

"Okay, Liza," the woman said curtly, flipping through a thick script. "You've got scene seventy-five. Why don't you just take it from 'I never thought I'd feel . . .'?"

Liza's eyes were burning by the time she and Travis sat down. Someone pushed scripts in front of them, but Liza pushed hers away. She knew every line. Her mouth began to tremble with feeling as she began.

"I never thought I'd feel this way about anyone, David," Liza began, a tear forming in her eye. "When I first met you, I'd been through too many disappointments. I didn't think I'd ever let anyone in again."

"'Then why did you do it?'" Travis read the line quietly.

"Please forgive me, David," Liza replied, the lines she'd memorized suddenly taking on a deeper meaning that was unexpectedly hers to give. Choking sobs rose from deep within her. "I'm not used to giving. I'm not used to having someone who needs me. Cares for me. Loves me for who I am—not expecting anything in return."

"'I did,'" Travis read on, a clutch in his throat.

Liza suddenly felt the familiar touch of his hand on hers.

"Please—can't we start over?" Liza pleaded, lifting her eyes to his. She knew he understood what she was asking. He knew it wasn't just an act. Suddenly she felt a tiny ray of hope.

"'I can't,'" Travis read the lines. "'Maybe a year from now. Maybe two. But not now. Not until you've learned how to love yourself as much as I've loved you.'"

Liza bent her head, her face contorted and streaming with tears. She felt Travis squeeze her hand gently, then withdraw it.

"*Thank* you," a woman in back spoke up, walking toward them, looking thoughtful and tapping a pencil to her cheek. Her long black hair was pulled into a ponytail, and her lips were painted a bright red. "I'm Donna Hillman, Geoff's casting director." She shook Liza's hand, then Travis's. "That was lovely. Better than I've seen anyone read that scene in days. Do you have experience on film?"

"Yes," Liza said quietly, looking over at Travis. It was funny to be saying that so matter-of-factly. On any other day she would have been blabbing to the casting director about her films with Waldo on the U of S campus. But now, suddenly, standing next to soft-spoken Travis, she didn't want to play L.A.'s self-promotion game. She was content simply to be herself.

"Look," the woman said after a pause. "We'll let you know tomorrow if we've got something for you in *Princess Beast*. But even if we don't, I'm casting several other teen films right now. I'm going to take a look at what I've got and get back with you."

"Thank you," Liza said quietly, pushing her chair out and standing up. She left the room quickly, too full of feeling to speak. When she reached the lobby, she paused and tried to calm her racing heart, unsure whether she was reacting to the thrill of the audition, or the pain of seeing Travis.

She walked outside and breathed in the fresh air. A moment later she could feel Travis behind her. She felt him touch her shoulder, and then she turned slowly around to face him.

Travis leaned carefully against a tree planter, his

hands stuffed into his pockets. Several pretty girls strode by in combat fatigues, and a shiny movie-lot cart sped by, carrying a guy talking on a cellular phone.

"Great reading," Travis said quietly. He was playing his knuckle along his top lip, not looking at her.

Liza felt a heaviness in her chest. She could barely breathe. Travis was four feet away from her—and he was a million miles away from her. Somewhere she'd crossed a line. And turning back seemed impossible. "Yours was great too," she said, her voice starting to crack. Why couldn't he just make the first move and grab her? Take her. Kiss her. Didn't he want to? She couldn't be sure. She cleared her throat, self-conscious. "Um. Good luck. I mean—getting a part."

"Yeah," Travis whispered, shaking his bangs gently out of his eyes and giving her a tender look. "I don't know why they think a crazy musician like me can make it in the movies."

"Wild," Liza said, biting her lip and looking down.

"Yeah," Travis agreed, "it was a wild idea. It came from you, I think."

Liza looked up, her eyes full of tears. "Then it was a good one."

Travis tried to smile, but the heaviness in his eyes made the effort fall apart. "Look—I guess we'll be seeing each other. You know. Well—maybe around here."

Liza nodded, trying to ignore the tear spilling down her cheek. "Yeah. If we get parts."

"Yeah," Travis said in a cracked voice. He coughed. "But if I don't . . . Well, we will, if it's meant to be."

"Yeah, Travis," she whispered to herself, "if it's meant to be."

Twenty-three

"**S**o you actually *broke* into the Sikes mansion last night?" April was demanding next morning, popping her pen up and down on the conference table. "You have a tape implicating Walker Ingham, but you had to commit a crime to get it? Where's Max?"

Lauren sipped her cold cup of coffee and closed her eyes. "No, April. Evan Sikes *gave* us the key. It's his *home*. And he directed us to the editing room in the basement."

Several staff members leaned forward, murmuring among themselves. Lauren's eyes darted desperately toward the door. When she and Max had parted last night, he'd promised to get the incriminating tape to a lab, so the water damage could be repaired in time for this meeting with April. Now they were a good ten minutes into it—and still no Max.

"What do you think, Harry?" April turned to a gray-suited man who was the show's chief legal counsel.

"Ms. Turnbell-Smythe," the lawyer began, making a steeple with his long fingers and staring at her, "I'm sure you must understand our position. Mr. Ingham is scheduled to appear on April's show tomorrow. But without solid proof of misconduct, April cannot possibly bring up the subject of fraudulent overseas programs. We run the risk of a multi-million-dollar libel suit."

Lauren felt sick. Just yesterday she'd been so sure she could pull off an Ingham scandal story for April. Now she realized she was in way over her head. April's staffers weren't like the inexperienced eager beavers on the university's weekly newspaper. They were tough, world-weary, and trained to look for trouble before it happened. They were the best in the giant talk-show industry. Her hands began to tremble from fear and fatigue. She had no business being there.

Where is Max?

"It's a great story, Lauren," Elaine soothed, sticking a pencil behind her ear and sighing. "If Walker's Institute and international relief effort are a fraud—I'd say bring him on the show and accuse him right there on the air."

April's eyes glittered.

"Publicity would go through the roof if we tipped off the affiliates just before it happened," said a young blond woman who was April's publicity director. "You can't buy that kind of attention. Ratings would definitely soar."

"But if the tape itself is a fake—assuming Max gets his butt over here so we can actually *see* it," another staffer complained, "then we look ridiculous. Actually, I'd bet it's the weirdo Sikes son playing prankster with you and Max."

Lauren's heart sank. "Yes," she said quietly. "You could be right. He's a troubled guy. He drinks a lot and has big problems with his dad. But when you see the tape, you'll realize it just couldn't have been faked. It's actual footage of Walker requesting special makeup effects. Complaining about a child actor. Arguing with the kid's mother."

"If we ever see the tape . . ." another older staff member named Jerry muttered.

"Okay," April boomed, leaning forward and resting her elbows on the table. She grasped her forehead with both hands and thought. "Just knock it off, Jerry. I think Lauren and Max are onto something very big here, and I'm not going to blow this gal off this morning because you ate the wrong thing for breakfast."

The man sat back, wounded, then glared at Lauren.

"We just need the tape," April suddenly shouted.

Lauren felt tears springing into her eyes. She

knew that if Max didn't walk through the door in the next few minutes, it would be over for her.

Knock. Knock.

Lauren looked up, her heart rising into her throat. *Max!*

April's assistant rose and went to the door. She opened it a crack. "No, Nancy," the assistant whispered. "April's sealed the meeting. Only Max Cantor is to be sent through."

Lauren slumped in her chair. It wasn't Max after all.

"What is going on?" April demanded, making a fist on the table and staring at it like a loaded gun.

April's assistant looked back over her shoulder. "Nancy says there are two men here to see you. They say it's extremely urgent."

Lauren frowned. She watched in shock as the door opened slightly, then all the way. Two uniformed policemen wearing somber expressions stepped in and took off their hats.

"April Webster?" one of the officers said quietly. "I'm Dan Montegue with the county sheriff's department."

Lauren felt dread welling up inside her. Something was wrong. Something was very wrong. Where was Max?

April stood up, one hand gripping the edge of the conference table. Her dark eyes flashed with fear. "What is it? What's happened?"

The first officer took a small notepad out of his

shirt pocket, flipped it open, and looked at it briefly. "At approximately two A.M. this morning, a Crescent Beach resident reported hearing loud crashing sounds in the vicinity of Pirate Cove, just below his remote cliff cabin. When he walked out on his deck, he saw a large fireball and called authorities."

Lauren's blood froze. *Max. Where are you?*

"We conducted a search of the area and pulled a white Jeep out of the water early this morning. We traced its registration to a Crescent Beach residence."

Lauren let out a gasp. Something was falling inside her. Something was falling and breaking apart. *Max. Where are you?*

"What?" April whispered, her black eyes getting round.

"Nobody was home by the time we got to the house. A neighbor told us the Jeep's owner, a Ms. Lauren Turnbell-Smythe, worked here at the studio," the officer continued. "I'm afraid we haven't been able to recover the body, but her chances of surviving a drop of nearly a thousand feet into ocean waters are negligible."

"Ms. Turnbell-Smythe is sitting right here," April shouted, getting up and storming over to the officers. "What is the meaning of this?"

Lauren drew her hands up to her face in horror. "Max," she heard herself scream in an eerie, high-pitched voice that wasn't her own. *"Max took my Jeep last night!"* she wailed, her heart banging in her chest. She couldn't breathe. She couldn't move. The room was suddenly spinning and hands reached out around her. "Max," she repeated, jerking her head up and looking the officer straight in the eye. "Max Cantor. He—he's *dead*?"

She watched in horror and disbelief as the two officers hung their heads.

"Oh, my God!" she heard April shout somewhere among the gasps and sobs in the room.

Lauren struggled for breath. She felt her body falling through space and felt someone calling for her from far away. Max couldn't be dead. She was with him just last night. He'd been so alive. He'd been so close. She loved him so much. "Maaaaaaax!" she heard someone wailing over and over. Where was it coming from? Arms reached out for her, and her body seemed to float down the hall toward the infirmary. "Maaaaaaaax!" the wailing started again.

It wasn't until she was lying down on the white sheet that she realized the wailing was coming from her.

"What's wrong?" Melissa yelled over the fray in the hallway. She ripped off her pack and flung it into the message room, sweat still trickling off her back from a five-mile ride. A moment before, she'd seen several staffers carrying Lauren from the conference room, followed briefly by two uniformed officers, who then turned and headed back in. *"What's wrong with Lauren?"* she yelled as the infirmary door slammed in her face.

"It's Max," April's secretary, Nancy, blurted as the tears began to stream down her cheeks. She struggled to regain her voice. "The sheriff's department found Lauren's Jeep at the bottom of Pirate Cove. Max was driving it. They're pretty sure he's dead."

"No," Melissa blurted back, her mind racing, unable to take it in.

"Listen." Nancy was sobbing, punching her intercom button. "We can hear everything that's said—in the conference room. The cops are in there with April."

"There were two sets of tire tracks at the scene of the accident," one of the officers was telling April. "It looks like Mr. Cantor went to the Pirate Cove location voluntarily. Maybe he was meeting someone he knew. Someone he thought he could trust. . . ."

Melissa sat up straight. Evan had left the beach house about a half hour before Max dropped off Lauren. Could he have been the familiar face Max followed into the night? *Evan was practically the only person in L.A. who knew you could drive into Pirate Cove,* she thought with growing horror.

"Dammit, I wish I knew what was happening," Melissa heard April shriek over the intercom.

"In any case," the officer went on matter-of-factly, "the tire-track evidence shows that the Jeep was forced off the cliff by another vehicle."

The sound of April's muffled weeping crackled through the intercom.

Melissa chewed her thumbnail, tears pouring down her face. It couldn't be true. Evan might be a little wild and confused, but he wouldn't deliberately hurt anyone. *Would he?*

The voice of the officer rose again. "What we need, Ms. Webster, is any information you may have about who Mr. Cantor associated with. Perhaps someone who was familiar with this secluded spot—this—Pirate Cove?"

Melissa covered her mouth with her hands and doubled over at the waist. A wave of nausea swept over her. It was true. Everything pointed to Evan. Evan knew Max was at the mansion. Evan knew he had the incriminating tape; he'd even told him where to find it. Evan knew about Pirate Cove. Why was this happening? She wanted to trust him. She'd put her heart in his hands. She *needed* to trust him.

Nancy grabbed her hand. "Melissa? What? Do you know something?"

For a split second Melissa gazed into Nancy's wet, startled eyes. Then she turned away. "No," she lied, standing up and rushing out of the room. "I don't know anything at all."

A moment later she had grabbed her messenger bike and was pumping full blast into the Television City parking lot. The roads were damp from last night's violent storm. Steam rose from the asphalt as the hot morning sun burned down. Ducking into the Santa Monica Boulevard traffic, Melissa stood on the pedals and raced as hard as she could, weaving through traffic and speeding through yellow lights. Her muscles ached. Her lungs begged for air. All she wanted was to lose herself in the effort—and block out all of her thoughts.

Continuing to pump full speed through the morning traffic, Melissa glanced over her shoulder before she turned right. A shiny red convertible was following her closely.

Honk.

Melissa swerved to the right and impatiently waved the car to pass her.

Honk, honk.

Distraught, her eyes raw from crying, she looked over to the left at the car. Then she stopped pedaling and glided behind the car in front of her. She looked again and saw a shock of light blond hair whipping in the wind.

Evan?

Melissa pedaled forward, shaking her head, tears streaming down her face. She decided this time she *was* hallucinating. How would Evan be able to track her down in the middle of the Santa Monica traffic?

Honk, honk!

Melissa's grip tightened on her handlebars. *Unless he'd been following her.*

"I've got to talk to you!" she heard a guy shouting above the chaotic noise of the traffic. His red car glinted in the sunlight. Several cars honked as he slowed down. "Toss the bike in the car. Come with me."

She looked back. It was Evan. Clutching the wheel of his car with one hand, he was waving the other wildly in the air.

Melissa bit her lip and shook her head wordlessly, nearly crashing into a van that had dodged in front of her in the lane. Every logical bone in her body told her to run. But she couldn't help her feelings. She was desperate to talk to him.

I have to trust him, Melissa thought, her mind reeling. *I can't live my life not being able to trust.*

"Please, Melissa," Evan pleaded, shouting. "If you won't stop—just meet me at Pirate Cove. Meet me there as soon as you can. I'll wait for you."

There was a clutch at Melissa's throat. Pirate Cove? Meet him at Pirate Cove? At Max's grave? Now? What was he saying? She turned and looked at him, suddenly terrified. Max had followed him there last night. And now Max was dead!

"Melissssssaaaaaaaaa," she heard his final call over the rising roar of screeching brakes and honking luxury cars. She pedaled faster, this time certain that she would never look back. She wanted to trust Evan. But trusting him was too hard. The facts were too clear. The risk was too great. She was certain now that she had to lose Evan. Her life depended on it. Weaving through traffic, she finally ducked into an alley and disappeared from his sight.

She stopped, exhausted and soaking with sweat, near a sidewalk pay phone a mile away. Then she leaned against it, sobbing. Trust. She'd trusted her father before he'd turned to alcohol and ruined her life. She'd trusted Brooks before he stood her up at the altar. The only person she'd ever been able to depend on was herself. It was the only way.

Punching in the studio phone number, she was quickly connected to the officers still meeting with April in her office. Her voice seemed far off, and she could barely see through her tears.

"Yes," she managed to speak, her voice cracking with emotion. "This is Melissa McDormand. I have information that may help you with the Max Cantor investigation." She held her breath for a moment, letting it out slowly as she spoke. "Evan Sikes—Evan Sikes spends a lot of time at Pirate Cove. Yes. Yes, he's Oliver Sikes's son. And he knows how to get there by car. I—I just saw him a moment ago. He wanted to meet me there too. You see, he—he's there right now. And—and I thought you'd probably want to pick him up."

Before the officers could reply, Melissa hung up. Her body sagged against the phone, and her bike fell over with a loud crash. Then she collapsed, sobbing, onto the pavement—alone, confused, and suddenly terribly ashamed.

Twenty-four

"Good morning, I'm Lisa Quinn with KWAT Action News," the television droned in Winnie's ears. "There was bad news yesterday for the staff of television's popular April Webster Show. One of the program's researchers is presumed dead this morning—the result of a tragic car accident just north of Santa Monica. Details after this message."

Winnie huddled in the flickering blue light of the screen, staring numbly at the newscast. The living room of the beach house, with its drawn drapes and piles of dirty dishes, was as barren and dark as the inside of her heart.

"I'm going to sit out on the beach," Melissa

murmured as she padded behind her, scarcely look-ing at the screen, "as soon as I find the thongs Liza stole from me. She's comatose over her split with Travis. Refuses to get out of bed."

Winnie blew a large purple bubble, then popped it, ignoring her. She didn't care about Melissa and she definitely didn't care about Liza. Anger swelled inside her, dark and out of control. It had been that way all night, since her narrow escape from Walker Ingham's slimy clutches. Fury would sweep over her, subside, then take over again until she thought she would suffocate. Instinctively, she rubbed the sides of her arms. Her skin crawled with the mem-ory of Walker's touch. Her feet ached from the wet run down two miles of coastal highway. Her eyes burned and tears began to spill down her face. Only yesterday she'd been filled with hope. At last she thought she'd found someone who seemed to really care. Someone she thought could give her life direc-tion and meaning.

She hugged her stomach and leaned forward, suddenly nauseated. Walker hadn't cared at all. Nei-ther had Randall. All Walker wanted was young, willing girls. And Randall was his willing agent.

"Bye." She heard Lauren's whispery voice be-hind her. "I have to go to work. I can't just stay here and think about Max."

Winnie turned around slowly and stared at Lau-ren's pale, swollen face. Her wispy hair hung flat, and her violet eyes were strangely lifeless and red-rimmed. Lauren stared blankly at the soap commercial dancing across the television screen. Then she lifted a tissue to her tear-streaked face and sobbed quietly into it, bent over at the waist.

"Walker Ingham's coming back to the studio today—the animal," Lauren finally said, her voice flat and hollow. "April's still going ahead with the second show, but now Oliver Sikes wants to show up too." Her words suddenly caught with emotion, and she balled up her fists in anger. Overcome, she sagged against the back of the couch, fell to her knees, and began to sob.

Winnie stared, half-angry, half-stunned at Lauren's display. Then she turned her attention back to the television.

"In a bizzare twist an anonymous tip has led to the arrest of Evan Sikes—the son of Hollywood movie mogul Oliver Sikes," the newscaster chirped. Pictures of Evan flashed onto the screen, followed by tape of Max's weeping parents. Winnie and Lauren watched silently. "Mr. Cantor had recently been involved in developing two episodes of *The April Webster Show* and an upcoming book with Sikes's close friend—internationally known humanitarian, Walker Ingham."

"Oliver wants to talk about Evan on the show," Lauren interrupted. She let out a short, bitter laugh. "Says he wants to talk about how *troubled* his son is. The show," Lauren spat, "is now Walker and Oliver talking about 'our troubled youth.'"

Winnie wanted to throw up. Oliver Sikes probably had a sudden urge to look as good as possible
this week. For all she knew, Oliver had his own teenage harem too. No wonder Evan was so screwed up.
The only people he had to look up to were Oliver
and Walker.

"According to county sheriff's detectives," the
newscaster went on, "Mr. Cantor was seen last night
trespassing on the grounds of the huge oceanfront
Sikes estate north of Santa Monica. Authorities
aren't revealing why young Sikes was taken into custody. But friends and acquaintances have told KWAT
Action News that Evan Sikes—known widely for his
thrill-seeking lifestyle and hot temper—may have
sought revenge on Mr. Cantor's trespassing. Drugs
are suspected."

"Can you believe it?" Lauren muttered. "Oliver
Sikes telling a national television audience how terrible we feel when a child *slips through our fingers.*
These clowns will do anything to twist this situation
to their advantage."

Winnie rolled her eyes and shot Lauren a harsh
look.

*Oh, really, Lauren? Wow, you know so much, Ms.
Big Shot talk-show journalist. You wouldn't think of
asking me what I know, would you? Even though you
know for a fact I was with Walker Ingham last night.
That I've spent every day for the last two weeks at the
Institute. You probably think I'm just a brainwashed,
airhead groupie who wouldn't have a clue, don't you?*

When Winnie didn't respond, a drained look swept over Lauren's face. She yanked out another tissue and pressed it to her eyes. "I—I just can't believe that—Max—is—gone. It's not real. I'm not—ready to—accept it."

Without another word Lauren turned and walked out the front door. A few moments later Melissa walked back in and stared quietly as the newscast displayed footage of Evan emerging from a police car, handcuffed and grim. Before Winnie could say anything, Melissa had quickly left through the sliding glass door to the deck.

"We're going to switch to Gus Lanahan live in Santa Monica, who's talking with April Webster about today's tragedy."

Winnie clenched her teeth as April's imposing face flashed on the screen. Touching the corner of her eye, April shook her head and looked down. "I guess you could say that all of us on the show's staff are in shock right now, Gus," April said in a cracked voice. "Max's death was senseless. He was a brilliant, tough, incredibly talented researcher—responsible for much of the freshness and vitality our show strives for."

"Lovin' that publicity, aren't you, April?" Winnie sneered at the screen. "Hey, yeah—why *don't* you and Lauren go ahead and use Max's death to boost ratings? Walker and Oliver are going to use it to boost their fund-raiser. You're no different."

"In Max's memory," April continued, this time looking straight into the camera, "we're devoting our show today to the troubled youth of America. A young man just Max's age was taken into custody this morning in connection with this death. His father has agreed to talk with us, along with philanthropist and spiritual leader Walker Ingham. What led to this horrible tragedy? Who's responsible?"

"Give me a break," Winnie shouted, throwing a sandal at the TV.

"What kind of a reaction are you getting so far?" the news reporter intervened.

April's mouth fell open in feigned surprise. "It's been incredible, of course. People feel emotionally needy at times like this. And I think Walker Ingham will provide the kind of relief valve we desperately need. He'll be answering questions from our studio audience."

"Oh—yeah—right," Winnie ranted, springing to her feet and pacing the room. She switched off the TV with a violent jerk. "Let's have Walker give us advice. He's probably ripping off millions from an unsuspecting public. And he's probably conned hundreds of teenaged girls. But let's listen to his wise words."

Somebody has to do something!

Winnie stopped in her tracks. Then she drew open the drapes and stared out at the pounding surf. A swift wind was blowing away the storm clouds, and sunshine was sweeping across the sand. A tiny voice in the back of her head spoke. She recognized it, then let out a loud, bitter laugh.

You have incredible power within you. You are the only one responsible for your happiness. All you need are the tools to unlock it.

Randall, Winnie thought, suddenly longing for revenge. She felt a swell of determination flood through her. Then she set her jaw and thought long and hard. Randall had spoken these words on her first visit to the Ingham Institute. Wouldn't it be sweet to put his hypocritical words into action—to destroy his leader?

She *was* responsible for herself. She *did* have power. And Walker had *definitely* given her the tools. She wasn't brainwashed. She wasn't lovesick, grieving, or helpless. She was ready to act.

Winnie rushed into her room, pulled on a pair of pants and shoes, then darted out the front door, grabbing Melissa's messenger bike. With a quick shove she was pumping up the hill to the coastal highway, heading to the *April Webster* studio in the heart of Santa Monica.

She pumped hard, but her breath came easily and her heart was full. Branches and clumps of wet grass were strewn over the storm-ravaged road. Cars whipped by, splashing her. But Winnie hunched determinedly over the handlebars and sped ahead, the breeze whipping in her ears and the sun glaring in her eyes. For the first time that summer she knew exactly what she wanted to do. What she had to do. She would somehow get into April's studio audience. And there, before millions of believers, she would tell the world who Walker Ingham and his goons really were.

A half hour later Winnie was maneuvering through downtown traffic, her eyes peeled for the entrance to Santa Monica Television City. She pushed her hot-pink sunglasses up on her nose. The blazing sun beat down on her head. Her sweaty T-shirt stuck to her back. Fear gripped her. She suddenly wished that nothing had happened. That she'd never come to L.A. That she'd never gone to the Institute. That she was the same old impulsive, self-destructive, nonstop Winnie who was majoring in life screwups at the U of S.

At least they were the screwups I was starting to deal with, Winnie thought, signaling right when she saw the huge *April Webster Show* billboard. A small sign on the wall of the Television City lot read Studio Audience Tickets. She put her right foot down on the pavement and bumped to a stop. Then she stopped and gazed at the long line winding out of the walled lot and extending to the corner. April hadn't been exaggerating. It was clear to Winnie that she had only a slim chance of getting into the show and challenging Walker on the air. But she was sure now that she had to try.

Walking her bike to the end of the line, Winnie stared at the women in broad-brimmed hats and the grim-faced men who'd obviously been waiting for hours. Lawn chairs dotted the sidewalk. A man carrying a cooler had cans of pop for sale. But after only a few moments, several uniformed guards proceeded down the line, and Winnie could see the crowd breaking up.

"Sorry. No more tickets for *The April Webster Show*," one of the guards was calling out. "Sold out. Sorry."

Winnie's heart sank. But as the crowd dispersed and the guards began to wander back inside the lot, she spotted an opening in the gate. Her breath coming fast, Winnie made her move. She pushed the bike forward, her head down, praying she'd be taken for a regular on the lot. By the time she had the nerve to look back, the guards were nowhere in sight. And up ahead she noticed a large loading dock at the rear of the studio.

She leaned her bike against the side of the dock and quickly climbed up. No one was working in the loading area, but she could hear a man shouting orders in the distance. Quick as lightning Winnie moved inside, ducking behind some office furniture. Keeping her head down, she scurried past two forklifts and hid briefly behind a potted office plant as a guy chugging a can of cola walked by.

Once inside the cavernous building, Winnie had no idea where she was. The air smelled of dust and diesel fumes. Her legs aching and her heart pounding, she jogged through a huge warehouse filled with sets, cardboard boxes, and lighting equipment. She plastered her back to a cement wall as a guy with a huge sound boom walked by. But as she pulled away, she realized that she was leaning against a small door. She tried the knob. It opened.

"What is this?" Winnie whispered, climbing a musty staircase. Light shone from above. At the top her feet hit a gridded metal platform, which was encased by the concrete staircase shaft. Aside from turning back, the only way out was a steel ladder clamped to the side of the wall. She gripped the railing and climbed up to another steel platform that hovered over a large metal grid, woven with power cords, lighting equipment, and ladders. Then she looked out over a steel safety bar and gasped with surprise.

Below, Winnie could hear the sound of a milling crowd. Lowering herself under the safety bar, she was able to crawl out on a narrow, gridded walkway. Below, studio lights flooded hundreds of seats, where an audience was settling. A brightly lit stage faced them, and camera operators on hydraulic booms were positioned everywhere.

It was *The April Webster Show!*

Winnie froze, praying she wouldn't be seen. Electrical cords hung in every direction. It was dark. And she had no idea whether the grid of metal bars was strong enough to hold her body weight.

"Okay, folks, taping begins in ten seconds," a technician in jeans was explaining to the audience below. "Please hold the applause until after April's done her intro."

Winnie stared, half in fascination, half in terror at

the scene below. She knew she had to do something. But what could she do from her precarious spot on the ceiling?

"Kids in trouble." April Webster's voice suddenly broke into her thoughts. Winnie looked below at April, standing before the audience in a stunning crimson pantsuit. "They're everywhere. They're hurting. And we feel helpless to do anything. Where have we gone wrong? What can we do? We'll be talking today with one famous father who'll be sharing his own personal family tragedy with us. And internationally known humanitarian and philosopher Walker Ingham will also be joining us. . . ."

The sound of Walker's name turned Winnie's indecision to rage and determination. Sucking in her breath, she scanned the lighting grid for a way down. She stared into the darkness, her eyes suddenly fixed on what looked like a figure in the shadows. There was a movement, and the figure shifted, turning toward her. A dark head emerged only about ten feet away, half lit by the stage lights. A pale face. Unshaven. Trembling.

Winnie's lips parted. The face. She knew the face. His eyes were pleading with her. His hand lifted, trembling, as if to beg her to stay quiet. She stared at the dark eyes behind the glasses. And then, in terror, she gripped the side of the grid with her fist. Was it a ghost? Was she dreaming?

Or was it really Max Cantor?

Twenty-five

auren had been hiding in the dark control booth for the last half hour, staring through the soundproof glass into the studio. Her hands were trembling. Her heart was breaking.

I thought I'd lost you, she kept hearing Max's voice call out over the beach after their narrow escape from the Sikes mansion. *I thought I'd lost you.*

She made two fists and buried her face in them, tears pouring down. Then she shook her head. Max was dead. It was true. And they'd both lost each other.

Lauren sat up, trying to distract herself from the pain. Excited audience members were filing down the aisles and searching for seats. Stagehands scrambled. Sound technicians made adjustments. The enthusiasm over April's "troubled teens" show starring Walker and Oliver Sikes was building. And taping was scheduled to begin shortly.

"We'll tape this baby in about ten minutes," the director told her, turning around and giving her a sympathetic look. "You can stick around if you want, Lauren."

"Thanks," Lauren whispered, a fresh flood of tears building behind her eyes. She twisted the button on her blouse, nearly popping it off. It was impossible to go downstairs. She knew that if she ran into Walker Ingham and Oliver Sikes, she'd probably start punching. Or screaming. Or crying.

That morning she'd gone to work, but as soon as she passed Max's old office in research, the grief and the guilt swept over her. Her hands shook terribly, and she could barely see through her swollen eyes. It had been only twenty-four hours since she'd heard about Max's death. She'd collapsed at her desk. And later Elaine had ordered her home.

Instead she'd wandered through the studio in a trance, trying to think about what had happened. The grief and shock must have done strange things to her memory. Nothing made sense anymore. There was the kiss in the Jeep. The promise that he would go to the lab to repair the wet tape. So how did he end up at Pirate Cove? How could he have hooked up with Evan? And why in the world would Evan want to harm him?

"Okay, three-two-one, go ahead, April," the director was murmuring in his headset.

Lauren raked back her hair, listening to April's warm and fuzzy introduction to Walker and Oliver Sikes. A hundred dials and switches glowed in the dim room. On the other side of the window the technicians hovered over their cameras and equipment as if this were just another show. Just another day of digging into the truth about things with April.

Suddenly filled with disgust and impatience, Lauren sprang from her seat, rushed down the staircase from the control booth, and headed for the wings of the studio set. She couldn't just stand by. Max was dead, couldn't they understand that? They didn't have enough time together! She needed him!

"Please welcome Walker Ingham and Oliver Sikes!" April's voice was thundering over her microphone when Lauren reached the edge of the set. Stepping back into the shadows, Lauren leaned against a backstage ladder and watched, sickened, as the two men walked onstage to the crash of applause.

"Don't look too happy, Oliver and Walker," Lauren whispered to herself. "Remember, you're onstage. There's been a death."

As if obeying Lauren's thoughts, Oliver and Walker clipped their waves short and issued only somber smiles before sitting down at the small round table with April. A camera operator on a boom moved in for a close-up.

"First of all," April began, knitting her eyebrows with concern, "we need to remind our studio audience that Oliver Sikes is here in a state of what must be impossible anguish. His son, Evan, was taken into custody last night in connection with the death of a talented staff member here on *The April Webster Show.*"

April paused, swallowed, and made an obvious effort to control her emotion.

"But," April began again, "Mr. Sikes is willing to share the story of his son, Evan, in the hopes that he might help other desperate parents. He's here with his close friend and partner, Walker Ingham, who's going to help us sort through the maze of difficulties our young people face today."

Oliver nodded, biting his lip with drama. Lauren could see from the nearby monitor that his eyes were wet.

"What we've heard, Oliver," April went on, folding her hands in front of her on the table, "is that your son is now in the custody of the Los Angeles County Sheriff's Department?"

Oliver nodded sadly. Wearing jeans and a denim shirt, it was clear he'd made an effort to look sincere and youthful for the national television audience. "Evan," he said steadily, as Walker looked on, "suffers from many things that happened in his early childhood, when I was deeply involved in the entertainment industry."

Lauren thought she was going to be sick. How could April possibly go ahead with this show? She'd told her only yesterday that Walker and Oliver were almost certainly frauds. She and Max had seen the tape that proved it. And now Max was mysteriously dead. The tape was conveniently gone. Why couldn't April see the truth?

Walker leaned forward, looking intense. "You see, April, before Oliver joined our Ingham Institute, he'd spent little time with his son. Oliver felt that what Evan needed were outward signs of success. A big house. A big bank account." As cameras zoomed in for a close-up, Walker's face became luminous, his eyes penetrating. "Now Oliver has spurned that existence for a new and richer one. He spends much of his time on international relief efforts. And fortunately he can spend precious time with his son—though we now know it may be too late."

"Yeah, right," Lauren muttered, a bitter taste in her mouth. "The only thing between you two clowns and the state penitentiary is that videotape."

She buried her face in her hands. It was impossible to think of Max gone. She was suddenly flooded with thoughts of him. Their long walks on the beach. The unexpected intensity of his kiss in the Sikes's wine cellar. They'd connected so quickly, so completely. His death wasn't real. *Couldn't* be real.

"*Aaaahhhhhhh!*" There was a shout from a member of the studio audience, interrupting April's interview. April swung around. More shouts and gasps from the audience. Lauren's gaze flew up to the monitor. The picture suddenly switched from April's stunned face to a section of the studio audience, where people were scattering in confusion. Someone had apparently fallen down from the lighting grid above the seats.

"I want to talk to Walker Ingham!" a voice was crying out in the midst of the commotion.

Lauren leaped to her feet, squinting at the screen. In the grainy black-and-white picture she could see several people scurrying away from a slender girl, who appeared to be helping another person down from the grid. Then the girl turned toward the cameras, her eyes blazing, her hands planted on her hips in anger.

Lauren gasped.

It was Winnie!

"Cut to commercial, April," Elaine was barking at April through her headset at the edge of the stage. *"Cut!"*

April shook her head, her eyes glinting and full of delight. She pointed into the audience and rolled her fists, motioning for the cameras to stay on the subject.

"Winnie!" Lauren shouted, rushing toward the stage, guarded by two of the show's security technicians. "Winnie," she yelled again, before she felt her elbows being grabbed and pulled back. "Let me go," she screamed.

"Hold it right there, young lady," the guard was shouting in her ear.

Lauren wrenched away and rushed onto the stage. The entire audience was on its feet, and several people were climbing over seats toward the back exit, apparently fearing a riot.

"Winnie!" Lauren screamed into the audience.

For a split second Winnie looked up at Lauren. Her face was hard. Her eyes flashed with anger. Then Winnie rushed up to the set and stood boldly in front of Walker, the camera still running. Lauren watched in amazement as Walker recognized her. Slowly, his face paled. His whole body seemed to shrink in Winnie's powerful presence. Lauren watched as Walker rose slowly from his seat and staggered back, away from Winnie. Then a panicked look consumed his face. He turned and tried to run off the set, directly toward Lauren.

"Stop!" she heard herself shout, sticking her arm out to block his path. Behind him she could see the cameras following eagerly, and April watching with pure delight on her face.

Winnie rushed up and twirled Walker around with her strong, wiry arms.

"What's the matter?" Winnie demanded. "Recognize me? Afraid of what I'll say on national television?" She ripped the microphone from his shirt and held it up to her mouth. "You live with the Sikeses in their fabulous mansion, don't you, Walker? And do you think you're an inspiration to Evan, Walker?

Do you think you're a great example for this poor, troubled boy?"

Walker looked terrified. Winnie shoved the mike in his face and he drew back, his eyes scrambling around the room. His face was covered with sweat and his lips were trembling. "I—I don't know what you're . . ." he stammered.

"Maybe he felt a little funny about the romance-for-spiritual-guidance gig you had up there in your Sikes mansion suite," Winnie taunted, her eyes blazing with hatred. "Maybe he got a little tired of hiding the truth from the impressionable teenage girls your Institute would send up to your luxurious suite at the mansion, *Mr. Spiritual*."

There was a gasp from the audience.

Winnie turned and looked bravely at the audience, who were now riveted in place, some sitting, some standing, some halfway up the aisles. "My name is Winnie Gottlieb, and I've been interning at Walker Ingham's so-called Institute for several weeks now. The night before last I was ushered up to his room for some close, spiritual advice. Only he didn't want to give any advice, he just wanted to seduce another teenager!"

April lumbered forward across the stage, a mike in her extended hand. "We'll give you a chance to answer, Walker. Is this true?"

Walker blanched. "I—uh—I . . ."

Before Walker could answer, there were more gasps of alarm from the audience. Another person was dropping down from the grid onto an empty seat. Lauren shaded her eyes from the intense camera lights. All she could see was a silhouette. A glint of glasses on his face . . . She reached her hands up to her face to muffle her scream of joy.

"Max!"

She watched, frozen, as Max rushed up to the stage. Their eyes met as he walked toward her, his expression full of love. He was still wearing the clothes he wore during their narrow ocean escape from the Sikes mansion. A dark, two-day stubble covered his face. His bloodshot eyes were wet and tired. But he was alive, Lauren thought joyfully. Alive.

A smile lit his haggard face, and all at once his arms, real and solid, were wrapped around her. "Lauren," he said in a cracked whisper. "Lauren, I'm sorry."

"Max," Lauren sobbed, the weight and the sorrow and pain lifting away. "I thought you were . . . I thought I'd . . ." Lauren stammered, before Max pulled away from her and smiled, hardly able to contain his joy. A second later he turned and faced the rolling cameras.

"Max Cantor," April was breathing into her microphone, looking at him in wonder. "You're alive."

Max pulled away from her and slid the precious videotape out of his windbreaker pocket. He held it up and rushed across the set toward April. "This is the proof we were looking for, April. Put it on the air now. It shows in detail how Walker Ingham's relief efforts are fraudulent. They're only carefully directed videos—directed and produced by Oliver Sikes."

April's eyes widened. She grabbed the tape and held it up. "Run this tape, Dan," she shouted to a nearby technician.

Within minutes the tape was rolling on national television. Tears rushed down Lauren's face. There it was. All of it. The makeup artists on the faked third-world street. Walker slapping a child's face. By the time the tape had run, the audience was booing Walker and Sikes, who were being held by studio security guards just off the set.

By this time April had moved toward Max and Lauren on the set. As she watched the tape, she moved between them and linked her arms with theirs. When the tape was over, Lauren could see the tears in April's eyes, and the red light on the camera pointed directly at the three of them.

"How did you get the tape?" April said, her voice thick with emotion. "What happened to you, Max?" She looked up into the camera. "As everyone here in L.A. knows, my fine researcher—Max Cantor—was presumed dead after his car plunged into the Pacific the night before last."

"Let me go!" Oliver was shouting behind them as the guards tightened their grip. Swiftly the light on the offstage camera lit up. April's show was documenting everything.

"Oliver Sikes's son, Evan, gave us the key to his dad's mansion," Max explained. "He told us to look in the editing room. So we found the tape, but barely escaped. Sikes and Walker had security goons on our tail with loaded firearms."

There was a rumble from the studio audience.

"After I dropped off my friend Lauren at home," Max went on, glancing at Lauren, "I took off for a friend's video lab. The tape had gotten wet and needed reprocessing. But just as I was pulling out of the Crescent Colony, a guy in a car waved me down." Max glared over his shoulder at Walker in the wings. "It was a guy named Randall Stuart, one of Walker Ingham's operators. Randall told me to meet him at a place called Pirate Cove—out on the cliffs just south of Malibu. He said that Oliver Sikes was extorting funds from the Institute, and that he wanted me to know the whole story."

Lauren gasped.

April turned to Max and held her mike close to his lips. "Tell us what happened, Max."

Max shrugged. "I knew I was taking a chance. His story was a little bit strange, since I'd already seen the tape that clearly showed Walker was a fraud."

"But you went," April breathed, gazing out at the studio audience with disbelief.

"Parking at Pirate Cove is tricky," Max went on. "By the time I realized I was at the end of the remote dirt road, the Jeep I was driving was perched right at the edge of a cliff. It made me nervous waiting there for Randall, so I got out. Then I stuffed my jacket and hat to make it look as if I were waiting behind the wheel."

"Nooooooooooo!" Walker's wail echoed across the studio.

Max glared back at him. "Oh, yes. And then I saw *you*, Walker Ingham, coming down that narrow road in your pickup. You were coming pretty fast, weren't you? You aimed your bumper right at the tail of that Jeep and shoved it right over the cliff, didn't you?"

"Stop it!" Walker yelled over the commotion in the studio audience. "You're lying! Lying! Lying!"

"I have all the proof the police will ever need," Max said, victory shining in his eyes.

Suddenly Lauren was engulfed in Max's embrace. April wrapped both of them in her two gigantic arms, whispering loudly. "Oh, my God, I'm glad you're safe. Max, you did it. You really did it. Nothing like this has ever happened on any talk show. Any news show. Thank you. Thank you." She turned her wet face to the camera. "We'll be right back after this message," she whispered.

"Yeeeeeaaaaahhhhhhh," a huge roar rose from the audience.

"Yes!" April shouted, thrusting her fist into the air and dancing across the stage.

"Oh, Max!" Lauren breathed, wrapping her arms around his body and pulling him close.

Twenty-six

"Beautiful night," Evan was saying, taking Melissa's hand as they walked across the soft sand to the water. The waves swelled, broke, and rolled in, shining white in the darkness. On the horizon Mel could still see a faint blush of light.

"Yeah. Stars out."

"Can't see the stars in jail," Evan said with a half smile. "Know that?"

"Never really thought about it," Melissa answered, biting her lip. Behind them yellow light poured from the beach house windows. A warm breeze blew down from the grassy hills above Malibu. She leaned against Evan's solid shoulder, then slipped her arm around his waist.

"I'm sorry, Evan," Melissa said, trying not to cry. "I'm sorry I doubted you. And I can't quite believe you're here, still talking to me."

Evan looked down at her, then drew her tightly to his side. His face seemed to pale beneath the weight of his sadness. They stopped when they reached the wet sand. "What have I ever done to make you want to trust me?"

Melissa nodded. Evan hadn't exactly been a model of trustworthiness. He'd lied about who he was. He'd challenged her to dive into the rocky waters at Pirate Cove, then parachute into the clear blue sky over Santa Monica. Still, she knew that if she'd listened to her heart, she never would have turned him in to the police.

"People don't trust me," Evan said over the roar of an incoming wave. He looked down at her, and his eyes had that intense, longing look that always made Melissa's heart beat faster. "They never have. Maybe that's the way I've wanted it. It's kept me from getting close. It's kept me from being hurt."

"You did the right thing—giving Max and Lauren that tape," Melissa reminded him. "Maybe you're on a new track."

"Whew," Evan whistled, shaking his head. His white-blond hair blew in the wind. "I wish I felt like celebrating. But my dad's life is over. The house is empty. There isn't even anything left for me to fight."

"You're free," Melissa tried to sound hopeful. "You can go home and live in peace."

Evan looked down at his bare feet; then he turned and drew her close, brushing a stray lock of hair off her forehead. "I can't go home now. There's nothing there for me."

"Where's your mother, Evan?" Melissa asked, leaning into his grasp, feeling secure and dizzy all at the same time.

Evan's expression turned grim. He turned away a little and pulled her into a slow walk south, down the beach. "Oliver was married to a woman named Greta when I was adopted. One of his little blond starlets, you know. She didn't last. I don't even remember her. All I remember is a series of young girlfriends and old nannies. To them I was either a nuisance or a job."

"And Oliver . . ."

"Oliver was the only constant in my life," Evan said slowly, stopping and pressing one hand over his eyes. Melissa could feel his body shudder with quiet tears. "He was a jerk, but at least he was something I could call my own. Mr. Big Shot Producer. My dad. Maybe that's why it took so long for me to expose him. He's all I have."

Melissa looked over at Evan. "If Oliver was such a hotshot, why was he scamming with Walker?"

Evan's brown eyes searched the moonlit water. "His films got bigger and bigger. And then they started flopping. The studios saw big losses. Suddenly Dad wasn't so hot, but he'd bought the big house and had a lot of girlfriends with very expensive tastes. He needed money."

Melissa nodded. "So Walker was a face-saving move."

"Sure," Evan replied, gritting his teeth and sitting down on the sand. Evan gave her a serious look and pulled her down next to him. His bare feet dug into the sand. He picked up a pebble and threw it far out into the sparkling water. "He met Walker at a party in Beverly Hills. Back then Walker was a charismatic nobody who had a small-time counseling service in Santa Monica. They hit it off, and then Walker came up with the idea for the fake documentaries. They devised the Institute. The fund-raising scams. Everything."

"So your dad got to make the documentaries," Melissa thought out loud, "and all Hollywood thought he'd turned into a humanitarian."

Evan tossed a handful of sand. "Yep. Dad turned into Mr. Good Guy. Except he and Walker kept every penny of the money."

"How could he live with himself?" Melissa wondered.

"He figured he was doing his Hollywood friends a favor," Evan explained, slipping his arm around Melissa's waist. "He was giving them another way to feel good. He knew success made them feel a little guilty. Now they had a way out."

"Amazing."

"I didn't know how the scam worked until last summer, when I started working on the Institute's film crew." Evan shook his head and buried his face in his hands. "It made me sick. I'd believed in my father, and suddenly I realized everything was a lie. I didn't know what to do, except drink and throw myself out of airplanes a lot. Nothing made any sense."

Melissa felt a clutch at her heart. "I know. I felt that way too—once." Evan gave her a desperate, questioning look, and Melissa knew she had to explain. "It was my wedding day . . . Brooks . . . he didn't come. Everyone was waiting."

Evan stopped and looked at her for a long moment. Then he pulled her to his chest. His arms encircled her and his cheek pressed hard against hers. "I'm so sorry."

"Everything was gone," Melissa sobbed softly. "I wanted to push all the life away. Friends. School. All I wanted was to win on the track. I stuck needles into my arms. Steroids. I didn't care. I just wanted to . . ."

Evan caught her lips with his own and kissed her. It was a long, soft, open kiss that seemed to move to the music of the waves and the wind. He drew away gently. "I know, Melissa. I know. It's like everything you thought was real—was really only an illusion. All of it false."

"*I'm* not an illusion," Melissa whispered, holding him tightly. "We'll work it out together."

Twenty-seven

as anybody heard *anything*?" a girl in a low-cut leotard said in a loud voice. "We've been waiting on this movie lot for *two solid hours*."

Liza stirred from her spot on an overturned wooden box near the set of a suburban street. She'd painted her nails a bright shade of hot orange and was now blowing them carefully. Sweat trickled down her back, and her beehive was starting to shrink in the midday sun.

But her heart was soaring.

Just that morning she'd received a call from Geoff Hansen's casting director, who had loved Liza's audition. Would she report to the Megastar

Pictures lot at noon sharp? Mr. Hansen needed her for a key role in a picture he was directing.

Today was the first day of her life as a Hollywood actress.

Look out, Mr. Director. I'm going to blow you away, Liza thought, wielding her nail brush, a huge smile plastered on her face. *I'm gonna make your career, Mr. Director.*

"I don't even know what this flick is about," a guy with curly blond hair mumbled from his spot on a folding chair a few feet away. Clamping on a headset, he made a face and crossed his arms over his bronzed chest.

"Give me a break," a girl wearing bluish makeup grumbled, walking toward Liza and flopping down next to her. "Classic."

Liza frowned. "Classic?"

Taking a tissue out of the pocket of her jeans, the girl began to wipe the blue tint off her lips. "Do you realize what we're doing? I've just done my bit in the studio. This film is called *She Walks with Dead Dogs.* Talk about low-budget crap."

Liza cleared her throat delicately. "Did you say, She Walks with Dead Dogs?"

"Yeah." The girl shrugged, checking out Liza's hair. "Maybe you'll get to be one of the dogs."

Liza glared at her. "Thanks, doll. I'll keep you in mind when I hit it big in this town."

"Okay, everybody." A young guy wearing jeans and a tank top had walked around from the other side of the trailer. He was shouting through a megaphone, looking down at a piece of paper.

"He's the assistant director," the girl whispered, crossing her legs and lighting a cigarette. "What a jerk."

Liza glared at her again. "You'll die if you smoke those, you know."

"I want all of you over on the set in five," the assistant shouted. "We need extras for a background shot. "And—uh—Liza Ruff. Will you report to me? I need to give you part of the script to take a look at."

Liza followed the guy into a hangarlike building, hung with massive lighting equipment, cluttered with props, and scurrying with extras. Finally they reached a dimly lit set inside the building, built to look like the inside of a decrepit barn. The assistant told Liza to sit on a plastic chair, and then he disappeared.

Another hour passed, and Liza began to wonder if they'd completely forgotten her. Then, just as she was about to look for someone, Travis and the other extras entered and were put in position around a beat-up fence in the middle of the set.

For a second her eyes met Travis's. Just looking at his tired and disgusted face made her want to run into his arms. Still, she sat like an obedient slave, wondering what they would make her do. Liza's neck ached. Her nose was running from the hay. She was starving. Finally, after what seemed like hours, the assistant director walked over and handed her a piece of paper.

"The yellow highlighted lines are yours," he said, rubbing his eyes tiredly. "I want you to walk over to the fence in the middle of the set, look down at your feet in horror, and say them."

Liza took the paper carefully and stood up. "It smells like puppy puke," she read without thinking. Her mouth fell open. She looked up, shocked. "That's it? *It smells like puppy puke*?"

The assistant director gave her an irritated look. "Try emphasizing the word *smells*."

"It *smells* like puppy puke," Liza obeyed, feeling suddenly sick.

"Work with *puppy*."

"It smells like *puppy* puke," Liza said, feeling something between tears and wild, crackling, crazy laughter rising from within.

"Go with that," he snapped, walking away toward the camera, which had rolled toward her. "Okay, walk over to that chalk mark and say the line."

Slowly, Liza stood up and walked toward Travis and the others sitting on the fence. When she saw the line, she stopped and contorted her face in a look of sheer terror.

"It smells like *puppy* puke," Liza emoted, looking with horrified intensity at her feet.

"Cut," the director shouted, looking away. "Okay. We'll take fifteen, then shoot the next scene. Anybody got any gum. Mints? Something like that?

Liza sat in shock. The assistant director was actually walking away, talking intently to the cameraman. The extras relaxed and walked over to the pop machines. It was as if nothing had happened. She sat down with a thump and felt her face screw up with tears and frustration. It smells like puppy puke? This was her first spoken line in Hollywood? This was the big break she'd practically broken her neck to get? This is what Geoff Hansen had in mind when she sang and danced for him at the fabulous Sikes party? Was this one, huge horrible joke on her?

She sat stone faced, thinking. Then, slowly, she felt a faint tickle in her side. Soft giggles began to well up from somewhere inside her. She bent over and clutched her stomach, suddenly howling with wild, sidesplitting laughter. She took a deep, thirsty breath. Through her wet eyes she detected a still figure at the entrance to the set. She focused and saw that it was Travis, at first just staring in wonder. Then he walked over, smiling. By the time he was in front of her, he was laughing too.

"Puppy puke," Liza said solemnly.

"Puppy puke," he repeated, trying to keep a straight face. He threw his head back. *"Puppy puke,"* he howled, grabbing Liza around the waist and pulling her backward into the hay.

"Puppy puke!" they cried out, reaching for each other, rolling wildly on the hay, laughing together until Travis was suddenly looking straight into her eyes. He paused to stare at her, his eyes twinkling. Then in a single, swift move, he pulled her to his

chest and kissed her furiously on the mouth.

Liza let her head fall back with joy. She kissed him back. Somehow they'd crossed over the canyon. Somehow they were together. And somehow she knew they wouldn't be apart ever again.

"We'll miss you, Winnie," Lauren said softly, linking arms as they clicked down the wide corridor toward Gate 24 at the Los Angeles International Airport.

Winnie popped her bubble gum and hiked her travel bag on her shoulder, setting off a jangle of twelve clattering bracelets. "Hey, I'll miss you knuckleheads, too." She shrugged, stopped, and clicked her plastic sandals together three times, a spacey look on her face. "But you know what they say. There's no place like home. There's *no* place like home."

"Merely one of the greatest lines Hollywood ever came up with," Max said with a quick grin.

"Yeah," Winnie agreed, stepping forward. "Because it's probably true. I mean, I spent all that energy trying to reach out and feel loved at the Walker Institute. Why did I have to do it among complete strangers?"

"Look," Lauren said quietly, staring into Winnie's eyes, "I really mean it when I say I'll miss you. I—I've wanted to know you better, Winnie. That was the whole point of this summer. But I—I didn't stop to give you a chance. And I'm sorry."

Winnie's eyes grew soft. Her tiny, nonstop body actually stopped. Then she reached her arms out and hugged Lauren. "I didn't give you a chance either, Lauren. I was too jealous. I was too wrapped up in my own problems."

Lauren pulled away and looked at her, then at Max, who gave her an understanding nod. "Jealous?"

Winnie shrugged. "Yeah. You had this big job on a national show. You immediately found this cute hunk here." Winnie nudged Max playfully in the side. "I couldn't just let you enjoy it. I had to feel left out."

Lauren's eyes welled up with tears. There was something so honest and brave about Winnie. She had always admired her. Sure, Winnie did some crazy things, but she had great instincts. And great courage.

"All summer I kept thinking I was completely alone in the world," Winnie explained, linking her arm into Lauren's and heading down the gate. "But I've got a mother," she said, as if in awe of that basic fact. "and a new stepfather I barely know. And I've got my closest friends, KC and Faith, right there in Jacksonville. I want to start all over again with everyone who's close to me."

They walked into the gate waiting area, and Winnie handed her ticket to the agent. Lauren took Winnie's hand and squeezed it. "I'm sorry I—I, you know, gave you such a bad time."

"She just got a little uppity," Max teased. "Jumping April Webster's Nielsen rating will do that to a person."

Lauren nudged him. "Knock it off. Walker Ingham fell into our laps. Winnie was the brave one. And I'll never forget it."

Winnie gave her a funny, tender smile. Then she shook her head, took her ticket back from the agent, and strolled to a chair. "I do some pretty crazy things sometimes, Lauren. It's partly because I can't help myself. But it's also because I'm sort of fixated on not wanting to be like everybody else. I'm zany, wild Winnie. Fun, eccentric Winnie. But most of the time I end up looking like a fool."

"You didn't look like a fool to me, Winnie," Max said with a sincere smile.

"Good-bye," Winnie said quietly, hearing her flight announced. "We're going to have lots of time together sophomore year. Okay, Lauren?"

"Okay, Win," Lauren said, reaching out for a hug.

Standing up, Winnie gave Lauren and Max quick kisses and turned on her heel, wiggling her fingers over her shoulders as she walked to the gate.

When Winnie had disappeared into the plane, Lauren turned to Max and touched him on the cheek. Ever since she'd seen him walk up to April's stage, alive and well, she hadn't been able to stay away from him. "I guess we'll be saying good-bye like this in a month."

Max's face softened. His eyes shone as he took her face in his hands. "Not for a month."

Lauren gulped. "I have to go back to school in the fall."

"And I have to keep working for April," Max said, tenderly slipping his arm around her waist and guiding her out of the waiting area.

Lauren walked next to Max, hugging him tightly. Dash would be back in the fall too. Before, she'd been so sure of Dash. But now she knew that nothing was sure. She'd just have to wait and see where her feelings took her.

"Maybe what we have can't last forever," Max admitted, "but we've got time, Lauren. We've got the beach. The ocean. We could even get really corny and take in Disneyland. We have a beautiful, golden month ahead of us."

"Yeah." Lauren let out a short laugh. "And April breathing down our backs twenty-four hours a day."

"True," Max said, nudging her playfully as they pushed their way through the hurrying crowds. "What you say is always very, very true."

▄ HarperPaperbacks *By Mail*

Join KC, Faith, and Winnie as the three hometown friends share the triumphs, loves, and tragedies of their first year of college in this bestselling series: